These extraordinary stories offer a rare and
ca's longest conflict, and invite us to share t
ferings of war-weary Afghans. J Malcolm
bridge our world needs, and an essential ch
—BRIAN CASTNER, author of *Th*

J. Malcolm Garcia's impressive book of nonfi
extraordinary everyday people in Afghanist
fiction I've read in years, full of plot twists, l
Part Dickens, part Studs Terkel, the book re
with a refreshing candor I defy anyone not to
—HELEN BENEDICT, author of *Wolf Se*
and *The Lonely Soldier*

J. Malcolm Garcia's latest book exploring the l
of the American war in Afghanistan is profour
icans to read right now. While American lead
and news pundits glorify street vigilantism a
cal violence, Garcia reminds us what war actu
als, culture, and society. This isn't the Hollywo
meme. In real war, no one wins, no one gets
everyone is tortured by the things they saw and
—BEN BRODY, author of *Attention Ser*

It takes a unique combination of moral seriousn
and wild honesty to bear witness to war's devas
convey to those who weren't there what it was
Malcolm Garcia is such a writer. His tremendo
nary Afghans trying to endure two decades of d
tion deserves a wide readership."
—MATT GALLAGHER, author of *Empire City*

MOST DANGEROUS, MOST UNMERCIFUL

STORIES FROM AFGHANISTAN

J. MALCOLM GARCIA

SEVEN STORIES PRESS

NEW YORK · OAKLAND · LONDON

SEVEN STORIES PRESS
140 Watts Street
New York, NY 10013
www.sevenstories.com

College professors and high school and middle school teachers
may order free examination copies of Seven Stories Press titles.
Visit https://www.sevenstories.com/pg/resources-academics
or email academics@sevenstories.com.

Library of Congress Cataloging-in-Publication Data

Names: Garcia, J. Malcolm, 1957- author.
Title: Most dangerous, most unmerciful : Afghanistan stories / J. Malcolm
    Garcia.
Description: First Edition. | New York : Seven Stories Press, [2022]
Identifiers: LCCN 2021047334 | ISBN 9781644212035 (Hardcover) | ISBN
    9781644212042 (eBook)
Subjects: LCSH: Afghan War, 2001-2021. | Afghanistan--Social life and
    customs--21st century. | Afghanistan--Social conditions--21st century.
Classification: LCC DS371.413 .G47 2022 | DDC 958.104/7--dc23/eng/20220314
LC record available at https://lccn.loc.gov/2021047334

These stories first appeared, some in different versions, in *Alaska Quarterly Review*
("Mother's House"); *bioStories* ("Farmer by Day"); *Fourth Genre* ("In Those Days");
Guernica: A Magazine of Art & Politics ("Book Lady," "Old Guns"); *Huck* ("Weight of
the World"); *Latterly Magazine* ("Grave Digger"); *The Massachusetts Review* ("All That
Is Yet to Come," "Displaced Persons"); *New Letters* ("Animal Rescue"); *Tampa Review*
("Feral Children"); *VICE Magazine* ("A Mercy Killing," "Fire in the Hole," "Weather
Did Not Destroy This House"); *The Virginia Quarterly Review* ("Most Dangerous, Most
Unmerciful"); and *War, Literature & the Arts* ("Maybe One Day").

Some names were changed for privacy.

For David Littlejohn
1937–2015

Only the dead have
seen the end of war.

—PLATO

CONTENTS

NOT THE WEATHER

The man beside me drops a pill in his mouth and swallows it with a sip of green tea, and together, from beneath a thin angle of shade, we stare out at the dirt road and beyond it to the smog-heavy skyline of Kabul. The stony ground beneath our feet stinks of dried dung. Chickens scramble around us and flies dart above our heads.

"Your hotel?" the man asks me and raises his chin toward Kabul.

"Yes, I'm staying there."

He nods, says nothing further. A boy urges some cows forward and they pass us wide-eyed and lumbering, their heads lethargically thrusting back and forth with each step forward.

This morning, I woke up and decided to take a bus out of Kabul. Any bus to the first village it stopped at, just to leave the city. Its congested streets and thick layers of smog had begun to bear down on me like a weight. I needed a break from what in my mind was a boomtown in the midst of war.

Near my hotel, the Hazim Supermarket sells washing machines when just months ago it sold only laundry buckets.

An Italian restaurant will open soon in a local hotel two doors down from a new Chinese restaurant. International aid organizations pay up to $10,000 a month for housing.

After making several stops in the city, the bus I boarded drove into the village of Bini Sar. I got off and saw a man brewing tea in a kettle over a pile of smoking coals beneath a tree. Behind him stood a closed shop. Other men sat nearby smoking. I offered the man brewing tea a dollar. He waved my money away and poured me a cup. I sat beside him. From an envelope, he shook a pill into his hand and reached for his tea. I drank from my cup and looked out on the road.

"English?"

"American," I tell him." Journalist."

He nods, tells me his name, Nasir. He says he had worked as a translator for American troops in Helmand Province south of Kandahar. He quit two months ago when an Afghan soldier on patrol with American forces stepped on an IED. He heard the explosion and ran over and saw the body lying crookedly on the ground and the blood and torn pieces of flesh like chipped paint strewn about.

Two days later he could still hear the explosion, still see the dead man and the blood and body parts. So he left and returned home to Bini Sar. He continues to hear the explosion, see the body. He takes tablets for depression. He shakes some pills into his hand and shows them to me and then puts them back in the envelope and his pocket. Later in the morning, he will open the shop behind him. He repairs hunting rifles and sells petrol.

"More tea?"

"No, thank you," I tell him and slap at flies collecting above my head.

Most mornings, Nasir wakes up, makes tea, and drinks it

with other merchants. Then he changes clothes, opens his shop. He organizes the guns that need to be repaired and inspects his gas pump. At night, he returns home and sits with his wife and five children. They eat dinner. The sky darkens, the day concludes. They sleep. There is nothing more to do. He feels he is wasting his time with his shop but he can't find other work.

"Does he know what will happen in our country when the Americans leave?" a vendor asks Nasir and raises his chin at me. Nasir translates.

"I don't know what he knows," he says.

He takes an apricot from his pocket, splits it open, and tosses the pit into the road. We watch it bounce through the wheel spokes of a cart harnessed to a donkey. Flies buzzing in clouds above the animal's head break apart and swarm the pit.

Nasir tells me that as a translator he earned about eight hundred a month. The American soldiers he worked with were involved in mountain fighting. The Taliban would shoot down at them and the Americans would move to the side of the mountain and crouch down seeking cover. Rocket-propelled grenades, mortars, IEDs set beneath bridges. It was very loud. The noise would thrust Nasir backward. The Pakistan Taliban always attacked American and Afghan forces. The Pakistan Taliban trained the Afghan Taliban to fight.

During combat, American soldiers yelled a lot. They seemed very scared. For Afghan soldiers, combat was like a game. After all, the country has been fighting wars since 1979, when the Soviet Union invaded. Then the Soviets left in 1989 and civil war followed and after that the Taliban. For a while, it seemed the fighting would stop when the Americans invaded a month after September 11th and toppled the Taliban, but then as the years passed the war dragged on and the US began seeking a way out and the Taliban became strong again and the fighting continued.

"Do you want a biscuit with your tea?"

"No, thank you."

One time in Nuristan Province two Afghan soldiers were blown to pieces, Nasir says. He thanks god he did not see this. They were put in coffins and taken to their families. The families were given nine hundred seventy dollars apiece and enough food for three days of mourning and no more.

Sometimes when there was no fighting, American soldiers wearing only shorts and T-shirts would visit with Afghan soldiers. The Afghans had to explain that for a man to show so much of himself was a violation of their culture and they would ask the Americans to leave.

Nasir worries that life will become difficult when the Americans withdraw from Afghanistan in 2014. There are places the Afghan army can't reach but the Americans can with their planes and helicopters. You can't do anything without air support, he says.

"What do you think is next for Afghanistan?"

"I don't know."

"Cigarette?"

I don't smoke but I take it hoping the smoke will ward off the flies. Nasir waves a hand and the flies scatter. He points to the broken walls of a mud-brick house across the street.

"I was born there," he says.

In the mid-1990s, feuding Afghan factions destroyed the compound. Pashtun and Uzbek forces pounded Bini Sar with mortars and grenades. Nasir and his family left the village and built a new home a few miles away.

He stands and we cross over to the house. An enormous padlock gathers dust on the massive front doors. Peeling wood curls into clumps the size of fists. Dogs ramble out an open side door, leaving paw prints in the dust and scattering chickens. I step around the chickens and peer inside. Nothing but a ruined staircase and balcony, and broken pottery and wooden beams. The scarred earthen floor bears the remains of the broken roof and a ruined fireplace. A shorn wall reveals a weed-clotted courtyard and empty animal stalls. The buzz of insects rises from the ground.

"As a boy, I made snowmen there in winter," Nasir says.

The house was built almost two hundred years ago. His great-grandfather died there, as did his grandfather and father, and his mother and two cousins. Nasir will die in the home he now occupies outside Bini Sar. It was cheaper to leave and build a new house rather than repair the old.

"There is no room for sentiment," he says.

He runs a hand over the mud-brick walls bristling with bits of straw. I ask him how homes built from mud withstand rain. The walls are very strong, he explains. The family of his great-grandfather stomped the mud with their feet and then cut it into squares and baked it and made bricks. After one or two years, they sometimes had to patch the roof, but nothing more. The bricks held.

"Afghans," Nasir says, "have an expression. When someone asks, 'How long will your house stand?' the answer is, 'As long as people don't destroy it.'"

"Weather," he tells me, "did not destroy this house."

A man approaches us and asks Nasir about me. Nasir tells him I'm an American journalist. The man wants to know what Afghan president Hamid Karzai will do about education, health, and other social problems once the Americans leave. I shake my head. I don't know.

"What is the United Nations?" he asks.

"Representatives from countries around the world meet and discuss the problems of the world," I tell him.

"It is not my fault that I ask you these questions," the man says. "I didn't go to school. Now I know nothing. I have nothing. The Americans support Karzai but he does nothing. Everyone is angry at the Americans. As an American you are a target of people's anger."

"Please, there will be no more fighting," Nasir says. "Not today."

We watch the man walk away. Somewhere a generator coughs and starts, and I look toward the noise. A merchant has opened his shop. He stands on his toes and turns on the one bare bulb hanging above a counter stacked high with bags of rice. Behind his store, shadows retreat up a rocky hill, exposing a barren graveyard where the parents, grandparents, and great-grandparents of Nasir lie buried beneath nameless slabs of stone shaped like large arrowheads.

Nasir and I wander back to our spot outside his shop. He withdraws his envelope of pills, looks inside it, and counts silently. He folds it and puts it back in his pocket. Flies collect on our feet and legs. Nasir waves his arms but I don't bother. The flies won't go no matter what we do. They gather in bunches on my knees but I ignore them. I watch them spin in circles, uncertain without the threat of my hand hovering above them.

OLD GUNS

The antique-weapons dealer remembers me from my visit last spring.

"You were the American reporter who bought a pistol."

"Not a pistol. Flintlock rifle. 1852."

"Yes," he says.

"On my way back to the States, I was stopped at airport security in Pakistan, Dubai, and London. They were worried about the gun."

"They thought you were a terrorist with an ancient rifle?"

"I guess. No one stopped me here."

"Why would they? After thirty years of war, why we would we care about an old gun leaving Afghanistan?"

I follow him up some broken stairs to the second floor of his shop. He points to a rug and we sit on the floor near an open balcony. Rifles and pistols, decorated with ivory and tin, hang from the cinder-block walls beside circular shields and swords brown from rust and age. Knives and spiked battle flails lie tangled in the corners.

Below us on Chicken Street, Kabul's tourist district, laborers slap cement on the walls of a new apartment building. American soldiers cradling AK-47 rifles roam the jammed sidewalks. Merchants call to them, point at the old red and yellow carpets hanging outside their shops. New carpets lie on the muddy street and passing trucks and cars flatten them, grinding in dirt and stones. This quick and easy aging process fools the unsuspecting foreigner into believing that the worn, dusty carpets harken back to bygone eras. There is a common expression among carpet merchants: Three days on the street, three hundred years old, three hundred dollars.

"Please come look," they shout. "No charge for looking."

The antique dealer calls to a boy and tells him to bring hot water for tea. The boy rinses two glass cups with steaming water from a kettle. He offers the cups to us and sits beside the antique dealer, pouring us green tea from another kettle. Sunlight spills into the room from an open balcony, the sky a brilliant blue, and we shift our positions to keep the sun's relentless heat off our backs. The lumbering weight of trucks outside shakes the shop, and the antique dealer, the boy, and I put our hands on the floor until the building stops trembling.

The antique dealer's father opened the shop in 1939. At first he sold old clothes and furniture, but when it seemed that war in Afghanistan was a thing of the past, lost to history and memory, and the guns and pistols seemed to have no purpose other than as souvenirs, he began selling those instead.

"In this time, the 1950s and '60s, there were many tourists in Afghanistan searching for old things," the antique dealer says. "Why is this? I think some countries move too fast and the people do not know who they are and so they come here. Here our history is all around us."

I sip my tea, listen to the noise of bicycle riders frantically ringing their horns on the crowded street below us, racing past buildings that still bear scars from the civil war that nearly destroyed Afghanistan in the mid-1990s.

When I watch BBC news reports from Syria in my hotel room and see the shorn remains of buildings in Aleppo, I have a small sense of what the fighting here must have been like during the Soviet occupation of the 1980s and the later civil war, the Taliban and the post–September 11th American-led invasion. Eleven years later, fighting continues. The United States has learned, as did the Russians and invaders before them, that Afghanistan won't yield to would-be conquerors. Plans now call for all American combat forces to draw down by 2014 with no pretense of victory.

Today, the Taliban controls large swaths of Afghanistan, areas that function not unlike independent city-states. Maidan Wardak Province, for instance, just a forty-minute drive from Kabul, is dominated by the Taliban. As is Logar Province, a ninety-minute drive from Kabul, and Nangarhar Province, a two-hour drive from Kabul, and so on. The Taliban governs southern Afghanistan so thoroughly that the divide is nearly as stark as that between North and South Korea.

But on Chicken Street the war feels far away. The laborers dip shovels into mounds of stones mixed with cement and cover their faces with prayer shawls to protect themselves against the dust the cement mixers produce as they turn in slow circles. Donkey-drawn carts haul bricks, and men pull wagons stacked with wood. Above them, signs on nearby buildings—Baha DVD Store, Kabul Computers, A. B. Samey Hamayoun Desk Top Publishing—promote a new Afghanistan rushing to catch up with the twenty-first century. Boys fly kites from rooftops near billboards advertising "Afghan Wireless: Your connection to the world."

"When I was young, the foreigners were not like they are now," the antique dealer says. "They were not soldiers. They came here to see Afghanistan. They slept outside in tents and no one bothered them. My shop was open until one o'clock in the morning and I never locked it. The police were not like they are now. They did not take bribes. They were not former militia. The police in that time would stop by and I'd asked them in for tea."

Two American soldiers in desert fatigues walk into the shop. They nod and smile, and the antique dealer stands and bows slightly, pressing his right hand over his heart. One of the soldiers picks up a pistol, drawing cobwebs with it. He makes a face and puts it down, slapping dust off his hand. The antique dealer stands and points to other guns.

"Very clean, no problem," he says. "Two hundred years old."

The soldiers stand over the guns whispering to each other, and the antique dealer sits beside me again. He watches the soldiers put the guns down and move into another room filled with swords and knives.

"Without peace, we can't live here," the antique dealer says. "During Talib time, I lived in Pakistan selling rugs. I returned when Karzai came to power. But now the fighting has come back. The rocketing has not stopped. We are waiting for tourists like before, but I think we will be waiting a very long time."

The boy takes our empty cups and rinses them, tossing the water out on the floor. He follows the soldiers into the other room with the cups and two kettles. He comes back out seconds later, drying his hands with a rag.

"They are gone," he says.

The antique dealer and I peer into the room. I see a rear door open to a narrow stairwell. We listen to the soldiers clomping down the steps in their heavy boots, look at one another, and shrug. The boy sits down.

"I hope every day becomes better in Afghanistan, but I don't know," the antique dealer says. "The Americans are leaving. There will be big problems, big fighting. Our soldiers, the Afghan National Army, are not completely strong yet."

I look out the balcony and watch merchants dragging carpets off and onto the street. I listen to the sound of jackhammers and the rumble of traffic. A laborer pulls bags of cement off the backs of two donkeys, and rips one bag open, emptying it into a cement mixer. He washes his hands in a bucket of muddy-looking water. He shakes his hands dry and dials a number on his cell phone.

"Come, I'll show you something," the antique dealer tells me.

He takes my hand and leads me into the room the soldiers just left. He closes the door to the stairwell. He pulls a cord to a ceiling light and parts a curtain, revealing a closet protected by an enormous padlock. He unlocks it with a long slender key and opens the door. Hot, moldy air washes over us and I taste dust in my mouth. A ribbon of gray light shines through a crack in the mud walls. About a dozen Russian Kalashnikov rifles lie in a pile on the floor, scratched and worn. Duct tape holds several of the rifle butts together.

"Relatives gave these to me to sell for them, and some of them I bought myself," the antique dealer says. "But it is too soon to sell. Maybe in ten years if there is no more fighting, I can sell. Not for killing but for decoration. For now, I will keep them here and we will see what happens."

The boy picks up one of the guns and points it at the crack in the wall, squinting through the sight. Behind us, rising up over the balcony, I hear the high-pitched noise of a drill. The boy puts the gun down. It slides off the pile and clatters to the floor.

"If the fighting comes to Chicken Street, I would say to Karzai, 'I have the guns. Take my chair so I can no longer sit and I will help you defend our country,'" the antique dealer says.

I imagine the new building going up across the street being destroyed by an army of men who, like this antique dealer, would believe they were fighting for the good of Afghanistan. I think of the Aleppo footage again and try to picture what happened here, but the pandemonium on Chicken Street interferes with my thoughts, and then I hear someone enter the shop and the antique dealer hurries to close and lock the closet door.

He pushes the boy ahead of him and looks at me and presses a finger to his lips. He reaches back and pulls the curtain and shuts off the light. We move toward the white-hot glare beyond the balcony and the noise of construction outside.

MOTHER'S HOUSE

PART ONE

I

The Taj Begum restaurant stands behind a gate on an exhausted dirt road in Kabul, the crumbled asphalt exposing rocks and tree roots and gaping potholes. Passersby, burdened by the intense heat of an August afternoon, walk on the road until they reach a stretch of sidewalk that has somehow survived its own ruin. On rainy days, muddy water fills immense craters that cars can do little to avoid, slaloming around one only to sink into another with a horrible bang of the undercarriage sending up geysers of filth and dowsing anyone—on this morning me—outside the closed metal gates of the restaurant. Upon seeing me drenched and dripping, sunlight blinking off the wet concrete drive and my own soaked body, a guard hurries to let me in. He offers an apologetic smile and hands me a towel.

Wiping my face, I enter a courtyard. The high white walls

reduce the street noise to a whisper and it would be easy to think that I am no longer in Kabul but some peaceful place without war or strife of any kind. Cats dart across a lawn, and iron lanterns with stained glass throw a wavering blue and orange light that provides minimal heat for other cats to bask in, and roses stand in pots to one side of the lanterns, ready to be planted. I watch a barefoot man step across the grass with a hose and amble around tables and chairs that another man washes and stacks on a brick patio, and I'm reminded of scenes from a fairy tale where elves scurry in preparation for their monarch. I intend no pejorative, but there is just something so acquiescent and submissive about their conduct, hurried and stooped over. The restaurant, a two-story, brown brick building with white columns like something out of America's antebellum South, casts a long, broad shadow over the laborers, enforcing the morning's stillness with the quiet solemnity of its vacant windows and empty dining hall.

As I hand the towel back to the guard, Laila Haidari, the proprietor, approaches me, wrapped in an orange and red sari. A scarf of the same color covers her black hair. She has a firm handshake and a warm smile, and I feel her tired eyes search my face as she sizes me up, determining whether I can be trusted. Men, I will soon learn, have not treated Laila well. I follow her to a set of lawn chairs and we sit in the sun and observe two men emerge from within the restaurant to assist the other two tending the grounds. They are all graduates of an alcohol and drug detox program Laila founded across town. The profits from Taj Begum keep the program open. Before I became a reporter, I had worked with homeless people in San Francisco. When I heard about Laila's work with addicts from a friend with Amnesty International, I decided to look her up.

Don't forget the rose bushes, Laila calls to the man watering the grass.

Yes, Mother, he says and jogs to the roses.

All the recovering addicts call Laila Mother. She compares them to eager children who want to make their parent happy. Grown men behaving like needy kids discomfit her, but she understands. Few people care about addicts. The men cling to the ones who do, their affection something so rare that it becomes almost as addictive as the drugs the addicts once used. They can't let her go. Some refuse to leave even when they complete the program. They have become so used to her care that they make their way to Taj Begum and insist she continue to watch over them.

C'mon, Laila tells them. You're sober. You have your shops and families to return to.

No, you're our mother; we're your kids, they tell her.

She insists they go but they resist and she absorbs their profanity, their rants like spoiled brats, until, exhausted, she relents and lets them stay, assigning them tasks at the restaurant.

Her brother, Hakim, also cursed her but for different reasons. He became envious of her success. Hakim had been an addict for twenty-two years, hooked on heroin and hashish. As a family, Laila and her parents experienced the shame of his addiction until their father banished him from the house. She remembers seeing him on the street passed out. Alive or dead, as an addict her brother no longer existed, no longer mattered, an unwanted non-person just like other addicts, whom she would chronicle in the early 2000s as a documentary filmmaker. However, Laila became increasingly disillusioned with making movies. A film did not change lives. In 2010, she put aside her camera and established a thirty-day drug and alcohol recovery program. She offered a house, three meals a day, and Narcotics Anonymous meetings. The first few clients began calling the program Mother's House, and the name stuck. Hakim stayed for a month and now he no longer uses. After he left he started his own program. He considers Mother's House competition. They haven't spoken in years.

Laila tried to help addicted women after Mother's House opened, but she received so many death threats that she dropped the idea. The women and their children transported drugs and guns for the dealers they lived with, most of whom were their husbands and fathers, and the dealers confronted Laila and demanded that she stop encouraging their women to leave.

You're interfering with business, they told her.

One night someone kicked in the door of her home. She woke with a start but saw nothing. Then two men emerged from the dark and one of them jumped on top of her and began choking her with a wire. Laila pushed the fingers of one hand beneath the wire and with her other hand reached for a gun she kept by the bed. The second intruder grabbed the gun and they struggled. Laila pulled the trigger once, twice, blasting holes in the walls, and her assailants beat her until she released the weapon and passed out. When she opened her eyes, the men were gone. Above her stood a neighbor who'd heard the commotion. When he entered Laila's house, the startled intruders shoved past him and ran outside. Laila did not call the police. An attack on a woman, even in post-Taliban Afghanistan, was of no consequence.

Another time, a taxi driver offered Laila a ride as she walked to the restaurant. Three men sat in the back seat. It is not uncommon in Afghanistan to share taxis with strangers. Laila opened the passenger door and got in. One of the men grabbed her scarf and jerked her head back and punched her while the two other men demanded that she stop helping addicts. Addicts bought their drugs, they shouted, hitting her again and again until they told the driver to stop. One of the men then stepped out and jerked Laila from the taxi, throwing her on the ground. This time she went to the police, but they did nothing. Drug dealers, she suspects, paid the police to stay out of their way.

To this day, the threats have not stopped. Her phone rings in the middle of the night. When she answers, she hears only a taunting silence. She began to worry about her two sons, eighteen-year-old Murtaza and thirteen-year-old Mustafa, and her fifteen-year-old daughter, Zakia. It was one thing when they were small and stayed home, but now they are old enough to wander about Kabul as they choose. These crazy people might kidnap them or worse. In addition, the children's stepmother wanted Zakia to marry a man Laila felt was mentally unstable. Her children were just four, six, and eight when Laila divorced their father, but they stayed with him because according to Sharia law, Afghan children belong to the father. He married their stepmother a short time later. She resented having the responsibility of children not her own. Some days, she would lock them out of the kitchen and refuse to feed them. Eventually she persuaded her husband to let them stay with Laila.

As the menacing phone calls continued, Laila grew obsessed with worry until she arrived at a plan: She must get her children out of Afghanistan. Avoiding any mention of his wife, Laila told her ex, who had recently moved to Iran, about the threats on her life and how their children might be affected, convincing him they should leave for Europe.

Laila then paid a smuggler to make the arrangements. She put in fifteen hundred euros; her ex-husband, eight thousand.

She coached her children on what to say at the borders they would cross. Don't tell anyone your father is alive and lives in Iran, she warned them. Say he disappeared. If border agents know your father lives in Iran, they might deport you to Tehran. Afghanistan is dangerous; Iran is not. The Europeans might think it's no problem to send you there. That would be terrible, Laila knew. Their father was a mullah. The Europeans would not understand how hard it would be for her children, especially her daughter, to live with a conservative man and his crazy wife. And because the children are part Afghan, they would suffer discrimination. Iranians consider Afghans inferior. Their father could not protect them.

Murtaza, Mustafa, and Zakia left by bus two days before I stood soaking wet outside Taj Begum's gate. If they were on schedule, they would soon cross into Turkey. There a man the smuggler knows has promised to help them reach Austria.

You will have a hard journey, Laila told Zakia before she departed.

After what we went through with our stepmother, this trip won't be so bad, Zakia replied.

2

The gardener whom Laila and I watch watering the grass is named Ali. Like many Afghans, he does not have a last name. Long tangles of hair curl around his ears. He wears a light brown salwar kameez spattered with stains. After he finishes watering, he rolls up the hose and leaves it beside the roses. He then turns his attention to some chairs that need new legs and ruminates about his life and how he became an addict when he started using cocaine and heroin as a construction worker in

Iran, where many Afghans travel to find work. His experience has led him to the conclusion that people get addicted for so many reasons: joblessness, curiosity, associating with the wrong people. You see other people using and think, Hey, let me try that. At least that's how he thought at the time. He had no idea that an impulsive notion would lead to a drug habit.

Ali left Iran for Afghanistan after the Taliban fell, joining the newly formed Afghan National Army because it was the only institution offering work. He spent eight months in the field near the Pakistan border in Paktika, Sharana, Morgah, Barmal, Khatr-kot, Gomal, and so many other places, fighting remnants of the Taliban. He saw friends shot and blown up. He got depressed and kept using, not for the fun of getting high but for the need to cauterize his mind from troubling thoughts. He liked the painkiller Tramadol, the way it numbed his whole body so that he felt nothing other than the emptiness of his mind, like a placid pond without even a ripple disturbing its surface. When he quit the army, he found he could easily buy Tramadol on the streets in Kabul. Opium too. He was jobless and joined other addicts who lived under the Pol-e-Sokhta bridge downtown. The name means burned bridge, and indeed the people gathering beneath it had burned every bridge that had nothing to do with their addiction. Men and a few women would lie passed out on heaps of putrid trash and torn plastic bags spilling more spoiled garbage, and families walking across the bridge would look down and point at the addicts as if they were an exhibit for their entertainment, the addicts jerking awake and stumbling over sacks of refuse, falling and rising, falling and rising, like marionettes in the hands of a distracted puppeteer, staggering barefoot across black, muddy ground, twitching from invisible currents, unable to keep still until they found someone with a pipe or a syringe who could join them to sink into oblivion again, their skeletal bodies grimed and foul, and when they spoke in croaking voices, spittle sprayed through the decay of what remained of their yellowed teeth.

It was under the bridge in 2015 that Laila discovered Ali sprawled between rank, deep puddles of water. One month later, after he graduated from Mother's House, he found work as a laborer. However, those kinds of jobs became scarce as the economy faltered under a revived Taliban insurgency. He asked Laila for help and she hired him at the restaurant. He lives here in a room with one window that looks out on a stack of chairs in need of repair. Every day, he concentrates on his work as the on-site maintenance man, avoiding thoughts of hash, opium, and Tramadol, as well as recollections of combat. Memories such as that of an officer who left his base in Wazir with six soldiers. Seven hours later only one soldier returned alive; the rest were dead, killed by a roadside bomb. The surviving soldier alternated between laughing hysterically at his good fortune and sinking into a deep silence tormented by thoughts Ali could only imagine. In his dreams he saw the soldier weeping until he would wake up crying himself. He'd wipe his eyes and try to fall back asleep, but he had his own horrors to dream about. Like the time he was on patrol and a roadside bomb exploded under the armored vehicle in front of him, enveloping it in flames—boom!—just like that. One minute it was there, the next minute it wasn't, and he knew before he fully comprehended that the four men inside—the kid he'd sat beside at breakfast, the guy who'd shared cigarettes, the other guy who'd laughed at his jokes—were burning alive, if not dead already.

Thinking about things he'd rather not remember, his brain

a torn screen with the bad memories entering like flies, he recalled one morning when his commanding officer told him, We have to leave on a mission. He instructed Ali to ride with the communications officer and three other soldiers. They drove through desert and then crossed an invisible line where, for no reason Ali could discern, nature allowed the ground sustenance, and grass and trees emerged from the sand, so many trees that the trees soon became an overgrown wood so dense that Ali could not see through the low-hanging branches swiping at the windshield. The patrol stopped at an intersection and then turned left. They had not driven more than three hundred feet when the commander's vehicle exploded, pieces of metal and body parts falling onto the hood of Ali's car. He and three other soldiers with him started yelling and one of them vomited and the driver shifted into reverse and floored it, the rear wheels spitting dirt, and then he stopped and no one said anything for a long time while the commander's vehicle burned and charred chunks of metal and pieces of uniformed flesh smoldered on the ground. Ali and other members cleaned the puke from their vehicle and then collected all the body parts they could find before they returned to base.

When such a thing happens, Ali has concluded, a man goes crazy. Soldiers see their commander and friends die, they can't bury them completely, because they can't find their legs and arms, or they find their arms but their hands are missing, and at that point of helplessness and futility they want only to kill the insurgents who set the bomb. No more searching for body parts. No more burials. No more anything. Just kill and kill and kill. Nothing removes the pain of a soldier seeing comrades die other than more killing.

Ali gathered the body parts of the commanding officer but

could not find his left leg. That night, the officer came to him in a dream and said, You're not a good friend. You did not bury my leg. Ali woke up determined to find the missing limb. He returned with a patrol to the spot where the explosion occurred and after three days he found the remains of the leg in some bushes, rotting and maggot-filled and partially eaten by animals. He wrapped it in cloth and dug a small grave and buried it. The officer no longer appears in Ali's dreams. He rests in Paradise and has given Ali peace, but not so much peace that Ali doesn't dream of explosions and of dead soldiers whose body parts he never finds.

3

This evening, Laila can't sleep. Her children called in the afternoon to tell her they'd reached the Turkish border. They were shutting off their phones to conserve power and she has not heard from them since. Her blood pressure rises with worry. She wonders, Did they cross into Turkey yet? Were they stopped? Arrested? Are they well? She doesn't want her daughter, Zakia, harmed—her sons either, of course, but a young woman is so vulnerable. Laila can only wait for them to call again. Waiting is so hard. Oh, God, she hopes her kids make it to Europe. Most Afghans who leave end up in Germany, but Laila would like them to live in Sweden. She has heard wonderful things about Sweden. If they think the journey they're on now is difficult, just wait until they have to adapt to a foreign land, a foreign language, a foreign people. Laila knows how it feels to be uprooted. She was born to Afghan parents in Quetta, Pakistan, after they left Kabul during the Soviet occupation. Tired of the antipathy Pakistanis felt toward Afghans, they later moved to Iran, but there, too, Afghans were treated as second-class citizens.

As a child, Laila wrote poetry to express her feelings of dislocation. However, as she grew older, she became disillusioned with verse. Her words did not adequately convey the pain she needed to express. How it was to live in a country and be treated as inferior. Laila saw Iranian police slap Afghans for no reason, shove them to the ground and kick them. It scared her because she was an Afghan. Would she, too, be pushed around and punished for being from somewhere else?

When the Taliban fell in 2001 to a US-led military coalition following the attacks of 9/11, her family returned to Kabul. It was there she met dozens of addicts under the Pol-e-Sokhta bridge as she searched for her brother, Hakim. The addicts reminded Laila of zombies. She stepped gingerly down broken steps that led beneath the bridge, the stench of garbage and unwashed bodies and human waste fogging her senses, and she almost turned back. When she reached the bottom, the mud beneath her feet oozed thick and foul and she shook with disgust and fear. The addicts approached her like feral dogs, suspicious, curious, hesitant. To her surprise, they assumed she was an addict like them. What are you using? they asked. Crystal? Hash? Opium? Heroin? Nothing, Laila told them. I just want to help you.

The addicts didn't believe her. They accused her of being with the government.

You are using us to campaign for office, they said. You are trying to manipulate us for your gain.

No, no, Laila protested. I am a simple person. I just want to help you.

One night, she wondered aloud to a friend how she could

assist addicts. Her poetry and films wouldn't help them. What would? Laila determined she'd need a place to get them off the street; a house where they could stay for at least four weeks and that would provide them basic necessities and daily Narcotics Anonymous meetings. If they needed more time, they could stay longer, providing they helped to maintain the house and did not use. She spoke to landlords but no one would rent to her, because they considered addicts criminals, useless people, animals. Laila looked and looked until she found an empty wreck of a house far from downtown. Birds nested in the rafters, darting in and out of rooms wet from rain and filled with the rubble of collapsed walls. The owner agreed to rent to Laila, but she would have to finance the repairs herself.

She raised money from friends. To get started, she intended to take only five addicts from under the bridge. Instead, she loaded as many men as could squeeze into her rented van. Struggling to close the door against the press of their bodies with one hand, with the other she waved off more men pleading to go with her. Encouraged that so many addicts wanted help, Laila drove to a public shower owned by her uncle. Shopkeepers stared with mouths open as twenty filthy men stepped out of Laila's van. She bought them soap and shampoo, and while they bathed, she walked to a secondhand store and purchased clothes. Bathed, shaved, and dressed, they were unrecognizable. Their skin so white, their hair wet and shining in the sun. Laila took them to a kabob kiosk and fed them.

The addicts and some of Laila's friends helped repair the house. They borrowed ladders and tools and patched the roof, installed windows, laid carpet. Laila had little money left over for food so she boiled the parts of chickens that butchers had thrown away and made soup. What is this? the addicts asked her. Eat it, she told them, until I can afford to buy real food. That first winter, the house grew so cold the carpet froze and made crackling sounds underfoot.

A former Taliban fighter stood out among Laila's first clients. His name was Esmat and he was a short, thin man with dark hair and piercing blue eyes. He told her he had beheaded so many people at the orders of his commanders that he had lost count and could cope with the memories only by smoking opium. Without drugs, he slept little. Every night at Mother's House he patrolled outside Laila's window. What are you doing? she would ask him. Don't be afraid, I'm protecting you, he replied. She believed him because he called her Mother like everyone else. Laila has not heard from Esmat for some time. When he left, he worried the Taliban would kill him.

A few of her first clients tried to leave without completing the program. They had gained weight and felt much better but their nerves were fragile and they resented being cooped up. Laila stopped them as they were walking out and shamed them for what she called their ingratitude. All the money I spent on you, all the time, she scolded before she locked them in a room so they could not try to escape again. Later, she beat them with an orange rubber hose so they felt pain, a metaphor in her mind for the hurt they'd inflicted on their families, as Hakim had inflicted on her own. They stretched out on their stomachs and she struck their backs repeatedly. They cried out, but they never tried to stop her. She warned the other addicts, Don't let them leave or I'll beat you too.

At night, she listened for anyone unlocking the front door or climbing a wall, bolting out of her bed without bothering to put on her shoes and a scarf to chase after them. Sometimes she called them Hakim. Who? they asked her. A few men did escape and fled to Chil Dokhtaran, a nearby mountain. Laila searched among the boulders for their hiding places until she found them.

Back at Mother's House, she would try to sleep again but could not. She listened to the men tossing and turning on their mats, haunted by nightmares. Laila's own dreams were filled with images of the dead addicts she'd come across, especially in winter when temperatures in Kabul plummet to well below freezing. She'd look under blankets and sheets of cardboard and see a hand or a leg, the skin dark and frigid. Upon closer inspection, she would come across a body curled into a ball, barefoot and in tattered clothes, bare hands jammed between its legs, like something found in an archaeological dig. Sometimes the body was days old. No one cared about addicts when they were alive, why would anyone care about them dead? Because Laila was not related to the deceased, the police refused to allow her to bury them. She paid the police to make the appropriate arrangements.

I don't ask much, she told the police. Just care for the bodies.

She had no way of knowing how they spent the money she gave them.

Laila's phone rings, interrupting these sad memories. It's her daughter, Zakia. Are you in Turkey? Laila asks. Just past Turkey? In a village but you're not yet in Istanbul? OK, call me again from Istanbul. She hangs up, the call kept short so Zakia would have enough units to call again. Laila sets the phone down, relieved. Her children are OK. Maybe now she can sleep.

4

The manager of Mother's House, Naser Amini, knows all about the journey Laila's children have embarked upon. He was one of her earliest clients, and she trusts and confides in him. He listens but rarely comments because he knows that nothing he says will ease her concern. She needs his ears, not his mouth. She thanks him for listening and he bows his head slightly. Listening to her is a small thing he is happy to give. He would be dead if it were not for Laila. As a client at Mother's House, he never fawned over her like the other men. He never tried to manipulate her affection. He thanked her not in words but by mopping the floors, repairing the electrical wiring, holding NA meetings and performing other tasks without asking or expecting anything. When she talks about her children, he nods, says, Yes, Mother, and nothing more, as if it would be inappropriate for him to comment further. Her problems, he knows, remain hers alone. He can no more share them than she can his. They live in the solitude of their own struggles.

Naser began using drugs when he joined the police in 2004 during the second administration of President Hamid Karzai. A fellow officer introduced him to opium. Every officer Naser knew, including commanders, smoked opium, heroin, or hash. If they used, why not the rest of us? Naser thought. He was stationed in the Taliban stronghold of Ghazni and he got high regularly.

In one town, Salon, the Taliban attacked a military supply convoy and Naser saw more than a dozen soldiers struck in the face by gunfire. Among all the fleeing civilians, Naser could not tell who was a Taliban fighter and who was not. What are we doing? he screamed. Who are we fighting? He watched cars burn, ducked when a truck exploded, hunks of metal spinning overhead. He can describe how each person died: how this one had his shoulder shorn off, how that one lost his right arm at the elbow, how another one fell and convulsed for a long time before he lay still, blood oozing from his mouth.

The fighting made no sense. As a police officer, he swore an oath to protect civilians, but it seemed everyone saw him and his fellow officers as the enemy. They always were attacked by the people they wanted to help. The Taliban had ruled districts in and around Ghazni for years, so perhaps the people were afraid they would be killed themselves if they helped the police and army. For all he knew, they may have liked the Taliban. The Taliban railed against the Karzai government through static-filled speakers of nearby mosques. Afterward, when he patrolled the streets, Naser sensed the space that existed between him and the quiet houses and the suspicious eyes he imagined peering at him.

One morning, high on hash, Naser caught a bus into Kabul to celebrate Eid, a religious holiday that marks the end of Ramadan. A police officer called him to say a firefight in Maidan Shar in Wardak Province, about thirty miles outside Kabul, had left twelve dead policemen. An officer sympathetic to the Taliban had been on guard duty. He had called his Taliban contacts, and they shot the policemen. The bodies had been removed by the time Naser arrived but he saw the blood-stained room where the men had died.

Naser returned to Kabul and didn't eat for three days. He drank Pepsi to control his nausea. He had dreams of the dead policemen drowning in their own blood. Some people said the traitorous police officer had grown disillusioned because nothing ever changed. The police arrested the Taliban and the Taliban killed the police and the fighting dragged on and on. What was the point? What is the value of a life? Naser didn't know the answers to these questions but he knew he didn't want to die. He quit the police force and spent all his time and money buying drugs. He recycled cans to pay for his habit and stole food to eat. He lived under the Pol-e-Sokhta bridge. One day he ran into a friend with whom he had smoked opium. The man had changed. His eyes were clear and his clothes clean and he had a deliberate stride that told Naser he had plans, goals. What happened to you? Naser asked. I've been to Mother's House and stopped using, his friend said. When you see a small woman with a van stop here, go with her. She'll be your mother and help you get well. The next time Laila made her rounds under the bridge, Naser followed her out.

5

Laila's daughter, Zakia, calls again, this time in the middle of the night. She and her brothers have arrived in Istanbul. They'll stay one or two days. It's their good luck that Laila has Facebook friends in Turkey—Afghans who left Kabul years earlier and who are willing to shelter them. However, the worst part of their journey awaits: from Istanbul, they must use a raft to cross part of the eastern Aegean Sea to reach Greece. From news reports, Laila knows hundreds of people have died trying to reach Europe in an armada of flimsy rubber dinghies and rickety fishing boats.

Get some sleep, Laila urges Zakia, choking back the worry in her voice.

When she gets up four hours later, Laila drives to Mother's House. She lurches along the crumbled roads, swerving one way and then another in a failed effort to keep the bottom of her car from slamming against the ground as a wheel dips into a hole. Muddy water splashes the windshield and she turns on the wipers and a man driving past curses her.

Woman, he shouts, do you not feel shame for driving?

Is being a woman a crime? she shouts back at him and then swears. Do I not have the same right to drive as a man? Then she laughs, recalling how one addict she had helped moved to Canada where his family lived. He became so Westernized that he had forgotten how it was to live in Kabul. When he returned for a visit, the noise of so many blaring car horns, the endless traffic jams, and the furious drivers drove him to distraction.

You're no longer Afghan, Laila scolded him.

After maneuvering through traffic for half an hour, Laila parks outside a rutted alley. Runnels of sewage flow through trenches made by recent rains. A few clouds linger in an otherwise blue sky and the hot air steams her face. Laila walks down the alley, skirting the filth, and approaches the heavy metal door of Mother's House. Concertina wire unfurls from one end of a wall to the other to prevent thieves from entering and addicts from escaping. Laila presses a buzzer. As she waits for someone to open the door, she recalls years ago when she questioned the wisdom of buying a dilapidated house, as derelict in its way as the addicts she brought to it. Together the addicts and the house improved, and while some of her clients started using again, reducing their bodies to a new state of decay, the house remains, a testament to Laila's determination.

Naser opens the door—Hello, Mother—and Laila smiles, pleased as always to see him, and walks inside, slipping off her sandals. Men with shaved heads, some bleeding from small cuts made by the hand razors used to remove their hair, converge on her in the narrow hall where photographs of these same men as they looked when they first arrived—filthy, emaciated, covered in sores—look out at them as a reminder of who they'd once been and could become again if they resume their drug use.

Who are you? Laila asks one man who won't let go of her hand.

The one getting better every day, he says and points to a photo on the wall. It shows a gaunt figure with a sunken face and a hollow stare, his collarbone and ribs protruding.

That was you?

That was me, the man says.

Laila turns to another man.

And who are you?

I'm the one with the pregnant wife.

Ah, and I beat you.

Yes, Mother, the man says and looks at the floor.

When Laila accepted him into Mother's House, he told her he had a fifteen-day-old baby. Laila became enraged. You would rather smoke opium than take care of your child and wife? She told him to get on the floor. She covered him with a blanket and thrashed him with the rubber hose.

And how is your family? she asks him now.

They are good. My wife comes with our baby to visit.

You're lucky she stays with you. You remember the pain from your beating?

Yes.

Think of it as their pain so you don't feel sorry for yourself.

Laila continues down the hall like a ward boss greeting grateful constituents. She pauses by two men sitting on the floor chained together at their ankles. They had attempted to escape a few days earlier before some of the other addicts stopped them. They'll remain chained together 24-7, even when they use the toilet, until Laila trusts them to complete the program.

He goes to the bathroom too much, one of the men complains of his partner.

If you had not tried to escape, you would not have this problem, Laila says.

Do they not understand what's involved in operating Mother's House? Laila wonders. Of course not. Addicts have no sense of responsibility to anything other than their habit. To live here, they must think differently. She has rules and regulations. They must live like a family. Nothing else matters: ethnicity, religion, none of it. They all have addiction in common, and that makes them brothers, and like brothers they will argue and like children they will disobey, and like a mother she will discipline them. She has become so used to being called Mother that she feels toward them, even the new ones, as if they had emerged from her own body, their suffering her suffering, their struggles her struggles.

Laila turns her attention to another addict, a short, lean man who resembles a teenager, with rumpled hair and the smooth face of a boy. His name is Mohammad Nadir and at twenty-seven he has long left his childhood behind, his adolescent appearance notwithstanding. He sits beside the two shackled men, tapping the air with his feet with nervous energy, and when he speaks, his words rush out of his mouth, revealing his impatience with his confinement.

How do you feel?

Very good, Mother, Nadir answers.

You look good.

Thank you, Mother.

Do you still have nightmares?

I dreamed I had a pocketful of heroin and was caught by the police. Please go away from me, I told the drug, you'll get me in trouble, but the heroin would not leave me.

Have good thoughts during the day and then you'll have good thoughts at night.

Yes, Mother, Nadir says, feet tapping ceaselessly.

Nadir lived a nomadic youth. His mother was Iranian, his

father, Afghan. The family moved back and forth between the two countries when he was a boy. After the Taliban fell, they stayed in Kabul. Mohammad served in the Afghan National Army in 2005 when he was seventeen and saw combat in Helmand Province. One time, a rocket-propelled grenade struck his commander's vehicle. After that day, he decided that movie directors didn't understand war, at least not the war he experienced. When his commander's vehicle exploded that hot afternoon, everything came rushing toward Nadir as if each bullet and rocket and piece of shrapnel was intended for him and him alone. He never saw anything like that in a movie.

He stayed in the army for one year. Then, as his parents before him, he moved between Afghanistan and Iran finding jobs in construction. In 2014, he began reading Facebook posts that said ISIS was destroying Shia shrines outside Damascus. The posts showed videos of ISIS fighters beheading Shia people. As a Shia himself, Nadir decided he must fight for his religion. He took a bus to Iran, an ally of Syria's, and enlisted to fight ISIS. Officers with the Iranian army showed him how to shoot, use a grenade launcher, fire missiles. Nadir knew how to do all these things from his time in the Afghan army but he pretended not to, because he did not want to upset the officers. After two weeks of training, he flew to Damascus with other foreign recruits.

Despite his service in Helmand, Syria left him feeling off balance, uncertain. No one appeared to know what they were doing. Foreign fighters without orders wandered around like children. His unit used three or four scouts and sometimes they made mistakes. They'd say such and such an area was clear and then when Nadir and his unit arrived, ISIS fighters would rise up from the ground like a myth and the fighters beside Nadir would panic and forget their training, flee, and die. This sort of thing happened often. One time, a scout told Nadir that ISIS fighters had left a particular camp. Nadir entered with five other Afghan fighters. A tank stood amid the rubble and ISIS fighters materialized from behind it and began firing. Then the turret of the tank turned and Nadir and his men dashed into a building with a collapsed roof as the tank shelled it. Three men with Nadir died before he was able to withdraw. The scout answered to Nadir's commander. Nadir presumed he was executed.

Nadir considers ISIS fighters to be more like rabbits than people. They seemed to breed on the battlefield. When he shot one, another fighter appeared. No matter how many he killed, more followed, walking over the rising piles of dead comrades. Nadir estimates he killed one hundred, no, two hundred ISIS fighters. Some of the men at Mother's House smirk when they hear him, but he won't back down. He may have shot more, he insists. He used crystal to be hyper alert in battle and he smoked heroin at night to sleep, and the next day he killed ISIS fighters and killed them again and again for seven months before he returned to Kabul to see his parents. He continued using drugs, however, and Laila found him living under Pol-e-Sokhta bridge, a man who had fought for his faith in Syria now devoted to staying high. Nadir intends to return to Syria by way of Iran once he collects enough money. Fighting ISIS, standing up for his faith, gave him purpose. At Mother's House, he attends NA meetings, eats, sleeps, and kills time with a gnawing unease. He worries that if he leaves Mother's House without the money necessary to reach Iran, he'll use again. He hopes his father will help him.

Laila, Nadir knows, does not want him to return to Syria. She opposes killing of any kind. Returning to a war makes little sense, she has told him. Stay in Afghanistan if you need a war. Practice the twelve steps of NA and pray. Only when you feel secure in your recovery should you decide your future.

Where my heart steers me, I will go, Nadir said.

PART TWO

I

After an hour, Laila leaves Mother's House for Taj Begum. She drives through a bazaar and then onto a street in Pol-e-kote-e-sange, a district of Kabul crammed with vendor stalls and open-air markets not far from Pol-e-Sokhta bridge. Addicts collect on the median strip dividing the highway, caught in the eye of a swirl of plastic shopping bags that bounce through traffic and cling to them. They cover themselves with prayer shawls in a failed effort to conceal the syringes they stick into their wrists, or the pipes they smoke. Other addicts sprawl out on the ground passed out, their faces red and blistered from the sun, their bodies peppered with highway residue, their lips cracked and open, their lungs filled with exhaust fumes—the rancid odor of their bodies amid the heat and the diesel fumes becomes almost intolerable. Still they sleep and get high—young and old, bearded and shaven, clothes dust-covered and unwashed, oblivious of the funk of this strip of wasteland, a settlement of their own making—and when they stir, bleary-eyed but alert, they recognize Laila creeping forward in the stalled traffic and they rise, waving their arms and lurching toward her like toddlers learning to walk.

How come you're here? one man asks. Are you collecting people?

One week from this Friday, Laila shouts above the noise of

beeping cars. I always come once a month.

Put me on your priority list.

I have no list.

Will you be here before twelve o'clock or after?

After.

What is your place? another man asks, pushing aside the first man.

It's a place that protects you. All of you need such a place.

Traffic breaks and Laila speeds forward to fill an opening between two cars.

One of us died, the first man says, hurrying to keep up with her, shouting above everyone else and the noise of traffic.

What's his name? Laila asks.

Zahir. He was hit by a car. Tell the family, if you know them.

He stops running and Laila glances in her rearview mirror at his diminishing figure and then another knot of congestion forms. As she waits for traffic to move again, more addicts approach. One man with no shirt holds a syringe, the needle stained with blood.

When are you coming, Mother?

Friday.

Do you have money? he demands, holding out a hand.

I don't. I have no medicine, no food. I'll give you a house to live in. That's all I have.

Traffic rolls forward again and Laila accelerates, the hands of the addicts dragging off her car streaking the dusty windows, and they watch her leave and then shamble back to the median and the dust and the smell and their need.

When Laila reaches Taj Begum, Ali, the gardener, opens the gate. A sheep stands tied to a post, a metal pail filled with water beside it. Laila bought it for Mother's House. The men will butcher it. Its meat will last just one day, but it will be a nice party for them.

Laila's phone has been silent all day and in the quiet of the courtyard, away from the neediness of the men at Mother's House and the addicts on the street, away from traffic and noise, the worries she has carried with her, briefly submerged beneath the tumult, rise to the surface. Why has Zakia not called? This morning, they were to have started traveling to an island between Turkey and Greece. Her children have never been on a boat. What if they get stuck in the middle of the sea?

Sitting at a table, Laila waits for Ali to bring her tea. She wearily concludes that she will have to contact her ex-husband for money if her children require more than she can provide. He isn't a bad man; he had loved her in his way. She had goals and could not live with a man who wanted her to remain in the house. A house can be like a box, Laila told him. If she must live in a box, then the world will be her box and nothing less. It wasn't her nature to live only for the love of a husband. She needed more: her poetry, her documentary filmmaking, her work with addicts.

Sipping her tea, she wonders how long her children will stay on the island. One day, one week? They're so young. Pray for my children, she says aloud to no one. Leaving your country is the worst thing in the world. On one side is Afghanistan, where the insurgents threaten Kabul every day. On the other side is Europe. The people there don't want Afghans or any foreigners. Stuck in the middle are the refugees. They want only to live.

2

At nine o'clock that evening, Mohammad Nasim walks the hall

of Mother's House, looking in on sleeping clients. Like Naser, he also works for Laila and helps maintain the program. In the quiet of the night, Mohammad considers his life. He has concluded that what he calls gaps in his childhood contributed to the problems he would have later with drugs. The parents of children he knew as a boy loved them. They played with their children, took them to bazaars. His parents, however, showed little tenderness. When he came home from school, his mother would slap him. What were you doing in school so long? she'd admonish. Who were you spending time with? You're to come home and help me around the house. He first tried opium as a teenager. It made him happy in a joyless home.

Funny how something so long ago remains so vivid. He shakes his head at the vagaries of memory, walking stiffly in the dark, swinging his prosthetic right leg forward, lurching to one side with each step. He was a second lieutenant in Afghanistan's police force in Kandahar in 2005 when he lost his leg. Every night, he heard rocket fire, and while he knew he might die in the abstract way that the living imagine something as inconceivable as death, it never occurred to him he would lose a leg.

Mohammad didn't enjoy being a policeman. He felt confined within the station. No one was permitted inside unless an officer knew that person. A stranger might be a friend, might be an enemy, who knew? Sniper fire, roadside bombs, and assaults on the station interrupted the monotony. One hundred twenty officers died during his time in Helmand. Mohammad and his colleagues smoked crack, opium, hashish, whatever became available. They had no trouble rationalizing their need to anesthetize themselves from war.

He remembers once being on a patrol when his pickup

struck a roadside bomb. He had just left Mussakala, a village in Helmand. An elder had told him, We don't want you and we don't want the Taliban. Mohammad and four other officers were smoking hash when the bomb exploded. The explosion filled his ears and his head felt as if it were inflating, and he was thrown about fifteen feet from the car, landing on the ground like a broken sack. The severed hand of another officer lay by his face, the fingers moving. When he tried to get up, he fell. He saw his right leg attached by a few strips of muscle and flesh but he didn't feel pain. It was almost as if the leg no longer belonged to him. The army evacuated him to a military hospital in Kandahar. When doctors examined his leg, sharp, electrical-like jabs convulsed his body and he screamed. He remained in Kandahar for two months before he was sent to Bagram Airbase outside Kabul. There his leg was amputated. He had three subsequent operations. It took months for doctors to wean him off morphine.

After his discharge from Bagram, he stayed with his parents in Kabul, just one of many war-wounded in the capital. No one commented on his sacrifice. Mohammad felt lost in his parents' house, resenting their pitying looks. He found comfort smoking opium and moved out. Making his way to the Pol-e-Sokhta bridge, he lived among people equally alone as he—outside of it, they appeared to live in another universe, and he sought that other dimension with them. It was there that Laila found him.

Come with me, she told him, penetrating the fog of his intoxication and extending a hand. Live again.

3

Mohammad Nadir listens to Mohammad Nasim make his nightly rounds. Nadir can't sleep. Troubling thoughts come to him unbidden, keeping him awake. He considers his service with the Afghan National Army and his time fighting in Syria. He does not think fighting the Taliban compares with combating ISIS. He knows some of the men think of him as a braggart. The ego of an addict, Mohammad Nasim has cautioned him, can get you in trouble. It is not ego, Nadir insists, but the truth of his experiences. He had fought in Helmand, but Syria proved much more difficult and he makes no apologies for the skills he honed there. He could shoot any object as far away as two thousand feet. He dampened the ledge where he rested his gun so dust would not rise and give away his position. The enemy would shoot and run, and Nadir would follow and shoot them one by one. He'd watch the man's head drop to his chest in the silence that followed his pull on the trigger, and then he would shoot four or five other ISIS fighters who tried to help him. Sometimes he struck a target in the arm or a shoulder, and he presumes they lived. At other times, he missed completely, although this was very rare, and then he would run to another spot so that when the enemy returned fire he would be elsewhere and he could shoot again and this time kill them. His commanders handed out pills. He didn't know what they were but they made his heart race. He had no problem fighting high. Being high killed the stress. When the target got close he would shoot without thought, his trigger finger doing his thinking for him.

Drones took photos, and based on those images, Syrian commanders picked neighborhoods to attack. Every time

Nadir fought, it seemed to him that more than one hundred ISIS fighters would fall, but they would not stop shooting until they had all been killed. It was good for Nadir that they fought so hard, because then he could kill more of them. ISIS often attacked in one massive wave and Nadir fired his weapon until the hot barrel burned his hands. The assault, Nadir concluded, was not a tactic but a sacrifice. Afterward, he watched dogs and cats gnaw on the dead while he rubbed water on his long rifle to cool it, and then he collected the belongings of dead ISIS fighters he'd killed: their guns, clothes, food, and photos. He examined the pictures and sometimes acknowledged that the dead man had a good family, a beautiful wife. He rubbed his thumb over the faces as if somehow this would help him learn more about them, and then he threw the pictures away. He did not need the eyes of a widow or an orphaned son or daughter watching him while he slept.

Nadir fought alongside other foreigners: Hezbollah, Iraqis, Pakistanis, even women from Chechnya who carried military supplies on their backs. All foreign fighters enlisted with units organized by the country they came from, and all of them behaved like warriors. For each month Nadir fought, he and the other foreign fighters earned five hundred sixty dollars. When they took a town or village, they collected a bonus of three hundred dollars. Nadir sent his salary to his family. He fought not for money but for his beliefs and he killed with all his heart on behalf of his Shia faith.

You're taking too much fire. ISIS can see your position, his commander told him one afternoon.

It's OK, Nadir replied. I'm here for Shia. I will kill whomever I can until I'm no longer alive.

It is your life, his commander said. I'll see you in Paradise.

4

A Friday morning. Laila prepares to pick up new addicts for Mother's House along the highway in Pol-e-kote-e-sange where she saw them gathered on the median days earlier. A rented van stands in the driveway of Taj Begum damp with dew. Ali will drive. As Laila prepares to leave, her daughter, Zakia, calls. She tells her mother that she and her brothers had a good night's sleep. But the excitement in her voice suggests something more is on her mind than small talk. In a few hours, Zakia explains, they will leave for Greece in a raft. The smuggler will not travel with them, however, because he knows no one in Greece or Europe. That worries Laila but she says nothing to Zakia to ruin her mood, her thrill that she will soon be in Europe. Once she gets off the phone, Laila calls the smuggler.

All I have are my kids, she tells him. I want them alive. Take care of them. Put them in the center of the raft.

It doesn't matter where they sit, he explains. It will still be a very dangerous journey.

I know, but for some reason I think they will be safer in the middle.

OK, the smuggler agrees.

Whatever happens, no matter how tragic, tell me whatever you hear about their journey, Laila insists.

Yes, the smuggler says.

And get back to me with someone you know in Greece.

I don't know anyone.

Think! You must! Laila insists.

Her mind conjures all sorts of horrors that might await her children, but Zakia's high spirits, even if unwarranted, leave her feeling optimistic. Everything will work out. Zakia would not be this happy if crossing to Greece was as dangerous as Laila has heard. She must control her worry so her imagination does not carry her to a place where all the scenarios end in disaster. Just get to Europe and Sweden, she thinks.

Laila slips her phone in her pocket and steps inside the van, her mind racing with thoughts of Zakia and her sons and the day ahead of them. She tries to refocus on the drive to Pol-e-kote-e-sange and the task ahead. Sometimes, she feels she should do things differently. Rather than treating addicts, she should increase understanding of what addiction is, to stop people from using drugs in the first place. But then what would happen to the people already addicted? A philosopher should consider these questions, not her.

The drive to Pol-e-kote-e-sange takes forever. To avoid traffic, she should have left before eight o'clock. It's after ten now. Congestion leaves roads in a twisted gridlock of cars and trucks jockeying for position. Laila curses while Ali maneuvers the van like a snake edging between cars and inching forward and blasting his horn as loud as the other drivers around him. Ali and Laila look at each other and laugh and then curse again. Ali moves forward once more, brazenly cutting off other cars, closing his window against the drift of sooty exhaust and wind-stirred dust.

An hour later, they reach Pol-e-kote-e-sange. They both feel as if they've been driving for hours. Before they even stop, addicts recognize Laila through her open window and swarm the van. Other addicts peer out from beneath prayer shawls and Laila returns their stares and tries to place names to their haggard faces. Has she seen them here before? Have they been to Mother's House?

Ali parks on the road, turns on the emergency lights. Drivers blast their horns, furious that he has blocked a lane, adding yet another barrier to the tangle of traffic. Laila gets out to a chorus of woes.

Mother, we need money!

Mother, the police come here and take our money and our drugs and kick us out. They beat us. The police even took our cigarettes.

Mother, the police took us to Logar Province and left us in the desert. We are treated like criminals.

A policeman, overhearing the complaints, tells Laila that he does not target addicts. He jails only those people who behave badly. He complains that she is causing a disturbance. The next time she comes here she should alert the police so they can prepare for all this commotion. Laila ignores him as the addicts surge around her. She resembles a politician campaigning for votes, the policeman scolds. She pushes her way through the crowd. The policeman does not follow her, instead turning to face the onslaught of drivers leaning out of their windows and raving about Laila's parked van.

Who wants to quit drugs? Laila shouts, ignoring the problems she has created on the highway. Who wants to come with me?

I will, a woman cries. I will!

No, Laila says, I can't take you.

The woman's eyes tear up. She wipes her face, smearing dirt across a cheek, and dabs her nose with a corner of her torn blue burqa. Holding up her worn, pebbled slippers, she looks at Laila without speaking another word.

Give me your phone number, Laila says. I'll find a place to help you.

No, the woman tells her. It is always the same for women. I'll stay here and take care of myself.

Suit yourself, Laila says. I'm looking for a man with an injured leg.

I don't know such a man, the woman says.

The crowd shifts. More people vie for Laila's attention. Mother! Mother! Mother! Laila appeals for order, waves her hands against knots of flies drawn to the odor of feces and the funk of sweating, filthy bodies, and the heat drills down on all of them from a sun unhindered by clouds.

Mother, children kick us.

Mother, hospitals won't take us.

Mother, we need food.

Laila looks to see the faces behind each shout, but their pleas and pitiful expressions blend into one long stream of words, and among all the eyes turned toward her, she can't identify even one speaker.

Whoever wants to leave, follow me, Laila says to them all. Understand, I'm taking people with no family. Families expect to be supported and I can't do that.

What is the medicine you use?

Cold water and food, Laila shouts. For one month, no more. I can't support you for the rest of your life.

Do you have a psychiatrist?

No.

Is treatment free? I went somewhere else but was beaten.

I won't beat you unless you break the rules.

The woman who spoke earlier pushes her way to the front of the crowd again.

This is the fourth night I haven't slept. I can't sleep here. Under the bridge was better for me because no one saw me. Find me a place, Mother.

I can't take you to my program, Laila says, and you wouldn't let me call anyone for you.

Laila rummages in her pocket and offers the woman fifty afghanis, about one dollar.

This money is for my lunch. Do something good with it, Laila tells her.

Only fifty afghanis. Is that all I'm worth? the woman asks.

Can we go this afternoon? a man yells. I have a broken leg and have to see a doctor first.

No, come now or wait thirty days, Laila insists. If I take you, I'll make you a real human being.

But I need a doctor.

You say your leg is broken but earlier when you asked me for money you were walking just fine.

You confuse me with someone else.

No, I see very well, Laila says.

She makes her way back to the van and opens a side door. Despite the mob that follows her, only six men get in. Laila slams the door, pulls herself into the passenger seat, and Ali starts the ignition. The honking of indignant drivers rises as he turns into traffic, and as Laila leaves the addicts who have been left behind plead for money, their voices fading as their faces recede in the rearview mirror. Laila stares ahead without blinking and without once looking back. Brushing dust off her body, she makes a face at the odor of the men seated behind her. She still feels hands touching her, still hears the shouts of Mother, Mother, Mother so clearly that she almost wonders whether they have not left. Mother, Mother, Mother. Laila feels better about collecting people here than at the Pol-e-Sokhta bridge. Here at least she works in the open air, as fetid as the air may be. Under the bridge, she can't breathe. She wonders about the man who asked for a psychiatrist. He could have come with her, he didn't. His choice. At some point, she has to cut herself off from all the problems faced by addicts; otherwise she will never rest or have a moment's peace.

Laila recognized the woman she turned away. She sold her children to her landlord because she needed money for drugs, or so Laila has heard. Who else did she recognize? An old man with one eye and another man, an amputee. They always ask for money but they never go with her.

For no discernible reason, traffic lightens and Ali reaches Mother's House sooner than Laila expected. She tells the addicts to get out and they walk single file behind her down the alley to the imposing steel door. Nadir lets them in and Laila leads them to an enclosed concrete courtyard behind the house. In one corner, a toilet. A laundry line sags from the weight of wet clothes. Shade stretches from the walls, and some recovering addicts lounge in its coolness, watching the new addicts who stand uncertainly among them with half-closed eyes.

You will get a shower and haircut, and then you'll sleep, Laila shouts like a drill sergeant. You're still high. It will take five days to detox, to get rid of all the drugs in your bodies. You will sweat as if you've been exercising. You will take a cold shower every day to help with the sweats.

She tells them to strip to their underwear. They turn over their clothes and all personal belongings—cigarettes, money, prayer beads, drugs—to Nadir, who flushes the drugs down a drain. He then distributes clean clothes but tells them not to put them on. Not yet.

We have to wash you and cut your hair, he explains.

If we catch you smoking opium or using any other drugs, we will beat you, Laila warns. You can't leave for thirty days. There is no going back. Whoever breaks the rules, we will talk to them with this.

She raises an orange rubber tube and slaps it against the ground.

Nadir tells the new clients to stand in a line and squat. Stepping behind them, he puts on plastic gloves, picks up a hose and runs cold water over a man who holds his bandaged left hand away from his body so it doesn't get wet. Almost instantly, the man begins shivering, his body blossoming with goose bumps. Nadir shampoos his hair, massaging his head as the man washes his body with soap. When he finishes rinsing his hair, Nadir takes a hand razor and meticulously shaves the man's scalp, working from his neck to his forehead. Clumps of lice-filled hair fall and the man flinches at tiny razor cuts that Nadir inflicts—soon not even stubble remains, and blood runs down the man's neck and around his ears as Nadir rinses the now bald white head, water and hair pooling at his feet. The man stands when Nadir finishes and removes the bandage from his hand, exposing open sores from a burn.

What do we do? Nadir asks Laila.

Laila peers at the wound.

Apply some antiseptic cream, she says.

It hurts, don't touch, the man cries out, cringing.

Let me wash it with water, Nadir says.

It hurts!

Just suffer this once, Nadir insists, gripping the man's hand.

This is my second time here, the man says between gritted teeth. I worked here as a servant

We don't have servants, Nadir says. We all have chores. That does not make us servants. You were not special. If this is your second time, I will shave your eyebrows to show it is your second time.

Don't shave my eyebrows, the man pleads.

I have to, Nadir says. It's the rules, so that others will understand what happens if you start using again and come back.

The man closes his eyes and shakes with pain and cold as Nadir rinses his hand.

This reminds me of my first day, Nadir tells him. After a week or so you will feel much better.

How was it for you?

I tried to hide heroin in my cheek. I swallowed it, four and a half grams. Oh, I got so sick. Mother was angry, but I was too sick for her to beat me. I have seen other addicts try to hide their drugs in drains. They think they can take it out later, but when they look for it, it has been washed away.

Nadir releases the man's hand. Shaking almost uncontrollably, the man covers his face with a towel and Nadir leads him past the laundry line and a water tank to a corner where he huddles in the sun. Nadir gives him a hand razor.

You will shave your crotch and armpits. That is your responsibility.

When Nadir finishes bathing and cutting the hair of each new man, he throws away the razors and carries the towels to the laundry room. The new clients watch him and then squint at the clear sky, mouths open, reborn to the world. Beside them sit the two shackled men who had tried to escape.

Be careful here, Mother beats everyone, one of the chained men comments, without realizing that Laila is standing behind him. The other day, he continues, she beat a guy who looked for a key to escape out the front door. There's no humanity here.

No humanity? an enraged Laila interrupts, stepping in front of him and looking down at where he sits. Where is the humanity out there? Here, you're human again. We give you empathy. No humanity! I'm a mother in Afghanistan. I sent my children away so they could have a life! I know all there is to know about humanity!

The chained man leans away from her and covers his face and she spins around and storms into an empty office, pacing furiously. The day had started so well and then this stupid fool opened his mouth. That little, ungrateful ass! Everybody wants more from her. She is never good enough. Are her sacrifices not sufficient? Do they not see how she struggles?

Searching for her phone, Laila dials Zakia. She wants to hear the voices of her real children and to tell them how much she misses them and to listen to them say how much they miss her, but Zakia doesn't answer. Laila wipes tears from her eyes. Staring out the door, she sees the shackled men resume talking to the new clients. Let them say what they will. They'd been through Mother's House once before. Laila took them back only because their families begged her, and then they tried to escape, so she beat them. Their wives and parents had no complaints. Do what you must, they told her.

Everyone knows the rules and signs them with a thumb-print, Laila reminds herself. She doesn't like to strike anyone but she sees no other way. If you don't have a fresh stick, donkeys and cows won't do what they're told, and addicts can be just as stubborn as farm animals. She feels bad for two or three days after she beats a client, and when she sees him again, he apologizes to her or she apologizes to him, and he forgives her and she forgives him, as any mother would.

5

Two days after their arrival, six of the new clients kneel in the courtyard, naked except for their underwear, while Nadir holds the hose above their heads and rinses their bodies for twenty minutes. Laila believes cold showers help with detox and insists the men submit to this treatment their first week in Mother's House.

I get crazy with this, a man complains. You do nothing but wash us in cold water.

It is your sacrifice for being an addict, Nadir says.

No, there have to be other steps like medication to help us not get sick.

If I give you meds, you'll repeat your addiction.

Water splashes off the men's bowed, bare heads, and their pale bodies shine in the sun like waxed figures. Nadir remembers how he perspired every day of his first week at Mother's House and all the bone-chilling baths he took, how afterward he still sweated.

What is that cap you wear? one of the new clients asks.

I wore this in Syria, Nadir says. It's the color of the desert, as was my uniform.

Why did you fight in Syria?

Because I am Shia.

In Pakistan, the police told me I should not use drugs, the new client replied. Drugs, they told us, are not for Muslims, so I went to a church and said I wanted to convert. I went every Sunday. I didn't really want to convert. I was lying so I could use and not be bothered by the police, because I had become a Christian. I told the police I'd converted and they said, OK, it's not against the church to drink and take drugs. That's why Christianity is the faith of infidels. I told them I didn't care. I was tired of being Muslim.

Once the drugs get out of your body, you'll want to be a Muslim again, Nadir said.

There is enough fighting in Afghanistan. If I were you, I'd stay home and fight here. It would be simpler.

Mother tells me the same thing, but one does not fight for convenience.

The new client waits for him to continue but Nadir says nothing more, his mind elsewhere. He had no rank in Syria. Foreign fighters like him were given duties based on their abilities but received no special recognition. Nadir's skill: He could shoot. He carried a rifle and an Uzi. He especially liked the Uzi. The submachine gun fit his hand well and gave him confidence when he fired it. He didn't have to aim as he did with a long rifle. Just point and shoot. Other soldiers carried PPKs and RPGs and Kalashnikovs and sometimes he shouldered those weapons too, but always he had an Uzi.

Nadir saw no chemical weapons in areas Syrian forces took from ISIS, but he noticed empty canisters that Syrian officers told him had held chemical weapons. He found Yugoslavian arms—M16s mostly, and some M49s. Nadir fought well. He felt he was born for war. When he received an order, he'd carry it out without thinking. He yearns to fight again and feels he's missing something, like a boy who must remain inside while his friends play outdoors. His parents don't want him to return to Syria, but he has no money and he doesn't know anyone with a good job in Kabul. If he leaves Mother's House without work, he'll get frustrated and use again. Besides, no job would match combating ISIS on behalf of all Shia people. So he will return to Syria, fight and shoot, do what he does so well. He'll be provided with food, a barrack, a weapon. It's all he needs in this life. In some ways it will be like Mother's House, but instead of Narcotics Anonymous meetings, he'll consult with his commanders and do as they tell him. He won't get high. Using drugs in battle made him vigilant, but excessively so; he was too unstable. He assaulted everything. He attacked the door of an empty house one afternoon, shooting it so many times that nothing was left but splinters, and there was no one inside. More often, he didn't remember what he did when he was high, and when he did, they were things he didn't want to remember. Like wounded ISIS fighters bleeding from the neck, hands over their wound, blood pulsing between their fingers while Syrian officers executed them. Perhaps he just thought he recalled these things, because he was high. Perhaps he was hallucinating: he doesn't know. He thanks God he no longer uses, and for this second chance to reach Paradise as a clean and sober fighter.

PART THREE

I

Zakia sounds so exhausted. The signal on Laila's cell phone is weak but the weariness in her daughter's voice comes across clearly as her worried mother sits in the courtyard of Taj Begum. However, the important thing is she and her brothers are safe. They've reached the Greek island of Lesvos.

The crossing had been as dangerous as Laila had feared. The smuggler pointed to the horizon and told her children, This is the direction of Greece. Follow the moon and stay to your left. Then he was gone. Zakia, Murtaza, and Mustafa sat in a raft for eighteen hours with thirty-seven other people, mostly from Syria. Laila called Zakia during the crossing. Leave us alone, a sobbing Zakia chastised her mother. Water is coming into the raft and we have to concentrate if we want to live! As they neared Lesvos, Greek fishermen approached and followed them in. The fishermen pulled the raft onto a beach and Zakia and her brothers got out, soaking wet and aching with cold. They followed some Syrians to a police station where they registered as refugees and got bus tickets to a camp in Athens, where Zakia called her mother.

There are so many refugees, Zakia tells her. Even the parks are full. Laila advises her to find a church, but Zakia says the churches, too, are packed with homeless people, and a simple room costs ten euros. Greek families brought water, food, and pallets for the refugees to sleep on, but because so many people are in need, the throng became unruly with men and women grabbing what they could like dogs fighting over scraps, and in the confusion Zakia and her brothers lost what food they'd been given. After the crowd had settled, a woman with a baby offered them some bread.

The behavior of the other refugees infuriates Laila. She did not raise her children to snatch food from others, and as a consequence of their good behavior they now have nothing but bread. At least they reached Greece. Zakia promises to call again once she knows where they'll travel next.

Noticing the gardeners watching her, Laila asks for tea. Ali hurries off while the others get back to work. All of them know about her children. They think she is rich because she owns a restaurant and sent her children to Europe. They don't know she bought the restaurant on credit to support the work of Mother's House and that she borrowed more money to get her children out of Afghanistan. She trusts only a few people, and she wonders about them. The belief that she has money changes how people think of her, even her friends. She knows how quickly addicts can turn against her in the presence of money. Sometimes she wonders whether some of the men in Mother's House are police informers. The authorities wouldn't have to offer them much, maybe nothing at all. Or maybe they'd promise them drugs. The informers could tell the police who has entered Mother's House and the police could then pass on the information to drug dealers. To what end, she doesn't know, but just thinking about it increases her suspicion and paranoia.

In 2012, a mullah accused Laila of operating a brothel. She was an independent woman with a business. What business other than a brothel would such a woman operate? the mullah asked, preaching from a mosque. He offered one of her former clients, an eighteen-year-old named Mateen, one hundred dollars to kill her. On a Wednesday night, Mateen climbed the restaurant walls and crept toward the main building where Laila slept. Ali and a few other employees cleaning the kitchen saw a shadow stretching across the ground and were suspicious. They called to Mateen and he ran but the men caught him. What do you want? Money? She will help you. No, Mateen said, I wanted to kill her, and then he explained the mullah's plan. They told Mateen never to come back and let him go. In the morning, before he watered the grass, Ali told Laila what happened. It's not safe for you here at night, he told her.

Laila wept at the mention of Mateen's name. Of all people! She'd grown close to him. At Mother's House, he would hug her and sometimes curl up at her feet to sleep like a puppy. He had had a difficult life. A man who once quarreled with his father shot his parents dead when Mateen was a boy. He lived with relatives who felt obligated to care for him but did not love him.

Considering his life and his time in the program, Laila consoled herself with the thought that he was sick, an addict who had resumed using. He was no longer himself, not the clean and sober Mateen she had grown so fond of. He needed money for drugs. She has not seen him in who knows how long and would say nothing to him if she did. She has no doubt he feels shame for his actions.

Had he found work, Mateen might have ignored the mullah's offer. Addicts think detox is bad, but detox is nothing compared to leaving Mother's House without a job. Laila asks shopkeepers to hire her clients, but few people have a position to offer, or if they do, they don't want to bring on an addict. So many people tell her, This is a mistake, your helping these people. They aren't good. You should dig a hole and bury them. They are of no use. Yes, you are right, Laila agrees, to avoid an argument. She walks away and appeals to the next shopkeeper.

One graduate of Mother's House now owns his own shop and sells clothes and shoes, yet he remains as needy as he was his first day in the program. He came to the restaurant one afternoon and asked for money. C'mon, Laila told him, you should help me. You have a good job. No, the man insisted. You should help me. Laila shook her head. I have my own children, she admonished. Stop being greedy or you can go back to your real mother if you need so much help.

2

As Laila waits at the restaurant for Zakia to call again, the residents at Mother's House gather together after an NA meeting and kill time before lunch, leaning against the walls or sprawling on the floor, hands behind their heads. One man, Khalid, adjusts the dial of a TV but receives nothing but static. Five other men around him stare at the screen. They all know about Laila's children. Most of them made a similar trek to Europe only to be deported.

I was in Copenhagen when I started using, Khalid says. I was twenty-two. I went through Iran, Turkey, Greece, Italy, Germany, and France. It was 2005. There was too much fighting in Afghanistan. War, man, I didn't want to die.

The other men speak in turn of their trials leaving Afghanistan and confronting addiction:

I started using in Iran. My boss invited me to his home and gave me hash and opium. First only on Fridays and then later every day for seven years. When I returned to Afghanistan to be with my family, I used crack and crystal. I had a brother in the UK and I lived with him for seven months. I didn't use then, but after I was deported in 2011, I started using again, this time with heroin and crack too. I was depressed. I don't want to be this way. I have a plan. I want to get back to the UK and work construction with my brother.

I'm waiting to leave at a good time. I can't live here forever. My family is in Pakistan but they don't want me back. I got in a fight there and stabbed a guy. He was in a hospital for five months and twenty days. My family paid his expenses.

We all want to leave, but how many of us will do so successfully?

Maybe Mother's children will help us once they're settled.

If they make it, inshallah, Khalid says.

Inshallah, they all respond.

My family is in Iran, Khalid continues. My brother is in the UK. I'll go to Iran or the UK, you'll see.

My family is in Pakistan. I'll go to Pakistan.

My mother came here from Iran. Where she lives, I will live.

The conversation flows on without pause, their voices blending together with nowhere to go.

In Denmark, drugs were really easy to find, Khalid tells them. I was working in a casino and a cop turned me in. I had been living there illegally for five months. There're no rules in Denmark, man, it's real free. I tried going back and made it to Turkey but got caught and was deported again.

We all are thinking of leaving. If we stay, we'll use again. There's nothing here. It's no life under the bridge. You know, when you're high the time passes and you feel happy, but when you're not high, the time passes slowly. When you're high, you close your eyes, and when you open them again the day is gone.

I quit once four months ago. I had no job and started using again.

In Denmark, Khalid says, if you have work, you won't use.

I spent four years in Iran and never used any drugs. Just worked. It kept me busy. Eighteen months ago I was clean. I lost my job, started using. My family asked me for money but I had nothing.

I worked for a bodyguard. He got high for sex.

Our families, if we tell them we're clean, they don't trust us, Khalid complains. They don't accept us and we end up on the streets.

We should be given jobs, and if we use again, the employer can behead us.

I had a tailor shop, I made good money and I still used. I used for enjoyment. It's about self-control. If I'm too happy or sad, I use.

I can give the example of my uncle. His wife left him and his heart broke and he started using, begging, and stealing. For me, it started when I saw a friend shot and killed. His name was Hamid. I haven't forgotten. I fell down and prayed to God to help me forget, but I cannot.

I was in Iran with four friends. We were riding motorcycles and had an accident and three of my friends died. Ten days later, I started using again.

I had a friend who got into a fight at a martial arts club in Kabul, Khalid recalls. The other guy lost. I'll kill you, this guy said. My friend thought he was joking, but the next day, this guy shot my friend. My friend's brother killed him and his mother too.

We live in our own worlds of trouble. We don't know anything outside our lives. I didn't know we had an election. Now I see we have a new president, Ghani.

We're all disappointed, Khalid says. That's why we want to leave Afghanistan.

Mohammad Nadir listens to the conversation but offers no comment. He does not share the uncertainty of the other addicts. He has no doubts about his future. When he has the money, he will return to Syria. He assumes that he will have to train again in Iran since he has been away for so long, about thirty days of drills using a Kalashnikov and RPGs. He will have nothing to do with recruits who fight only for a salary. Those fighters are not worth risking his life to save—but the holy warriors, he will die for.

From his first time in Syria, he remembers men who never mastered the most basic concepts of being a fighter. After one month, they still couldn't hit a target or assemble a gun. You're too nervous, Nadir told them. You're thinking of what's to come. Think only of today. What's to come will be here soon enough and it will not be so bad. The first ten to fifteen minutes of your first battle, you'll be scared but then you'll get used to the noise, and after you fire your first bullet all fear will leave you. The recruits agreed to relax but, despite his encouragement, their fear continued to betray them, and they were sent home.

That time feels so long ago. Nadir wonders whether American jets continue to bomb ISIS. Their attacks helped Syrian fighters. He remembers his commanders ordering withdrawals while the Americans pummeled ISIS positions, supporting Syrian troops whether they meant to or not. No one talked about the Americans much. They were fighting a holy war and the Americans were infidels, but everyone appreciated American bombs.

3

On the second floor of Taj Begum, Laila and three women sit in a room stitching blue waitress uniforms with white trim. She feeds cloth into a sewing machine while cradling her cell phone against her left ear and shoulder. She waits for Zakia to pick up. No answer. She lets the phone slide into her lap and curses. The other women chuckle. Her children left Greece the previous night. She wonders now whether they'll make it to Germany next or stop somewhere in between.

You're sewing it upside down, she snaps at one of the women. You have to start from the other side.

Holland or Sweden, which one is better? Sweden, Laila believes. She has heard Holland treats refugees well. Maybe her children should stop there. Or Norway. Friends have told her good things about Norway. Perhaps Norway. But doesn't it get very cold?

A fight between government forces and the Taliban the previous day occupies her mind. Just a few hours north of

Kabul, the Taliban for twenty-four hours seized Kunduz, the sixth-largest city in Afghanistan with a population of nearly three hundred thousand. The government regained control but what does that mean? If it lost Kunduz once, can it not lose it again? She can envision the Taliban capturing Kabul. They did it before. She does not believe ISIS is in Afghanistan. As far as she is concerned, what people call ISIS is the Taliban under a different name. Her children worry about her.

What about you, mother? Zakia had asked her before she and her brothers left Kabul.

I'll be fine, Laila assured her, but she really does not know. She can't say what the future holds. She won't go. Her life is here. Maybe she'll fight. Maybe it will all come down to that.

Laila feeds more cloth into the sewing machine, glancing at her phone as if willing Zakia to call. She looks at the women seated around her. Their husbands are addicts. She knows the women think she should set up a house for them. She has explained why she can't, but still they expect her to. She has an upcoming meeting with the minister of health to discuss anti-narcotics strategy. She will tell him that addicted women need help as much as the men. A waste of breath, she suspects, but she'll mention it anyway.

4

At Mother's House, the men listen to updates about Kunduz on TV.

What kind of police force can be defeated by the enemy? Nadir asks. If I had been there, I would have killed twenty Taliban with my long rifle. It was not a defeat but a betrayal. How can a small number of Taliban take a city without the cooperation of the Afghan police and army? Sometimes in Syria, government forces took villages from ISIS, and ISIS would pay the villagers to let them return. He thinks the same thing happened in Kunduz.

I fought with the Americans in 2012 in Kunduz, says Ali Raza, a thirty-year-old heroin and opium addict new to the program. We fought for two days and two nights. I myself destroyed three guns. The Afghan National Army were good fighters then.

However, Ali continues, the Taliban fighters were just as good. He fought with them before changing sides. He had no choice because he grew up in Kandahar, where the Taliban was strongest and recruited fighters. On his fifteenth birthday, a Taliban commander came to his house and demanded one child for the insurgency, or his father could pay one hundred forty dollars as a protection fee. Ali was the oldest child and the only boy. His father turned him over to the commander. Ali knew this day would come, as he had seen the same thing happen to some of his friends. Still, it was all he could do to not cry. His mother wept and he did not look at her as the commander led him away.

From 1999 to 2001 he worked with the Taliban as a mechanic. He learned how to drive Jeeps, trucks, and abandoned Soviet tanks. His commander was a short man with a heavy black beard and a prosthetic leg who did not like to eat alone and often ate with his fighters. He was well connected with members of the Taliban government.

One day while he was patching a tire, Ali saw his commander take the guns of six prisoners from a Pashtun tribe that opposed the Taliban. The commander showed them into a room and through a window Ali watched him serve them tea.

Then he took them outside again and lined them up against a wall. He took out his PPK and faced them.

I have to kill you so others know that if they fight me, I will kill them, the commander said. He shot each one in the head.

Seeing his commander kill the six Pashtuns disturbed Ali. In his dreams, he saw blood spurt from their heads like water from a fountain. The dead asked him, How could you watch us die and do nothing? He had no good answer, and escaped them only by waking up. He smoked heroin and opium, and while he was high, he felt no need to respond to their questions, felt no responsibility to them or anyone. Some Taliban commanders owned poppy fields along the borders of Pakistan and Iran, and drugs were always available.

After 9/11, the commander told Ali and the other fighters that the Americans were coming to kill Osama bin Laden. Should we turn him over, he asked? No! the men shouted. When they heard that Pakistan was cooperating with the US, his commander stopped talking about bin Laden. Instead, he asked his men whether they should surrender. Never! they shouted.

That's right, we can't surrender, even though our friends have deserted us, the commander agreed.

Then he left for Helmand and never returned, and Ali's unit capitulated to American forces about a month later. Rumors circulated that the Americans killed the commander and examined his organs, because they wanted to see what made him such a good officer. Ali did not believe these stories, but the commander's nephew swore they were true.

In November 2001, Ali's unit received orders from a Taliban commander in Kunduz to attack Mazar-e-Sharif, a city in the north. His battalion flew by helicopter from Herat in the western part of Afghanistan to Kunduz, about 105 miles east of Mazar. Taliban commanders divided their fighters in two groups. The first group entered Mazar, but Abdul Rashid Dostum, a general allied with the American-led military coalition, annihilated the Taliban forces. He then surrounded the remaining group of Taliban fighters to which Ali was attached. Instead of killing them, Dostum ordered the one hundred fifty fighters into metal shipping containers pocked with bullet holes and locked them inside without food or water.

The heat and miasma of feces and urine drove the prisoners mad. They screamed and wept and prayed and clawed at one another to reach the bullet holes for air. The fighters remained in the containers for three days before they were shipped to Sheberghan prison, about a ten-minute drive away. By the time the containers arrived, dozens of prisoners had died. Ali does not remember being removed from the container. He awoke in a prison cell with a headache from heat and dehydration. About two weeks later, the Red Crescent provided medical care. When he thinks about that time, Ali does not feel anger at Dostum, because the Taliban did the same thing. He himself had put Mujahideen fighters in shipping containers in which they later died. Dostum had more humanity than the Taliban because he did not dispatch the containers as far as the Taliban had. Fewer Taliban prisoners died under Dostum than Mujahideen died under the Taliban. Ali feels grateful for Dostum's generosity.

Ali remained in Sheberghan for six months. After his release in 2002, he returned to his family in Kandahar. His parents told him that one of his cousins, a Taliban fighter, beheaded another cousin who had joined the new Afghan police force. I can't trust you if you kill members of my own family, Ali told a Taliban commander who asked him to join the resistance to the Americans. I can't even trust my own cousin now. He left Kandahar for Kabul and switched his allegiance to the newly formed Afghan National Army. He was stationed in Ghazni, and although he was no longer with the Taliban, people still wanted to kill him. There was always a reason to light up an opium pipe.

None of the addicts speak when Ali finishes his story. The misfortunes of their lives don't compare with being locked in a shipping container. Nadir, however, is not as impressed.

I have been in jail too, in Iran, he tells Ali.

When Iranians made fun of Afghans, Nadir fought them, because he was half Afghan. One time, he saw a woman being teased by two Iranians. Nadir was in a taxi and he told the driver to stop and he got out and brawled with the men harassing the woman. Then four more Iranians joined the fight and one man stabbed Nadir in his right shoulder and Nadir lurched away with the knife still in his shoulder. He fought on with one arm and the Iranians ran away. At a hospital, a doctor examined his shoulder, told him to look away, and pulled the knife out. Nadir fainted, but when he woke he felt fine.

Ali and the other men look at one another. A few have trouble keeping a straight face. Let Nadir talk, their smirks suggest. Sure, we don't believe him, but we all must live together.

Nadir, giving no indication that he is aware of their doubts, launches into another story. This time he tells of the Iranian police stopping him when he was drunk. You've been drinking, you dirty Afghan, one of the officers yelled at him, and the second officer slapped him. Nadir punched him in the nose and both officers fled. As Nadir chased them into an alley, an officer in a parked police car shot at him and Nadir stopped running and raised his hands. The officers arrested him and shoved him into the car. In the front passenger seat sat the policeman he had punched, blood spilling from his nose. Officers beat Nadir at the station, but he was so drunk he didn't feel any pain until the next morning.

Why did you punch an officer? a judge asked him.

I thought he was a thief, Nadir lied.

Well, you hit a policeman and broke his nose. You have to go to jail.

Nadir served two months and twenty days.

That's my story, he says.

His listeners don't respond. Perhaps he did punch a policeman. Who can say? Who will listen to their stories when they leave Mother's House? Who will care about their lives?

What else? Ali asks, and Nadir launches into another story.

5

As the addicts entertain one another with their tales, Laila holds a party at Taj Begum to celebrate Eid and raise money for Mother's House. More than one hundred fifty guests fill the courtyard, milling about the tables and drinking fruit juice and tea, the minister of health, Dr. Ferozuddin Feroz, among them. Laila pulls him aside and asks him to establish a home for addicted women. Dr. Feroz says he likes the idea but won't make a commitment. It's a matter of money and priorities, he explains. Laila urges him to speak with the minister of commerce and industry. He could ask businesses to contribute money.

In Islam, she reminds him, the prophet says the money you have that is not necessary for your survival should be given to the poor. Ask businesses to give me their extra money for a house for women.

Dr. Feroz offers her a thin smile but promises nothing. Laila suggests they drive to the Pol-e-Sokhta bridge so she can show him where addicts live, but he laughs and then gives another lean smile.

After an hour of mingling, Laila steps behind a lectern and asks everyone to be seated.

Afghanistan is facing a drug crisis, insecurity, and unemployment, she says, the microphone crackling, interrupting her with volleys of static and hisses. We as citizens have a responsibility to everyone, including addicts, both men and women. No one but us can help one another. The government is very weak, the private sector weak. Let this night, let this place become a place where a movement can start to strengthen our country by caring for the least among us.

She receives a strong round of applause, including from Dr. Feroz, but afterward, the applause nothing more than a fading memory, she sees him walking to the front gate without even saying good night.

Around eleven o'clock, when everyone has left, as napkins and glasses litter tables and the empty chairs form vague shapes in the darkness and the noise of idle chatter has given way to the hum of bugs, Laila stands to one side of the patio and wonders what, if anything, the night has accomplished. Little, she concludes. Her guests were happy to talk about any problem she mentioned, but they had no intention of dirtying their hands. Many of them did offer to make a donation. Today or tomorrow, they told her. So many promises. She'll see how well they follow through. Others saw no reason to give her anything, because they assumed donors supported her work. They looked surprised when she told them she used her own money and what little friends gave her. On Facebook, Laila posts appeals, Give to Mother's House, and people she does not know accuse her of begging. Well, she admits, she is.

She had her phone turned off during the party, and of course Zakia called and left a message. Good news: she and her brothers reached Vienna by spending all their money on a taxi that drove them from Athens through Serbia and into Austria. They'd wanted to take a bus but the driver insisted on seeing their visas, which, of course, they didn't have. In Vienna, they got into a shoving match with other refugees and lost their place in a food line.

In her message, Zakia promised to call again. They will need more money, Laila knows. Where will she get it? How many countries lie between Austria and Switzerland and how much will it cost to get there? Laila waits as if the noises of the night will provide an answer. Then her phone rings and she answers. Not Zakia, but the smuggler who took them out of Afghanistan. He wants to know whether her children reached Europe. Laila ignores his question.

Do you know anyone who can send them money in Austria? You do? Can you give me their number? Thank you.

She hangs up. The smuggler will call back with a contact. She hates waiting. What if he forgets to call? Or was lying to get her off the phone?

Laila's phone rings again and she snatches it up, expecting the smuggler, but instead she hears the voice of a woman she doesn't know. Her husband is addicted to opium. Can you help? Come here and we can talk, Laila tells her. After we talk, I'll give you the address to Mother's House. Before I accept your husband, I need to see you to know whether you're serious and whether you're willing to kick him out of your house. Then he'll feel vulnerability and see the consequences of his addiction. The woman says nothing. Call me again when you're ready, Laila tells her.

She no sooner hangs up when her phone rings again. It's Zakia. I talked to the smuggler, Laila tells her, and once I hear from him about how to send you money, I'll let you know. Ask people around you how they get their money; obviously they are getting some. Do they know anybody there we can send money to? You have to try to get answers as much as I am. She has many more questions she wants to ask: How are you holding up? Where are you staying? But the connection is poor and Zakia doesn't want to run low on minutes. I have to go, she says, and hangs up. Laila sets the phone down, half expecting it to ring again. When it doesn't, she closes her eyes.

I should sleep, she tells herself, but she knows she won't.

6

At Mother's House, Mohammad Nadir sits with Ali Raza, the former Taliban soldier, eating bread and fruit. A man near them, a one-time police officer, comments that he will never leave Mother's House, where he can eat, shower, and use a toilet. He won't go into the world and be a donkey again to everyone who thinks they can tell him what to do. He refuses to tell the other addicts his name. He trusts no one, believes people are looking for him.

Nadir does not question his fears. He has probably earned them; who knows? Nadir doesn't like being around crazy people, because he worries he could become like them. He has had bad dreams that distract him. He talks to himself sometimes, responding to the words of dead men. When he returns to Syria, the nightmares will go away. He'll be fighting and the images in his head will be real and he'll no longer remember bad things, because there'll be nothing to remember. The bad things will be all around him, leaving other things—good things, like his time at Mother's House—left over for his dreams. He just needs money to reach Iran. He hasn't heard from his father. Maybe he'll ask Mother.

Do you remember your first time in combat? Nadir asks Ali.

Yes, of course, Ali says. The Americans used heavy weapons that could fire from behind their lines. Taliban fighters died, their bodies in pieces. I wanted to run, but if I was caught I would have been shot. If you so much as duck, you're not a warrior, my commander told me, so I looked straight ahead, my neck stiff with tension, and chewed tobacco. I'd rather have smoked, but the flare of a cigarette might have given away our position.

Nadir nods. In his first fight, he entered a house and shot at an ISIS fighter but he missed and the man raised his hands and Nadir turned him over to his commander, who passed him on to an Iranian officer. Later that day, his commander gave Nadir a box: inside, a pair of amputated hands. Here is what's left of your prisoner, his commander said. Nadir dreamed of those hands for a long time. He knew men who, after their first battle, never returned to their units. I won't come back, they said. They stepped over bodies and kept walking until Nadir no longer saw them. He cleaned his weapon and stayed.

He remembers the first time a friend died, Khalid. Nadir had been shooting video with his cell phone during a lull in fighting outside Damascus when Khalid raised his head to watch. Get down, Khalid, I'm filming, Nadir said, and then Khalid's head exploded from a sniper's bullet and Nadir dropped his phone and began screaming and then he went crazy and fired an RPG in the direction of the shooter. Gunfire pummeled Nadir's position and someone shouted, Get down! and grabbed him by the shoulder and jerked him to the ground.

When I was shooting, I told myself it was bullets killing people, not me, Ali says. What do you think?

I think you and your bullets were killing people together, Nadir tells him.

When I was fighting with the government of Karzai, after we captured a Taliban fighter, we'd take them to Bagram and beat them, Ali continues. I beat them myself with my gun. We hated them because their bombs killed our friends. We beat them with pipes and with the butts of our rifles. One time we had a Taliban commander. We kept him prisoner for a long time. Whenever we heard about a dead comrade, we beat him. I can't blame bullets or anything else for that. I beat him.

I didn't harm prisoners, Nadir says. I just killed them. I told them, Face the wall, and then I shot them and released them from this life—not with one or two bullets, but with a complete magazine—but I never touched them. Once I had a hostage who said he had a key to heaven. I told him to keep his key and shot him, but he did not die. I said, OK, open the door to Paradise and I shot him again. I could never beat anyone.

Let's talk about something else, Ali says. I don't want to fight again.

Where will you go after you finish here? Kandahar? Will the Taliban recruit you again?

They will try, of course, Ali says.

Will you use?

I don't know. I am confused.

I went outside yesterday for the first time since I've been

here, Nadir says. I called home. I wanted to be alone when I talked to my family. My father was out. I told my mother, I'm not addicted anymore. Are you coming home? she asked. Not yet, I told her. I'm going to Iran and then Syria.

7

The next morning, Laila speaks with Zakia. Through a Facebook friend, Laila has found an Afghan family in Vienna willing to give her children a room for no charge. They can shower and eat. Zakia says they have not bathed since they left Turkey and have eaten only what food strangers have given them.

I will send you money, Laila said, but spend it carefully.

Do you think we're here for sightseeing? Zakia snaps, shocking Laila into silence. She knows Zakia is frustrated and tired, but Laila hasn't slept either, and her nerves feel brittle as sticks. She wishes Zakia could see beyond her stress and show a little appreciation. Afghans respect family and never talk to their parents this way. Is this the behavior of Western children? What will living in Europe do to Zakia and her brothers? Will their personalities change?

Some sleepless nights have felt like one hundred nights for Laila. She saw a video on Facebook recently of Afghan migrants in Germany. Two girls were raped, a pregnant woman was shot, and an eight-year-old boy jumped from a speeding car and was now in a coma. All Laila had wanted was to get her children out of Afghanistan to safety. But did she make the right decision?

She gets off the phone and decides to visit Mother's House. Some of the men, like Mohammad Nadir, are approaching their thirty-day mark and she needs to know what they intend to do. She'll let them stay longer if they have a plan, but they can't just linger. Nadir, she knows, intends to leave for Syria. To get sober only to die in a war not his own makes little sense to her. She wishes he would change his mind. But like her own children, he has to decide for himself.

As she prepares to leave, a man calls and asks Laila whether she has a room he can use for sex. I don't provide what you want, she tells him. If you're an addict, you can come here, but for no other reason. I heard you have prostitutes, the man insists. Laila hangs up but he calls back demanding she provide him with a prostitute. I don't have any girls, but if you have a wife, sister, or mother and send them to me, the next time someone like you calls I'll provide them with a member of your family. The man hangs up.

Just because I'm a woman running a business, Laila mutters to herself.

8

As Laila reaches Mother's House, Zakia calls again. She and her brothers are leaving Austria for Germany on a train. They've decided not to remain in Austria despite the offer of a free room. Tired of traveling, they want to finish their journey. Maybe they'll go on to Sweden, maybe not. They'll see. Zakia doesn't know when she'll contact her mother again.

Call when you're able, Laila urges.

Standing by her car, she stares at her feet. Germany. Why not push on to Sweden? But Laila can't make these choices for her children. They are traveling, not her. She takes a deep breath and locks the car. Another deep breath and then she walks down the dirt alley to Mother's House and rings the bell. Nadir lets her in.

How are you?

I am good, Mother.

Just for today, stay clean. Then tomorrow, you can look back on today and say, I have another day of success.

Yes, Mother, that's what I do.

Pointing to a new client, he says, This man wanted to escape this morning. I stopped him.

No, no, the man protests. I thank you for this place.

Never say you're going unless I tell you, or I'll beat you, Laila says.

I have no complaints, the man maintains.

Another new client grumbles about how cold he gets when Nadir hoses him down with cold water.

Wrap yourself in a blanket, Laila advises him, and drink hot tea until four o'clock, but not after or you'll be going to the toilet all night.

We're not getting as much food, another man complains. I never have a full stomach.

Accept what we have, Nadir interjects before Laila can respond. You're here for treatment, not to party. I have been here almost thirty days. I don't complain. I work hard to stay clean. Follow my example. Do as I do and you will stay clean.

Don't show off, Laila cautions Nadir. Don't say "I" so much. Whenever you say "I," it shows you have too much pride.

Nadir stares at Laila, a furious look on his face for being reprimanded in front of others, especially new clients.

You'll give me respect and do as I advise, she tells him, returning his angry look.

He holds her stare.

I'm going to Syria, he tells her.

When?

The end of this week. Money or no money. I'll walk to Iran

if I must.

I have my own children to worry about. Don't make me worry about you.

I'm sorry, Mother.

I wish you wouldn't.

Mother, it's all I know.

9

While Laila visits Mother's House, Ali finishes watering the grass at Taj Begum, as he does every morning. A thirteen-year-old boy, Rohalluh Hussini, follows him, unsnagging the hose from chairs and tables. Rohalluh has worked for Laila for about a year. One Friday night, he saw people outside the restaurant and asked them for money. He returned the next day and the day after that and the day after that and got to know the regular customers. Then he began washing Laila's car. After two weeks Laila told him, Come inside, and he began working for her.

Why do so few people come to eat here anymore? Rohalluh asks.

Ali shrugs.

The restaurant is not doing well.

Why? Rohalluh persists.

How do you discuss business with a boy? Ali asks himself. He tries explaining that jobs are a problem. So many nongovernmental organizations have left Afghanistan because of the violence. The fighting in Kunduz has only made the problem worse. The NGOs had hired many Afghans but now they've left, and people no longer have work so they, too, are leaving Afghanistan. Who goes out to eat when they intend to escape to Europe? Even Mother has sent her children away. When he turns on the news, all Ali hears about is Kunduz and whether the Taliban will retake it, and will Kabul be next? Most of Ali's friends, even those who still use drugs, have fled the country.

Ali thinks he'll stay and rejoin the army. Better than being jobless or leaving without any money. He can't work for Mother forever. She allows him a place to sleep and gives him food but she does not pay him. In the army, he'd have a salary and respect, but of course the army would have its problems too. The stress of being shot at and of losing friends—that does something to a man. Commanders provided him with opium so he would not dwell on death. Once he got used to it, opium became part of his routine. If he ran out of opium, his commander gave him Tramadol. The drug made him feel awake and powerful.

If I had money I'd escape to Iran, Ali tells Rohalluh.

Afghanistan is my country, Rohalluh says. We should stay and die here. I want to go to university and learn something.

What you say is good, but you can't always find the job you want. Whatever door you knock on, you get a no, and after a while you feel hopeless. You're too young to imagine failure or the future. You don't know whether you'll find a job or get in school. You are young and eager and ignorant. You don't know what it means to go hungry.

Everyone has his own ideas, Rohalluh says. You talk from your stomach. I talk with my mind.

Ali smiles. He won't argue with a boy. And who knows? Rohalluh may get lucky. Luck is for the young. The old must rely on endurance. Most recovering addicts like Ali have no family. If they stay, it is to join the army or fight in Syria. He has considered doing that too. He knows it's not a good thing to fight for a country not your own, but for the money, why not? He has spoken to Nadir about this. Nadir told him ISIS is very strong.

If you only fight for a salary, Nadir told him, you will not go to Paradise.

Then I will stay here and eat, Ali said.

He doesn't want to leave Laila. She counts on him and he likes being needed. The restaurant walls keep the world and all its problems far away. Ali enjoys this sanctuary but he can't live behind these walls forever. Yes, rejoining the army makes the most sense. If not now, next week, or maybe in two or three weeks. At some point he will tell Mother goodbye and walk out with nothing but his clothes, his plans to reenlist, and his recovery from drugs but not war. How can he do anything else in a country that has been at war since the 1979 Soviet invasion? War is as addictive as opium. In the army, his Kalashnikov was as much a part of him as his arms and legs. When he fired at the enemy, his whole body shook with anticipation. He'd put in earplugs, find a target, aim, and squeeze the trigger, and the Kalashnikov jerked in his hands like a living thing. So much pressure. M16, Kalashnikov, whatever weapon was available, he used. He especially loved the M40; he marveled at its power and how that power surged through him with every shot.

He would ask hostages, Why are you with the Taliban? They'd say, Why are you with the Americans? I fight for my country, Ali said. We don't want America to take our land, the prisoners told him. We fight for our country too. When Ali tried to help villagers with food, many refused to take it. No, it belongs to the Americans. We don't want it. Ali dismissed these people as ignorant. To refuse food made no sense to him.

He turns to Rohalluh.

You go to school and I'll rejoin the army, he tells him.

Yes, Rohalluh says. It's better than leaving.

10

When she returns to Taj Begum later that morning, Laila notices Ali and Rohalluh talking. She raises a hand and waves. She knows Ali may return to the army and she does not like that idea any more than she does Nadir fighting in Syria. She'll miss them. Young men at war who will probably return to her addicted again, if they come back at all. They should all leave for Europe. Friends tell her fighting will start in Kabul. It is only a matter of time. She hopes not. If the war comes to Kabul, she will stay. She has Mother's House and the addicts in her care, her children not by blood but by commitment, and she won't abandon them. It's in her nature to resist.

She prays her children have reached some good place by now. Are they in Germany or still traveling on a train? She listens to Ali watering the lawn. The sun shines and she sees miniature rainbows above the wet grass. She closes her eyes and waits for Zakia to call.

DISPLACED PERSONS

I am desperate for water.

"No shade," I tell my colleague Masood.

He shrugs and gets out of our car, and I follow him past a ruined metal gate into Sakhi, a camp for the homeless outside Mazar-e-Sharif in northern Afghanistan. A relentless July sun bears down on us. Row after row of square huts covered with sheets of plastic and burlap stretch as far as I can see until they blur together against the scorched sky and bleached sand. I watch women pump well water into empty cooking-oil containers. Barefoot children dance in place beside their mothers until enough water sloshes on the ground for them to cool their feet.

I have been in the country about a week now and have yet to accustom myself to the extreme summer temperatures that can reach one hundred ten degrees and higher. My bottled water is in a Mazar-e-Sharif hotel some sixty miles away, and unlike Masood, I don't dare drink from the well. This is my tenth trip to Afghanistan as a journalist. I know better. To have forgotten my water in this heat is beyond stupid. Masood and I left the hotel about three hours ago. We got lost on our way out of Mazar. Then we found the secluded road we had been looking for and followed it through the desert to Sakhi. I was parched when we arrived.

My mouth tastes like paste. My head swims from the heat, eyes sting, pulse races. I sit on the ground against the wall of a small shop no different in shape from the huts around it. The owner stands outside in a triangular sliver of shade, pulls at his chin, and considers me. I look up at him, squinting. The sun blinds me; I can't see his face. Bearded men wearing gray turbans gather around the shopkeeper and stare at me, their deep-set, dark-circled eyes wreathed in wrinkles. No one speaks, yet I swear I hear someone calling my name.

I lower my head between my knees and close my eyes. Masood and I are in Sakhi to report a story about Afghanistan's homeless—internally displaced persons, as aid organizations and government bureaucrats call them. The accuracy of the term is inarguable, but it has done nothing to alleviate the plight of Afghans uprooted by war with no place to live but makeshift camps like this one. It does provide a means of categorization, however, so that the people who study things such as homelessness in Afghanistan can submit reports and recommendations.

Masood hands me a pebble to suck on. I take it from him and put it under my tongue. I hear the well water splashing behind me. I keep my mind occupied by reviewing the trip thus far. After I arrived in Kabul, Masood and I drove to Jalalabad, an eastern city that was once a Taliban stronghold near the Pakistan border. The black highway from Kabul to Jalalabad drew in the sun. Hot air blew through our open windows, leathering my skin to a deep tan. We reached Jalalabad three hours later and checked in to the Spin Ghar Hotel. A painting of a machine gun with a huge red "X" across it hung by the front door.

No Weapons, it read. Welcome to the Spin Ghar Hotel.

A plaque on the wall near the front door commemorates three reporters killed not far from Jalalabad on November 19, 2001. The reporters—Maria Grazia Cutuli of Italy, Julio Fuentes of Spain, and Azizullah Haidari of Afghanistan—were executed. I remember looking at a grainy black-and-white newspaper photo of Cutuli when I was in Lahore on my way to Kabul. She had long, dark hair. Her head was turned toward the camera, a shy smile on her face. Beside her picture was a photo of three crudely constructed wood coffins being loaded onto a plane.

Cutuli and Fuentes began their journey into Afghanistan from Islamabad. They met Haidari at the Spin Ghar. Then they proceeded west toward Kabul. They were murdered near Srubee, a village about halfway between Kabul and Jalalabad. Masood and I stopped there to buy water. Masood accused the vendor of overcharging us.

"Idiot," he said of the vendor as we walked back to our car. "He goes home at night and tells his wife about all the people he's cheated. She is so proud of him. Srubee people are not to be trusted."

I had arranged an interview that afternoon with a local warlord, Hazarat Ali. He met us in the front garden of his massive three-story home, entwined with vines and exhibiting a virulent decrepitude in the wide cracks splitting its walls. Armed guards leaned on pillars that framed a wide entryway where I could see a long, vacant hall that narrowed into shadow.

The interview lasted less than twenty minutes. Ali quickly became upset with my questions about the opium trade and whether he and his men were involved in it. I knew that he was. On our way into Jalalabad, Masood and I passed mile after mile of poppy fields, the source of most of the world's opium and heroin. The fields could not exist this close to Jalalabad, let alone be harvested, without Ali's consent. I asked no more than five questions before he told us to leave. I objected, but his men swarmed around Masood and me and shoved us toward our car. They stood in the road and watched us leave.

About an hour later, a United Nations Jeep pulled in front of the Spin Ghar as Masood and I were leaving to buy food at the bazaar. The Afghan driver asked me whether I was the Westerner who had met with Hazarat Ali. Yes, I said. A man with a British accent then stepped out of the Jeep. Ali had called this man and accused me of disrespecting him. He wanted Masood and me to leave Jalalabad at once. The Brit said we should not take our imperilment lightly. He himself had been threatened by Ali's men for his efforts at persuading farmers to grow alternative crops to poppies. I told him we had just arrived. The Brit shrugged and said it was my choice. He shook my hand and got back in the Jeep.

"Good luck," he said.

I watched him go and then sat at a white plastic table shaded by a tall palm tree to discuss the situation with Masood. We decided to leave in the morning when the road out of the city would be crowded with trucks coming in from Pakistan, making it less likely anyone would try to stop and harm us.

Rather than go to the bazaar, we thought it best to stick close to the hotel. We walked up the steps to the lobby and I paused by the door to again read the plaque commemorating Cutuli, Fuentes, and Haidari.

In Memory Of . . .

If I remember right, Cutuli, Fuentes, and Haidari left Pakistan in a predawn convoy. They must have been very excited. The Afghanistan war was not just the hottest news story of the time but also an event of historic proportions that verged, in the words of some commentators, on the rhapsodic.

Abandoned by the world following the withdrawal of the Soviet Union in 1989 and destroyed by years of subsequent civil war, Afghanistan was to be resuscitated. It would lead a democratic insurgency in Central Asia. Free elections would be held. Women would have rights equal to men. International aid would flow and jobs would be plentiful.

Then somehow Cutuli, Fuentes, and Haidari were separated from their convoy. Afghan gunmen surrounded them—bandits or Taliban, no one seemed to know. What they last saw, if they could concentrate on anything beside the guns pointed at them, was a desiccated landscape like the one surrounding the homeless camp where I sit now, trying to keep my mind off my thirst by thinking about three dead journalists.

"Does the shopkeeper have bottled water?" I ask Masood.

"I bought Pepsi and other things from Mazar, but all the refugees borrow from me," the shopkeeper tells him. "They put it on credit because they don't have money. For a year I have worked like that. I trusted them and now I have little to sell and no money."

He unlocks the doors to his shop. On one shelf, withered onions and blackened tomatoes rot in the heat. On another, prunes. Dusty shampoo bottles, packs of cigarettes, soap bars, soda cans, candy, and playing cards with photographs of Indian movie stars are strewn upon a large faded rug, barely distinguishable from the earthen floor. I see no water.

The shopkeeper, his wife, and their three children moved here last year after the Taliban burned their farm. They walked three months from Helmand Province in the south, carrying their belongings on their backs. The shopkeeper tells Masood the long walk turned his hair and beard gray. The lines creasing his face deepened into crevices.

By the time he reached Sakhi, he had accepted the loss of his farm but was determined to earn a living in another way. He told his wife that even people in a homeless camp need to bathe, cook, smoke, and comb their hair. He bought supplies in Mazar-e-Sharif. With scraps of wood, burlap, and aluminum siding, he built his shop just off the rocky road leading into the camp.

"Ten days ago, I closed my shop," he tells Masood. "Unless I am paid, why should I stay open?"

The other men standing around me start heckling the shopkeeper. Their loud, derisive voices swim unintelligibly inside my head. Masood squats beside me and translates. I close my eyes, wipe a white film off my mouth, and imagine Cutuli, Fuentes, and Haidari surrounded by a similar, more threatening mob.

"Oh," a man yells at the shopkeeper, "we have heard all your complaints before."

"If we don't have money, you should give these things to us and wait until we can pay you."

"You wait for us to pay you, but look how long we've been here waiting to go back to our homes."

"You can wait for your money. My children need to eat and go to school. They need to see a doctor."

"I told you if you needed a room to sleep, I'd trade you that for cigarettes."

"The rooms here are free," the shopkeeper tells Masood. "What kind of trade would that be, eh? These people are crazy, aren't they? How can I open? They need to pay me my money and then I can get other stuff. I have just two carpets in my house. There was a time I had many carpets."

He shows Masood the curled pages of a notebook filled with the names of people who owe him money:

Golan: $10 cooking oil, thread.

Abdul: $20 shampoo, soap, flour.

Fayez: $17 beans and rice.

"I prefer being a shopkeeper and opening my shop, but they have to pay," the shopkeeper says.

My head pounds from all the shouting. I push myself up to stand, feel dizzy, and sit back down. The shopkeeper stares at me. He speaks to Masood. Masood listens and nods. The shopkeeper walks over to the well, dampens a rag, and wraps it around my head. He searches his shop and after a moment gives an exultant shout. Reaching across a shelf, he uncovers a lone Pepsi can partially hidden by a pile of dried figs. He opens the Pepsi and hands it to me. I hold the warm can in both hands as though in prayer and drink in gulps. When I finish, the shopkeeper takes the can from me. He turns to Masood.

"He wants money," Masood says.

I left my money hidden in a pocket of my duffel bag in the hotel. Masood tells the shopkeeper I'll pay him later. The shopkeeper gives us both a look of contempt. He tells Masood I am no different from everyone else who owes him money.

Masood helps me to my feet. I press the rag against my head, squeezing water from it. The men who had been ridiculing the shopkeeper drift away, break into groups. Some sit in the thin shade offered by our car and pitch stones. Others merely stand and stare at nothing, wraith-like in the heat.

The shopkeeper shuts the doors to his shop. He drags a chain through the door handles and padlocks it without a word. I stand up, still thirsty, but better. I look beyond the camp to the empty road stretching toward Mazar in a thin, wavering line. I imagine the sound of gunshots, the sight of three reporters falling. I hear instead the silence of the desert and see the distended shape of the arid landscape I am to travel, unforgiving and relentless.

ANIMAL RESCUE

The American reporter checks in to the Park Palace Guest House on a hot July afternoon. After the desk clerk gives him a room key, he stops in the hotel restaurant and carries a plate of food into the courtyard, a duffel bag slung over one shoulder.

He is in Kabul to write stories for a British travel and culture magazine. He looks around, but when he does not see what he is looking for, he whistles sharply. People seated at round, white plastic tables balanced precariously on the lumpy lawn glance at him but pay little attention otherwise. A young man and woman look and then turn back to the laptop computer between them. Several men sitting in a group on lawn chairs furrow their brows at what he might be whistling for, shrug, and continue talking. One of them, an Australian, complains about the bland hotel food. An Afghan merchant, displaying rugs along a wall, turns his back to the reporter.

The sun blazes down and the reporter hears the vague clamor of traffic beyond the hotel's walls. A patched, flattened water hose lies like shed snakeskin across the cracked stone walk. Armed guards step over the hose, and from beneath the young couple's table a gray cat emerges, ears pricked, pausing midstride until the guards pass. The reporter sees the cat and whistles again. The cat stares at him, then trots over and sniffs his shoes and pants leg. She cries and stretches out at his feet and purrs, flipping her body from one side to the other, unable, it seems, to keep still. The reporter squats down and pats her, his duffel bag slipping off his shoulder.

He wonders whether the cat remembers him and presumes by her behavior that she does. He had found her the previous year, or she had found him. He was sitting in the courtyard and the cat had approached him from some bushes. He had guessed her age at about ten. She had one long fang remaining in an otherwise toothless mouth. Her meow sounded like the screech of a rusted door hinge. He brushed dirt from her fur, felt her ribs and hip bones against his hand. He fed her some of his beef kabob, and she followed him to his room and stayed until he left four weeks later.

He thought of the cat after he returned to his Illinois home, how he had to chase her from beneath his bed the morning he left Kabul because she didn't want to leave. He tried not to dwell on the image of her waiting for him outside his door. He would remind himself she was just a cat. Still, he could not deny the comfort he had found in her quiet, affectionate presence, her uncomplicated desires, and the enjoyment he felt when she ran to him in the courtyard at the end of each day. He remembered how she feared the Afghan staff, how she froze at the sight of them. She was always friendly, however, with Westerners.

He pulls at the cat's tail. Here he is again; here she is. She has lost patches of fur, and she is thinner than he remembered, her stomach distended. The reporter stands and walks to his room. The cat follows.

His second-floor room overlooks the courtyard. A thin, brown wall-to-wall carpet is bunched up beneath a cabinet on the crooked floor. By the door is a TV, and across from it a small refrigerator and a desk missing one leg, propped against the wall. Barbed wire is unspooled outside the bathroom window, and he sees the boots of a guard walking past on the ledge. Mildew splotches the walls, and the toilet runs.

The hot afternoon air has cooled and he leaves his door open for the breeze. Turning on the television, he searches for an English-language station. CNN. Dr. Mehmet Oz is filling in for Piers Morgan and interviewing Cyndi Lauper. He checks his email but has no messages. The cat sits in the doorway. He stares at her for a moment and whistles, wiggling his fingers by the side of the chair. She walks in and rubs against his hand, and he gives her chicken from his lunch. He shuts off his computer, sits on his bed, and looks at the ceiling, listening to Piers Morgan's voice above the faint utterances of hotel staff outside speaking Dari, the language of northern Afghanistan, and a kind of isolation settles over him.

This is the reporter's tenth trip to Afghanistan since 2001. The Taliban has regained control of most of the south. It has also made significant inroads in the once secure north. The poor security situation has not deterred NATO from its intention to withdraw all its troops by the end of 2014. Many of those with a stake in Afghanistan's future fear that the billions in foreign aid the country received will leave as well. The World Bank has concluded that Afghanistan's economy, expanding by nearly ten percent annually, could see that growth collapse by nearly half or more during the withdrawal, but the only news the reporter can now find on TV is Dr. Oz asking Cyndi Lauper, "How do you stay so youthful?" The reporter shuts it off without waiting for her answer. In the gray afternoon silence, he lies still and awake, listening to the cat eat.

The next morning, the reporter awakens and sees the cat curled up asleep by the refrigerator. He whistles and she looks at him, eyes half closed. She watches him shower and dress, and then follows him outside and into the courtyard, where she settles in the shade beneath a table. A gardener waters the grass. The reporter stops in the restaurant, pours a cup of coffee, and takes two hard-boiled eggs from a basket. He returns to the courtyard and breaks off some egg for the cat. She eats, purring. The gardener notices and sprays her with water. The cat, hissing, flees. The reporter stands.

"Stop it. What are you doing?"

"You fed it?" the gardener says.

"Yes."

"Then give me money. I am hungry too."

The reporter offers him twenty-five afghanis, about fifty cents.

"A gift from America," the gardener says and puts the wrinkled bill in his pocket.

The reporter finishes eating and walks outside to wait for his colleague Aarash. The cat follows, but stops at the edge of the courtyard. A security guard closes a metal gate behind the reporter, and he waits for Aarash in the shade of the hotel, watching a barefoot man splash water on the pitted dirt road to tamp down dust, but the ground absorbs the water within seconds and dust rises as military vehicles jounce past. When the dust clears, the reporter sees Aarash parking his car.

Aarash is tall and thin and speaks English with a gravelly, almost gargled tone. His long hair falls to his shoulders and a patchy beard covers his narrow face. He still carries the scars on his neck from a car bomb in 1998, when the Taliban held power. He felt as if he had been smacked on the side of his face; the noise stuffed his head as helium inflates a balloon, and his ears filled too, as if he were deep underwater. He lay on the ground and stuck his fingers in the shrapnel wounds in his neck to stop the bleeding and then stumbled through black smoke and burnt metal and mangled bodies on the street in scorched clothes. He asked a taxi driver to take him to a hospital and once there waited for forty-five minutes, but no doctor saw him. Blood dripped from his neck, and he asked a receptionist to call his family and tell them where he was and that he was leaving to find another hospital. That hospital had no available doctor either, so he went to a third hospital. There, doctors treated his injuries.

He often thinks about the blast, especially now with the NATO troop withdrawal approaching. He has a wife and a two-year-old son.

"What will happen to them if I die?" he asks the reporter.

They drive no more than two blocks from the hotel before a policeman pulls them over. The officer asks for Aarash's registration.

"Why do you have a photocopy and not the original registration?"

"The original was very worn," Aarash says. "I went to the license department and they made a photocopy and gave it to me."

"I am ticketing you for having false registration," the officer says. "Give me twelve hundred Afs."

"Twelve hundred is too much," Aarash says.

"If that is too much, put what you have inside this," the

officer says and tosses a notebook on Aarash's lap. "One thousand Afs."

"I don't have that."

"Give me what you have. Hurry. I don't want to embarrass you in front of this foreigner."

Aarash slips five hundred afghanis, about ten dollars, into the officer's notebook and gives it back to him. The officer thanks him and leaves.

"This would not have happened if you had not been with me," Aarash tells the reporter. "He knew you would have money. You owe me five hundred Afs."

The reporter and Aarash stop outside NATO headquarters to interview children who sell scarves and bracelets to Western soldiers and contractors. One twelve-year-old boy who's missing his left leg and leaning on crutches says that when the Westerners leave, he'll have no work. "Afghans won't buy scarves," he says. The boy grew up on a farm in Ghazni. He often saw coalition forces shoot their guns at farmers. Maybe they thought the farmers were Taliban. The boy was hit in the leg last year. An American soldier came over with a translator.

"What are you doing here?" the translator asked. Then he said, "Oh, God, you're just a farm kid."

The boy asks the reporter why the coalition soldiers shot him. The reporter does not know what to say and does not answer. Aarash speaks to the boy in Dari.

"What are you saying?" the reporter asks.

"It is between this boy and me as Afghan people," Aarash says.

At night, the reporter feeds the cat using an ashtray as a bowl. Her swollen stomach sags to the floor. The reporter sits at his desk and checks for email messages. Mostly spam. He writes to a friend and describes his encounters with the policeman and the boy. It is about eight in the evening in the States and his friend responds almost immediately: "You think it's crazy in Afghanistan; it has been a crazy few months here. I went to New York City for a week and had a ball. Then I came back and drove to Lake Tahoe to hang out with my cousins. Then the day they left, I wound up in the hospital getting my appendix out. That was fun . . . Not! Be well."

On his Facebook page, an old acquaintance whom the reporter has not heard from or seen in years sends a message: "Is this you?" The reporter confirms and within seconds, he receives a friend request. He will be her four hundredth friend. The idea makes him feel small, and he declines to respond.

He stands and closes his windows against a hard wind that makes his curtains snap. Dust spins in small tornadic swirls, swiftly expanding into a full-on dust storm that fogs the air, its brown grit scratching at the windows. Then the room goes dark. Power outage. The reporter sits in the gloom until he can make out the shapes of the TV, bed, night table. He picks up the cat. She stretches, yawns, and demands to be petted. The reporter stares outside, sees nothing but the violently spinning dust engulfing everything.

A generator starts up, and the reporter's lights snap back on. He sets the cat on the bed, turns on his computer, and Google searches "animal rescue Afghanistan." He scrolls through the search results, stopping at a site called "Tigger House," an animal shelter in Kabul named after a dog its founder, the *Washington Post* reporter Pamela Constable, rescued in 2004. She has worked in Afghanistan for years; the reporter recognizes her name. He had met her at Kabul news conferences in 2001 and 2002 and again in Islamabad. Everyone called her

Pam. He calls the number listed on the web page and leaves a message.

The next morning, he sends a Facebook message to Aarash, telling him he wants to return to NATO headquarters. He showers, dresses, eats, and leaves his room. The cat follows him to the edge of the courtyard. He watches her turn around and jog up two flights of steps and sit outside his room until a maid chases her away with a broom.

A fifteen-year-old boy, paralyzed from the waist down, sits in a wooden wheelchair outside NATO. "I always heard my grandfather talking about the fights during the Russian time," he tells the reporter, "so when I was old enough, I faced an enemy, the Taliban, just as my grandfather faced the Russians, and this is what happened. It's worse now than in my grandfather's time. He never saw civilians die as they do now. In his time, it was just the Russians against the opposition. Now, it is the opposition, the Americans, the civilians—everyone is involved and dying. This is the worst fighting in our history."

Aarash disagrees.

"It depends how we look at our history," he says. "When the Russians came and bombed us, the people were angry. Then they left, and the Mujahideen came to power, but there was no security, so the people said the Russians were good; the Mujahideen are bad. Then the Taliban came. They made everyone pray. Women had to stay home. So the people said, the Taliban are bad and the Mujahideen are good. Then the Americans came. They kill civilians and the people no longer trust them. So now the Taliban are good and the Americans are bad. It will be the same story when the Americans leave."

The reporter's pen runs out of ink and he reaches into a

pocket for another one. The boy pushes his wheelchair closer to him and the reporter realizes he thinks he is going to give him money. Taking his hand from his pocket, the reporter shows he only has a pen and backs up. The boy pushes after him and more children approach until they encircle the reporter and Aarash. A girl reaches out to them and the boy pushes her away and the other children rush forward.

"Go!" a guard shouts, running toward them, "Go!"

The children flee, the boy pushing frantically on the tires of his wheelchair. The guard grabs the reporter by the arm and shakes him.

"What are you doing here?"

"Let him go!" Aarash shouts. "He is a foreigner and a journalist and is doing no harm!"

"After twelve years of war, we see many journalists," the guard snaps. "What good will you do for these children? You take pictures and leave. Give me money to give to them."

The reporter refuses.

"I never want to see you here again," the guard says.

Back in his room, the reporter starts typing his notes. He listens to his fingers moving across the keys of his laptop. After a moment, he pauses, leans back in his chair, and crosses his arms. He could have offered the children some Afs. But then the guard might have accused him of not giving them enough, or he might have wanted money, too. The reporter shakes his head. No matter what he said or did, it would not have been enough. I am a journalist, he reminds himself. Still he wonders. He sighs and resumes typing. The cat demands his attention and he picks her up until she settles on his lap and sleeps. He has noticed that she is not gaining weight, no matter how much she eats. Her stomach hangs beneath her like a long, half-deflated balloon.

As he types, he notices a young Afghan man talking to the gardener. The reporter stares at him for a long time. He has seen him before and then he remembers his name, Uresh Jawid. One of five war-orphaned boys he had befriended in 2003. They didn't know their birth dates, but he guessed they were about thirteen at the time. The boys polished shoes outside the Mustafa Hotel. He gave them candy. Then he took them to lunch. Then he enrolled them in school and tutored them in English at night.

When he left, he promised to return, but he did not receive another assignment to Afghanistan until 2007. About a week into that trip, he saw Uresh selling tea on the street. They met the next day at his hotel with the four other boys, who had jobs hawking pirated DVDs. All of them had dropped out of school to work. The reporter offered to wire his Afghan colleague, a translator and fixer named Bahar, money to give them every month so they could live at his house and return to school instead of working mind-numbing jobs that would lead nowhere. They sat huddled around him and nodded their heads, looking very serious. After the boys left, Bahar told the reporter to include money for him too.

"This is a job you are asking me to do, like translating," he said.

The reporter flew back to the States and wired the money, but Bahar said he never received it. The boys accused him of stealing and the whole thing turned ugly, and Bahar called the police and had the boys removed from his house. He never saw them again.

The reporter watches Uresh for a long while and then walks outside, the cat hurrying after him.

"Uresh," the reporter calls.

Uresh turns, cocking his head to one side, and a slow smile spreads across his face.

"It's been a long time," he says.

He stands a head taller than the reporter. A sweat-dampened T-shirt clings to his narrow chest. He says he is friends with the hotel gardener and had stopped to see him. He has no job, but sometimes shines shoes or sells tea. He has not seen the other boys in he doesn't know how long. He smiles again, but his eyes show little expression. Guilt intrudes on the reporter, and he looks away.

Maybe the money never reached Kabul, although his bank insisted it did. Maybe Bahar kept it. He doesn't know. He never will.

"It's good to see you again," Uresh says.

The reporter nods. Without another word he turns around and starts walking back to his room. He thinks of the children outside NATO, experiences again the fury of the guard. The cat darts past him and up the stairs to the door. He picks her up and holds her, resting his chin against the top of her head; he stands like that for some time and tries not to think.

A few hours later, Pam Constable returns the reporter's call. He tells her he wants to take a cat home with him. He also mentions that they have met before. From her reaction, he knows she doesn't remember him. About the cat, she says several steps will be involved, none of them difficult. The cat will need rabies and distemper vaccinations. The shelter's veterinarian can administer those. She will also need to be quarantined for thirty days. The shelter can do that too.

The reporter explains he has been in Afghanistan for three weeks and has to leave at the end of the month, one week before the cat would complete its quarantine. Not a problem,

Pam says. She will ship the cat to him. She does this all the time. The reporter agrees to bring the cat to her in a few days.

"Where do you live?"

"Winnetka, Illinois. Just outside Chicago."

"What's her name?"

"I haven't named her. I just whistle and she answers."

"For our records, I'll call her Whistle," Pam says.

Tigger House stands on a residential street of two-story cinder block homes, each one surrounded by high concrete walls. Tall, spiked metal doors seal them off like tombs. The reporter gets out of Aarash's car holding Whistle. She buries her head in his armpit, squirming. He pushes a buzzer, and a chorus of barking dogs responds; Whistle claws at his shoulder to escape, but he holds her.

Pam greets him at the door. She tilts her head back—light brown hair crossing her forehead, large glasses perched on her nose above an embracing grin—and leads the reporter inside. Large pens take up the front entrance, with three to four dogs in each pen, barking and eager for attention. One dog had been given to a farmer in a nearby province, but after two weeks the owner returned it. There was too much fighting in the area, he explained, and he could not keep it safe.

The reporter follows Pam into a house converted into a clinic and kennel. Several rooms line a hall; one is reserved for sick animals. In another room, cats and kittens roam within a wire-mesh pen. Pam takes Whistle from the reporter and puts her in a cage inside the pen. Whistle bunches into a ball, ducking her head in a corner.

"She will be released among the other cats once they get used to one another," Pam says cheerfully. "And then, after thirty days, she'll be off to Illinois."

Pam walks them to their car and Aarash drives the reporter back to the Park Palace. As he enters the courtyard, the reporter sees Bahar waiting for him at a table. He hadn't called, and the reporter was not expecting him. They shake hands, hug, and order tea. Bahar wears a dress shirt and black slacks. His dark beard has grayed since the reporter last saw him two or three years ago. A Japanese nongovernmental organization hired him. When the reporter returned to Afghanistan and needed a trans-lator; Bahar recommended Aarash, a friend of one of his sons.

"How much are you paying these days?" Bahar asks.

"Seventy dollars a day including meals and gas," the reporter tells him. "The same arrangement I had with you."

"You should have asked me to speak to Aarash before you hired him. I would have arranged a lower rate."

The reporter shrugs. He suspects what Bahar really wanted to know was whether Aarash was making more than he had.

"How is your family?"

"Not good," Bahar answers.

A recently married son had been laid off. Another son, afraid terrorists might follow him home and kill his family, quit his job at the US embassy.

"I am also unemployed. There is less work with NATO leaving. Everyone is cutting back, even the NGOs."

Bahar finishes his tea and stands.

"Seventy US a day?"

"That's what I pay."

"I should have continued working for you."

They embrace again and the reporter watches him leave. He can't help Bahar, Aarash, and Uresh. He can't help the street kids he's interviewed. But he can rescue a goddamn cat. He appreciates how pathetic that is, how reduced his expectations, but he can't help that either.

The reporter leaves Kabul at the end of August. In the first week of October, Whistle arrives at Chicago's O'Hare Airport. He takes her home and she walks out of the cat carrier and into his kitchen. He puts food out for her. When she finishes, he holds her.

Two days later, he drives her to a veterinarian, Ashley Rossman, at the Glen Oak Dog & Cat Hospital about ten minutes from his house. Dr. Ashley, as her clients call her, feels Whistle's distended stomach and carries her into a back room to administer a sonogram. The reporter watches grainy black-and-white images swirl on a computer screen. Dr. Ashley pauses, pointing to a foggy white circular mass.

"Tumor," she says, "in the lymph nodes."

A blood test reveals that Whistle has cancer and feline AIDS. Neither one will be immediately fatal. But eventually. Sooner rather than later. The reporter doesn't know what to say. He'd assumed she had worms, parasites, not this. Picking her up, he cradles her against his chest and closes his eyes. Dr. Ashley pouts and shakes her head. She hands him two bottles of pills.

"You'll give her these for the rest of her little life."

The reporter drives out of the parking lot resting an arm on the cat carrier, wind blowing through the open passenger window. Whistle sniffs the breeze. Ears perked, eyes wide. The reporter looks at the broad brick houses on either side of the quiet road, the lawns stretching toward the wide sidewalks. He stares through the clear air and tries not to think.

FERAL CHILDREN

I

A boy emerges from a narrow alley at dawn holding a bathroom scale. Channels of sewage discolor the ground beneath his feet. A barefoot girl, her legs mud-spattered, walks in from a side street where ancient-looking burros with rough, balding hides stand strapped to wagons. Red, blue, and yellow scarves hang off her shoulders. Another boy squats beside a closed kabob stall and sucks his fingers.

On this July morning in 2013, about a dozen children, their smudged faces still puffy from sleep, are converging from all points of Kabul to gather near a gravel parking lot across the street from NATO headquarters. Eight, maybe twelve years old. Missing baby teeth, some of them. They stare at the barbed wire stretching across Hesco barriers as if waiting for a vision. A soldier in the uniform of the Afghan National Army watches them.

Perhaps through habit or some hidden signal, the children merge and shuffle forward as one; exhaust from cars and trucks hangs in the humid air like a beaded curtain, and the children pause to wipe sweat from their faces before walking within shadows receding in the new day's light, passing a parking lot attendant waving cars into empty spaces until the children stand on the sidewalk near—but not too near—an Afghan guard pacing before the NATO's front gate. The guard rests a hand on his baton.

"Don't create a crowd so that the terrorists can slip in here and explode a bomb," he warns them.

The guard does not expect them to leave and they don't. NATO is their prime hustling turf, a stomping ground that will no longer exist when NATO withdraws most of its forces at the end of 2014.

Soldiers and contractors buy scarves for about two dollars apiece from some of the children, or, at a cost of less than a dollar, they weigh themselves on the bathroom scales other children carry. Many of the boys and girls have nothing to offer other than pleading eyes and an outstretched hand.

I watch them with my fixer Aarash from his car. I'm here on my own dime to write about the removal of NATO forces from Afghanistan through the eyes of Kabul's street kids. While the rest of Afghanistan worries about security, these children fear the loss of their livelihoods.

"Afghan people," one girl told me, "won't give us money like Westerners."

I pitched the idea to an editor. He liked it but wouldn't commit. He wants to see the story first, see what kind of kids I find. If I'm to make the sale, cover my expenses, and score a little profit, I've got to find a boy or girl who really pulls the heartstrings. An Oliver Twist sort of kid. I've been here three days. Thus far, none of the children will let me hang out with them, because they worry my presence will distract them from making money. Also, their parents, they say, would not approve of them spending time with a Westerner. So Aarash and I wait and watch, hoping to find an accommodating subject. Then we notice one sullen boy who stands apart from the other kids. He balls up the neck of a burlap sack in a fist. Black grime streaks his face and hands. He is smaller than the other children and impossibly thin. The annoyed look on his gaunt face suggests he wants nothing to do with anyone. That he would choose to be invisible if he could.

"Call that boy over," I tell Aarash, "the one with the sack."

The name of the Afghan soldier in the parking lot is Qudratullah. Like many Afghans, he does not have a last name. He is tall and wears a dark green uniform and black boots. His angular face with its deep, dark wrinkles looks as if it has been cut from parchment. The butt of a pistol juts out of his belt. He lights a cigarette and watches as a boy approaches a Westerner and his Afghan companion. Qudratullah is part of a security detail assigned to the parking lot. Sometimes he sees Westerners treat the children well; other times, not so much. "Go away," they say. But this Westerner appears to want to talk to the boy.

The other children converge on the Westerner surrounding him and the boy and clutch at his body, shouting, "Money, mister!" Then the guard begins yelling. Raising his baton, he rushes toward the children, fear and rage mixed in his contorted face. Qudratullah understands the guard's outburst. His terror. A large explosion near NATO killed six people and wounded many others in 2012. The Taliban took responsibility. A teenage suicide bomber set the blast.

But these boys and girls are harmless. They flee the guard, running into the street, and the guard chases them and kicks the boy who had been talking with the Westerner, and the boy screams and falls. The guard pauses in his tantrum. His face softens but his body remains tense. He lowers his baton and looks down at the weeping boy, at the blood oozing from an ankle where he had kicked him. The guard says something to the boy Qudratullah can't hear and then drops money on the ground. The boy's eyes narrow as he grabs the money like a lizard snatching a bug with its tongue, and shoves it down his shirt. A truculent look reassembles across his face and the tears resume. He stands and limps off in the direction of the other children. The Westerner and his Afghan companion stand a few feet away, watching.

"You come here and the terrorists try to kill us and then you leave. What do you give back to Afghanistan?" the guard shouts at them.

The Westerner says nothing. Qudratullah watches them follow after the children in the direction of Wazir Akbar Khan Park near downtown. He does not see the boy the guard kicked among them.

A sixteen-year-old boy named Jawad sits by his scuffed brown and white shoeshine box on a hill in Wazir Akbar Khan Park. Two vacant benches and overgrown grass flank him on both sides as he waits for customers. Black polish stains his red shirt and torn black pants. Soot layers his brown hair. Beside his bare feet, the sneakers he put on this morning, the cloth worn in places to a thin checkerboard pattern.

Jawad wiggles his toes in the dry grass. He has shined shoes since he was little. Even before his father died, he had to work.

He gets up at five forty-five, eats a breakfast of bread and potatoes and then leaves for school. When school lets out at two o'clock, he polishes shoes until seven. In the evening he studies until midnight. Sometimes he is so tired he skips dinner, doesn't study, and just sleeps. He would like to be a doctor but he gets sick at the sight of blood. Maybe an engineer. But he's not good at math. Perhaps a policeman like his father, but Jawad can't imagine shooting anyone.

His father fought the Mujahideen in the civil war of the mid-1990s. At that time of block-to-block fighting, Jawad remembers eating only bread with a little water. One afternoon, his father's driver was shot as he was driving his father to work. His father jumped out of the car just before it went over a cliff.

On a good day, Jawad earns six to ten dollars in an afternoon. He sets no price. His earnings depend on the generosity of those asking for a shoeshine. If he doesn't polish well, people won't pay him. Mistakes happen. Sometimes he misses a spot or leaves a smudge.

"What have you done?" a man snapped at him one day. "This is not what I wanted at all."

Jawad uses his money to buy cooking oil and food for his family. His older brother washes cars and pays the rent. His younger brother polishes shoes in the downtown bazaar and puts aside his earnings for emergencies, like last year when their mother came down with pneumonia.

After his father died, Jawad's mother stopped speaking. She has less feeling for life now. Sadness stains her eyes. Jawad and his brothers eat dinner with her in silence. Afterward, they sit together in their bedroom and talk about money. Their father's pension, how can they help their mother get it? Who do they know? How do they find the right person with connections to help them?

When business is slow in the park, Jawad walks a few blocks to Wazir Mohammad Akbar Khan Mosque. The mullahs there allow him to polish shoes and sandals when men answer the calls to prayer. As they worship, he sleeps on the marble steps. If he is not too tired, he sweeps and mops the mosque entrance.

The mosque reminds Jawad of stories his father told him about the Taliban. When the Taliban was in power, his father said, you could leave your shop unlocked when you answered the call to prayer. No one would dare rob you and risk arrest, because the Taliban would cut off one of your hands. Today, it's different. You have to lock your shop. Now, people would rob it. The mosques were full of people then. Now, not so much.

Jawad stands and brushes grass from his pants. He notices some boys and girls stepping over the collapsed iron gate that at one time opened into the park. They split up and walk in opposite directions around the base of a hill. Other boys remain in the alley that runs past the entrance and sift through dumpsters overflowing with garbage and swarming with flies. More children troll their hands through gutters. One of them hoists a tin can triumphantly, his arm black with muck.

A Westerner and an Afghan man enter the park after the children. The Westerner has long gray hair and a beard; the Afghan, too, has a beard, patchy in spots, and he wears blue jeans and a blue Western-style button-down shirt. The Westerner glances around as if he is looking for someone. Then he notices Jawad. Sensing a potential customer, Jawad cocks his head and smiles. The Westerner and the Afghan approach him.

The Afghan asks him whether he has seen a small boy dragging a sack. Jawad shakes his head and the Afghan speaks to the Westerner and Jawad recognizes the language is English, a subject he has studied a little in school but does not yet understand. He asks the Afghan whether he and his Western friend want their shoes polished. The Westerner declines, but the Afghan kicks off his black leather shoes. Jawad kneels and rests the shoes on his lap. Rummaging in his box, he finds a pair of sandals and gives them to the Afghan so he doesn't soil his socks in the grass.

The Westerner watches Jawad apply black polish to each shoe and rub it in with a soiled rag, moving his hand back and forth and around each shoe. Jawad doesn't enjoy polishing shoes, but he has no choice. In 2008, his father died of a heart attack. One morning at two o'clock, his father awakened and told Jawad's mother he couldn't breathe. His heart was racing.

"Bring me some water," he said.

The family took him by taxi to a hospital. Four days later, a doctor told them that Jawad's father's heart was too weak to treat and the family brought him home. He died the next day. Jawad was eleven. He wept for two days until an uncle told him, "Stop your crying. God has given you the blessing to suffer."

As Jawad polishes his shoes, Aarash thinks about the boy he and the reporter had tried to speak to at NATO. He thought surely the boy would follow the other children to the park, but he is nowhere to be seen.

"Come here," Aarash had called when the reporter pointed him out. The boy walked up to him with a look on his face as if he was in trouble.

"What is your name?"

"Ghani," he said in a voice barely above a whisper. Other

children clutching at the reporter's notepad and camera shoved Ghani out of their way in an effort to get from Aarash what they thought he might give to Ghani. But Aarash told them to settle and be quiet and offered them nothing. He asked Ghani questions.

"How old are you?"

"Nine."

"What do you do here?"

"Collect cans."

Pepsi and Coke mostly. He sells the cans to a recycling center and earns one dollar for every seven kilograms of tin and one dollar and twenty cents for every seven kilograms of aluminum. He doesn't understand why one is worth more than the other. He also gathers scraps of paper for fuel.

"How much do you make a day?"

"Two, sometimes six dollars," Ghani said.

He does not like the work. The other day, a restaurant owner told him, "Don't come here again," when he saw him sorting through his garbage. Older boys make problems too. "Go away," they tell him. "This is our area." But he puts up with the difficulties out of necessity. His father died of a brain tumor in 2012. As the eldest son, he must support his family. He has an infant brother just nine months old. Another brother who is seven was struck by a car this year and now has difficulty walking. A sixteen-year-old sister does nothing but stay at home.

Ghani stopped talking. His eyes teared up and he rubbed his nose and sniffled. The children around him grew quiet. Then the guard started shouting and swinging his baton. Stupid man, Aarash told the reporter on their way to the park. Afghans are afraid of one another. They hear rumors. Kids are Taliban spies.

People believe anything. Only the uneducated and unsophisticated work security jobs.

Aarash was just a year older than Ghani when he lost his father in 1995 during the civil war. He had climbed the stairs to the roof of their house to plug a hole when a bullet struck him in the chest and he spun around and stumbled back down the stairs and collapsed in the living room. Blood spread across his shirt and dripped onto the carpet. Aarash recited verses from the Holy Koran and asked God to save his father while his mother cried, "Please don't go. Stay awake. Don't close your eyes." But his father did close his eyes and about thirty minutes later he died. He was thirty-one.

The fighting outside their home prevented the family from burying the body in a cemetery. Instead, Aarash dug a grave in the backyard. Five days later, a cease-fire allowed the family to depart, carrying only their clothing, for the home of Aarash's maternal uncle in a less embattled part of Kabul.

Aarash disliked living with his uncle. In the morning, he and his younger sisters drank tea and ate bread while his cousins had milk and eggs.

"I want milk and eggs too," Aarash complained to his mother.

"They have new clothes, why can't we?" his sisters demanded.

"They have everything we don't have," Aarash said.

His mother did not reply. She was a young woman, but as Aarash considers that moment now, he believes their questions and obvious distress put a stoop in her back that remains to this day. In the weeks following his father's death, Aarash's mother began washing clothes and cooking for other families. Aarash offered to quit school and work too, but his mother told him no.

"You have to study and graduate," she said.

Aarash is married now. He has a four-year-old son. His mother lives with him. He doesn't let his mother talk about his father's death. If she tries, he tells her, "We've moved beyond that sad time."

After Jawad finishes polishing Aarash's shoes, I buy the three of us chicken kabobs. Then we walk to Wazir Mohammad Akbar Khan Mosque moving slowly in the heat, the sky seared white. A billboard promoting Safi Airways shows a plane rising above Kabul into a firmament of refreshing blue. Clouds spread beneath the plane, and under the clouds stand square buildings and the flat images of smiling men and women looking upward. We make our way through the crowded sidewalks, dodging bicycle riders clanging their bells and packs of dogs. Every so often, Jawad glances around, worried he might run into someone he knows from school; they would make fun of him if they were to realize he polishes shoes. One of his classmates washes cars. "Poor boy," the other students call him. "Beggar boy."

Jawad enjoys school but hates his math class. He broke a pencil sharpener for the razor blade inside and cut his left wrist six times when he received a low grade on a quiz. Furious that he was too small to help, he cut himself again when he saw an older boy picking on a weaker boy.

One time, his math teacher gave Jawad a ruler and told him to beat the hand of a student who had been copying another boy's answers. Placing his hand over the student's, Jawad struck it five times, wincing with each whack, but sparing the boy pain and humiliation by absorbing the blows himself. His father had taught him to do only good things so he would be well remembered after he died. Jawad is confident the student will not forget him.

When we reach the mosque, pigeons rise off its bright red dome in a squall of flapping wings. Jawad stretches out on the shined white steps and waits for the four-thirty call to prayer. Soon he falls asleep and Aarash and I return to my hotel and sit in the courtyard near my room. A fountain burbles and plastic tables have been arranged around it with umbrellas to ward off the sun. Armed guards walk the second-floor balcony and sandbag bunkers take up the four corners of the rooftop. Around us, peacocks roam. At night, the guards herd the peacocks into a bunker of their own.

"What do we have for the story?"

"Two boys," Aarash says.

"No, one," I say. "We have one boy, Jawad. We don't know if we have the first boy."

Jawad is good but, at sixteen, a little old. Still, no father, polishing shoes to help the family, that's not bad. He might work. But I want the first kid. Nine years old. Perfect.

"We'll go back to NATO tomorrow," I tell Aarash, "and look for what's his name."

"Ghani?"

"Is that it?"

"Yes, Ghani," Aarash says.

This morning, the NATO parking attendant tells us he has not seen a boy fitting Ghani's description. On a whim, Aarash suggests that we drive to Chicken Street, Kabul's tourist trap, where merchants cajole Westerners into buying their wares for three times what an Afghan would pay; where street children offer to shield visitors from beggars for a fee; and where a friend of his, Sanam Sadaat, manages a toy store named Qandolak. It means cute, she tells me when we stop in. Teddy bears, camels, and other stuffed animals from Iran, Turkey, and the United Arab Emirates fill the shelves. Bright white clouds parade across sky-blue walls. Music plays softly and a swivel fan stirs butterfly mobiles.

Sanam has a delightful smile, her eyes alive with humor and mischief. Although she covers her head with a scarf, everything else about her—her blue jeans and patterned blouse—shows a Western influence. I describe Ghani to her but she does not know him. Or maybe she does but he sounds no different from the dozens of boys she sees daily. Before she opened her store, she asked some street kids what they thought she should sell. The boys wanted Jeeps and tanks and soldiers; the girls, necklaces and bracelets. One boy who washed cars told Sanam, "I can't go to school. My father died and I have to feed my family." Another boy sold magazines. Both his parents were dead. He wept as he spoke. "Buy one and you will help me," he said. Sanam bought all of his magazines. Most of the time, she tries to ignore street children. She can't support all of them.

Aarash and I return to NATO. This time the parking attendant motions us into a space. Leaning through the open window on the driver's side, he tells Aarash that Ghani is here.

"Wait," he tells us.

Crossing the street, he disappears into the congested sidewalk only to emerge seconds later with Ghani dragging his sack of cans and wearing the same soiled clothes and pugnacious expression he wore yesterday.

"Where did you go after the guard hit you?" Aarash asks him.

"I returned to NATO about two hours later," he says.

It was the start of a bad day. An older boy, maybe fifteen,

took his cans, about two dollars' worth, that afternoon and punched Ghani. "These cans are mine, why do you come here? Go. Leave," the boy said before he beat him in the back with a pipe. Ghani cried and the boy laughed as he dumped Ghani's cans into his own sack, threw the empty sack at Ghani, and ran away.

Walking home, his back aching, Ghani collected just a dollar's worth of cans. Enough to pay for tea and some bread. He gave the bread to his siblings. Then he lay down to sleep. He dreamed about how he must earn money. His father had supported the family by driving a taxi after they moved to Kabul from Gorgi, a village near the Pakistan border. He was always advising Ghani to work. He rarely talked about anything else. He would say, "Go to school and work. Do both."

When Ghani attended school, he played with his friend Mohammad during recess. Ghani does not remember specific things about Mohammad other than he was fun to be with and they studied math and Persian together. Persian was difficult but the boys liked math, the calculation required when they added up long columns of numbers. Ghani has not seen Mohammad in months.

"My father was my hero," Ghani says. "He took care of us and I did not have to work. Now I have no freedom."

This morning when Ghani woke up, he thought about the boy who stole his cans. He worried he might see him again, but he had to work so he said to himself over and over again, "He won't come back, don't worry."

"Are you still scared?" Aarash says.

"No. Well, yes. A little."

"Tell him we want to follow him for a day," I tell Aarash. "From where he lives to here and back again."

Ghani agrees to let us spend time with him. He tells Aarash he lives in Kart-e-Now, a poor district in west Kabul. He says to meet him in the morning about six by a bus stop. He will take us to a recycler who gives him a sack every morning to collect cans. From there, we'll follow him to NATO. I tell him we want to meet his family too, but Ghani says we can't. The village elders would never permit it. Not a Westerner, no. They are very conservative.

I don't push it. We'll spend the day together first and I'll take it from there. I give Ghani a dollar and apologize for taking him away from collecting cans. He says nothing, folds the money into his fist. He leans forward and watches my hand shove my wallet back into my pants pocket. When he sees that we have no more questions, he leaves, looking one last time at where I put my wallet.

The name of the parking attendant is Hamood. He watches the Westerner and Aarash walk to their car after they finish talking to the boy. He has been a parking lot attendant for five months. He expects he will no longer be a parking attendant when NATO leaves but doesn't worry too much about it. That is for tomorrow, not today.

Every day he wears a gray salwar kameez to work, and sneakers without laces, no socks. The grit stirred by cars sticks to his face like heavily applied makeup. A relative helped him get the job. When he doesn't work, he attends school from eleven in the morning until four. After school, he works a part-time maintenance job at a hotel. He lives at home and takes care of his mother and father. His father had been a truck driver but now drives a taxi. He is weak and old and suffers from diabetes.

Hamood's family always needs something: cooking oil, rice,

bread, something. These needs make him think about today and not tomorrow.

In other countries, like the United States, where the Westerner is from, people have goals. Here in Kabul, people just try to survive. Even when Afghans have goals, they don't stick to them. They will drop a goal to make money for today. Afghans have a saying: God willing, if I'm able to do this, I'll do it. If not, I'll go back to my goal. There's no achieving anything in Afghanistan.

Jawad assumes his seat on the steps of the Wazir Mohammad Akbar Khan Mosque, his shoeshine box beside him, when he sees the Westerner and Aarash park their car. Shoe polish speckles his school clothes, a blue shirt and black pants. Most days, he changes behind the mosque into his work clothes, hiding his school clothes in a stone oven no one uses, but his little brother forgot to bring him his work clothes this afternoon. Jawad will beat him for his forgetfulness tonight.

"How is school?" Aarash asks him.

Jawad makes a face. He digs into his school pack and withdraws a sheet with his exam scores. Science (thirty-four correct out of forty), religion (twenty-four correct out of forty), English (thirty-six correct out of forty), Dari (twenty-three correct out of forty), and algebra (twelve correct out of forty). A score of twenty or less is a failing grade.

"I flunked my math exam again," Jawad tells Aarash. "My mind does not work with algebra."

He notices the Westerner looking at a fresh cut on his wrist, and he hides his arm behind his back. This time, he cut himself for a girl, not the exam. She is so beautiful. When he looks at her she smiles, but he can't tell her that he likes her because he is poor. Her family has money. Her father owns a good shop.

Jawad possesses only a shoeshine box. Money, he understands, means everything. As a poor boy, no one notices him.

Evening, and outside NATO headquarters in the parking lot, the soldier Qudratullah prepares to return to his barracks. A few children mill around the gate.

"You stink bad, you smell like garbage," he hears a fruit vendor shout at them. "Leave here."

Qudratullah has not seen the guard since he chased off the children. Perhaps he quit his job. The guard knows the Taliban will kill him for working with Westerners. Qudratullah understands the same is true for himself. An hour outside Kabul, beyond the safety of downtown, his life would be in danger. He has been married six years and has been to his father-in-law's house only once, because he does not want to put his in-laws at risk. He can't visit his wife and three children, attend parties, or mourn the dead at funerals. Even a taxi driver cannot leave the center of Kabul if he has accepted fares from Westerners. The Taliban has very good intelligence, better than the government has. They would kill the taxi driver too.

Qudratullah patrolled the Kandahar highway after he enlisted in the Afghan National Army in 2008. The Taliban would watch him and the other soldiers with binoculars. The bullets they fired made a sound like a zipper, hiss, hiss. One night in Ramadan, he and two other soldiers went home on leave. Later in the evening, a man on a motorcycle shot the two soldiers when they stepped outside to smoke. Some soldiers are advised not to leave their province, because it's too dangerous. Qudratullah's cousin received the same advice but didn't listen. He volunteered on a convoy out of Kabul to Khost Province in the east and the Taliban shot him and cut off his head.

Now with NATO leaving, Afghanistan is like a crowded room. Everyone is waiting to see what will happen. Afghans have a saying: Give an Afghan bread and don't shout at him and you can lead him by the ear. If NATO withdraws, there will be no jobs and no bread, but there will be a lot of shouting.

At four o'clock Hamood prepares to leave the parking lot for school, where he will pass the cemetery where his maternal grandfather is buried. His grandfather cooked for the Mujahideen during the civil war. One day, the Mujahideen robbed and killed him. At night now, blood runs down the stairs of his house. Girls hide behind his grave when boys bother them. A ghost killed one of those boys a few years ago. Everyone knows this and boys now avoid the cemetery.

That his grandfather had enough money for the Mujahideen to kill him amazes Hamood. What he earns from his two jobs, less than fifty dollars a month, would tempt only the most desperate criminals.

Working at the parking lot gives Hamood a physical but not a mental break. Yes, he gets to move around and work outside and he is not stuck behind a desk, but his mind feels tight, his head aches. It is clear to him he is killing time, killing himself with this drudgery

Sanam closes her store about the same time Hamood leaves the parking lot. On the crowded sidewalk outside, boys run up to her with their hands out but she turns away. If she gave to all of them she would have nothing. She was seven, not much older than some of these children, when the Taliban came to power and her family fled to Iran. But Afghans have a saying: The dust of your country calls you back. And her family returned to Afghanistan permanently after 9/11.

The other day in Kabul, a man poured boiling water over a woman for refusing to wear a burqa. These things scare Sanam. Other problems annoy and exhaust her. No one can do anything without paying a bribe. She needed a license to open her store. Being a woman, she paid double what a man would have paid.

Afghans have a saying: When there are problems, wait until the fifty-ninth minute. She will wait and see what happens after NATO leaves. If necessary, she will escape to Iran again, in the sixtieth minute.

After he drops the reporter off at his hotel, Aarash drives home. His four-year-old son, he knows, will demand that he take him swimming. Aarash anticipates the boy jumping into his arms and laughs, and then he stops laughing. He cannot feel happy without his thoughts turning to some dark place; his mind jumps to something totally unrelated to the image of his son greeting him, and he considers NATO's withdrawal. He does not want his son to grow up in the Afghanistan he knew as a child, one where the Mujahideen would shoot rocket-propelled grenades into his neighborhood at all hours. One afternoon, when his father was out and the ferocity of the fighting was particularly intense, his mother sent him to his uncle's house. She thought he would be safer there. Aarash saw dead people lying in the street and collapsed against fruit stalls. So many dead bodies. Even on backstreets he heard gunshots. He would stop, look, run. His uncle wasn't home. He ran back to his house but no one heard him knocking. Then his father came home and held him until he stopped crying and took him inside. That night, electric lines broke, snapping and writhing like snakes in the dark.

In September 1996, Aarash saw the body of Afghan president Mohammad Najibullah Ahmadzai, commonly known as
Najibullah or Najib, after the Taliban had hanged him. A crowd
gathered and people laughed at the slowly spinning corpse.
They shoved paper up his rectum and into his penis. "That's
good, the dog is dead," Aarash heard one man say. Aarash
covered his mouth to stop himself from vomiting. When his
stomach settled, he felt nothing, as if his soul had left his body.
From that day onward, a piece of himself was missing. Was it
compassion? Disgust? Anger? He doesn't know.

Aarash did not collect cans or polish shoes after his father
died. He stayed in school as his mother told him to do. "That is
what your father would want," she said. As the only son, Aarash
felt he should support his family, but his father had done everything. What would Aarash do? He learned carpet weaving and
embroidered burqas, and he studied English to be a translator
for Western aid agencies.

"Don't follow the behavior of bad boys," his father had told
him. "Don't learn bad words." One afternoon, while he played
marbles outside with his friends, his father came out of the
house and took him inside. "Today," he said, "you play for fun,
but tomorrow you'll be gambling. I'd never want to see that,"
and he beat Aarash on his head and back. Later that evening, he
apologized, but today Aarash sees the beating as a good thing,
the apology unnecessary. His father had guided him to lead a
good life and be a parent to his son.

II

Eighteen-year-old Enit has not been awake long when he sees
a Westerner and an Afghan man park across the street from the

camp where he and his family live in Kart-e-Now. He rubs his eyes and then runs his hands over his dirty and damp clothes. He pours water over his hands from a jug that originally held cooking oil and drags his fingers through his tangled hair. Six o'clock in the morning. Fruit and vegetable vendors have just begun arranging their stalls. Horses and mules stand roped to stakes in the ground and thin dogs sleep beneath them. Barefoot men gather in groups with no purpose. Enit squints at them squatting and pissing on the hard, rocky ground. Flies rise in swirling lines. Piles of horse shit and donkey shit. The sun glints off the rusted tin sidings supporting some of the tents and the reflected heat presses against the bodies of those nearby.

The Afghan locks the car and he and the Westerner approach a group of men. "Do you know a boy named Ghani?" the Afghan asks them. The men frown and shake their heads, and the Afghan and the Westerner move on. They walk from one group of men to another until they approach Enit. The Afghan tells him he is working with an American reporter who wants to interview a boy. The boy is supposed to meet them here but the Afghan does not see him. The boy's name is Ghani.

"Do you know him?"

Enit shakes his head. He does not know this boy. There are many boys in the camp and even more in the mud-brick compounds across the street. Perhaps someone in Enit's family knows him. He invites the Afghan to his tent for tea. The Afghan and the American follow Enit along a stone path. At the end of the path, they step over a drainage ditch and Enit folds back the flap of a tent. Hunching through the opening, they enter single-file. The ground inside is strewn with pots, pans, kettles, charred wood, and blankets. In one corner, piles of rice, tomatoes, beans. A naked six-week-old baby girl sleeps on a heap of blankets beside a pile of wet clothes. Flies suck at the edges of her mouth. Enit's brother and sister-in-law sit beside her with pieces of bread in their laps. Their faces gleam with perspiration. The stale, claustrophobic air smells of smoke and unwashed bodies.

Enit and his sixteen-year-old pregnant wife, Asal, share the tent with his father and mother as well as his brother and sister-in-law. None of them knows Ghani. They have lived here since they left their home in Jalalabad four years ago. Everyone had told them they'd find work in Kabul but instead Enit collects cans just as he did in Jalalabad. The United Nations erected sixty tents here for people like Enit's family—who had nothing but what they were able to carry. He has not seen a UN representative since.

"You can see with your eyes we live in shit," he says. "I am a young man. No one wants to live here."

Asal has blood problems, low iron, the doctor told them. Last December, she gave birth to twin boys but they died four weeks later. When he got to the hospital with food Enit had prepared for Asal, Enit's mother told him, "They are gone." Asal wept and Enit stood beside her bed and cried too. He buried them near the camp and visits their graves once a week, but Asal never does. It is forbidden for a pregnant woman to be in a cemetery; bad spirits will inhabit the baby. Neither Asal nor Enit knows when the child is due.

"Afghans have a saying," Enit says. "The people who die wait for their families to visit on Saturday."

He blames Kabul's frigid winters for the deaths of his babies. To pay for their burial, he borrowed money from the recycler who buys his cans and he still owes the man two hundred forty dollars. The bicycle he rides to collect cans also belongs to the recycler, who takes half of Enit's daily earnings. Lately, the recycler has told Enit that he and not the UN owns the land where Enit and the other families live. He wants them out but has set no deadline.

If he had the money, Enit would return to Jalalabad, because it doesn't get cold there. In Kabul, when snow covers the ground, Enit walks from house to house and asks for cans and bread. The bread he sells as feed for farm animals. On good days, when he has collected many cans, the weight of the burlap sacks on the back of his bicycle keeps him struggling for balance. Sometimes he falls and the cans fly out onto the street in a clattering wave. Enit scrambles to gather back what he can. Drivers beep and shout, "Crazy man! What are you doing?"

The Afghan says he and the American must leave to find the boy Ghani. They stand and Enit leads them out of the tent. He tells the Afghan it would be a big help if his American friend bought him a motorbike, because then he could make money offering people rides and be respected. People don't look at him with respect on a bicycle. To them he is of no more value than his cans.

The Afghan translates this for the American. The American says nothing. Across the street Ghani waves and the Afghan and the American hurry toward him and away from Enit.

Mohammed Tahir's family has sold wooden beams to construction companies in Kabul's Eighth District since the time of Mohammed Zahir Shah, the last monarch of Afghanistan, who assumed the throne in 1933. Tahir was born twenty years later. He grew into a big man with large hands and thick arms and a full black beard. With the help of day laborers, he stacks the beams on flatbed trailers. Tahir's office stands a few feet from a recycling dump littered with cans and plastic jugs and hubcaps. Spoiled watermelon rinds and bananas buzz with flies and dogs pick their way up through the piles of discard like mountain goats.

Every day, Tahir sees boys and girls stop at the shack of the recycler and ask for sacks to collect cans and plastic bottles. Tahir shouts at them, "Don't steal from here or other shops." Under the Taliban, this area had been clean, unlike the mess it is today. He didn't see children collecting cans then. Afghans have a saying: If you plant a tree and tie it straight, it will grow straight. But these children were never tied straight. They steal here and sell there. They are nothing if not thieves. Still, Tahir has a soft spot for some of these boys, especially those he thinks could amount to something if given a chance.

On this morning he is more than a little surprised to see a Westerner and an Afghan following Ghani. He walks up to them, as Ghani stops at the shack and speaks to the recycler.

"Where's my bag?"

"It's gone," the man tells him. "Another boy came before you did and I gave it to him. You can find one on the street."

"Yes, I'll find one."

Ghani turns around to leave. Tahir stops him.

"How are you doing?"

"I am fine."

"No, how are you doing?"

"Don't talk to me about it," Ghani says.

"How are you?" Tahir insists.

"Leave me alone!"

Ghani's eyes begin to tear. He waves his arms as if he is trying to shoo Tahir away like the flies buzzing around his face. Tahir turns to the Afghan.

"His mother died yesterday," Tahir says.

"What?" the Afghan says. "Died? No, his father is dead."

"And now his mother," Tahir says.

"He told us nothing about his mother," the Afghan says.

Tahir invites them into his office. He puts a hand on Ghani's back and brings him along. The four of them sit on a rug and Tahir calls to an assistant to bring them tea.

"Two days ago he came here for a bag and on his way out I stopped him and said, 'Why don't you study? You only make so little a day. Why aren't you in school?'" Tahir says. "And then he started crying and I asked him why was he crying. He said his mother had died that morning. I was upset. I couldn't believe God would do this to a family already so poor and without a father."

"Are you sure?" the Afghan asks him.

"That's what he told me," Tahir says. "Look at him."

Ghani dabs his eyes with his sleeve.

"Tell them what happened," Tahir says.

"After my father died, my mother said she had only a short time to live," Ghani says. "She had a tumor inside her head like him. She took me to the doctor with her and he said in front of me, 'She won't survive.' We went home. In the middle of the night, she started coughing and woke us all up. She told me to take care of the family. 'I believe in you,' she said. She closed her eyes and died in our tent. My father had coughed the same way and he died the same way. Some relatives from Pakistan buried her and then they went back to Pakistan. They asked us to come with them but I said, 'No. I am responsible for the family now.'"

"Go home to your sister and brother," Tahir says.

"I don't know what to do," Ghani says. "I have to live. I have to survive."

"God help you," Tahir says.

Hours later, I lie in my bed and stare at the ceiling. The death of Ghani's mother still surprises me. What a great, unexpected twist for the story. Horrible thing to say, I know. But it is. My editor will love Ghani. What a monster I am. No. Not a monster. I gave him ten dollars so he would not need to work today. I can still see how he grabbed the money from my hand, a hard look crossing his face, and then he began to cry again and hurried away.

What will he do once that money is spent? Collect cans, I presume. Ghani's life is beyond anything I've known. He falls so far below the radar that his life makes the premise of my trip here ludicrous. For children like him, it matters little if NATO stays or leaves. He works the outer edges of society, a feral boy beyond the reach of policy and diplomacy and its consequences.

Ghani will pull through. He knows how to live with nothing. What kind of person he will become raises an entirely different set of questions. But he'll survive.

Jawad, however, eases my conscience. He has the potential for a different future. He's social, motivated to please. I could see him working at the Chelsea Supermarket near my hotel, bagging groceries, much as my high school friends and I did when we were his age. But there the comparison ends.

The looks on the faces of the Chelsea cashiers leave the impression that they are not working in a supermarket among eager shoppers at all but rather at some great remove, observing foreigners like me spending money in a manner so beyond their means (canned tuna, three dollars; Tabasco sauce, five dollars;

Wonder Bread, five dollars; Snickers bar, two dollars) that they are rendered mute, and then someone sets a basket on the checkout counter and the cashiers start moving without expression, scanning cans and bottles and cartons and taking money and making change as in any Western supermarket, except that here shoppers are directed toward an exit where street children like Jawad wait for them.

The next morning, Aarash and I stop at the Wazir Mohammad Akbar Khan Mosque. We see Jawad mopping the steps, his shoe box and rags off to one side. Aarash calls him over. He jogs up to us smiling, eager to talk.

While we had been with Ghani the day before, a mullah with a long beard who wore a white salwar kameez and a gray turban asked to have his shoes polished. Armed guards stood on either side of him.

"How much?" he asked Jawad.

"Whatever you give me," Jawad said.

"Why are you polishing shoes?"

"I have to work."

"Where's your father?"

"He died."

The mullah told Jawad that he taught at Omar Madrassa in Kabul and offered to enroll him without charge. Jawad could live at the school and would not need to work, only study. The mullah would provide for him and his entire family. He gave Jawad his phone number. "Speak to your mother," he told him.

"What about the school you are going to now?" Aarash asks Jawad.

"I haven't been there since the second time I failed the math exam."

Men begin walking into the mosque and Jawad hurries after them to polish their shoes. I watch him make his sales pitch. A few men stop and kick off their sandals. Who was this mullah who spoke to him? In some cases, leaders of madrassas use their schools to indoctrinate would-be jihadists.

"What do you think?" I ask Aarash.

"Either he is a good man or he is recruiting them for the insurgency. I don't know. Afghans have a saying: You can't judge a man by what people say. All we know about him is what Jawad has told us."

At NATO that afternoon, we find Ghani sitting on a curb, an empty sack beside him. His left arm is swollen and wrapped in a bandage. Hamood, Qudratullah, and a handful of street kids are standing around. The heat beats down on us, the empty streets stark white from the sun. Insects hover in the air but make no sound.

"I was walking, slipped, and fell on my arm," Ghani tells us. "I was not able to get up. A nice guy helped me. He gave me money so I could take a taxi to a doctor. The doctor said it would cost fifty dollars to X-ray my arm."

We stare at him without speaking. Who among us has fifty dollars? I do. Aarash looks at me. What did he say when he saw the body of Najibullah? It felt as if his soul had left his body. But not so completely that he doesn't expect me to help Ghani.

I reach for my wallet. Ghani leans forward, eyeballing me with that disturbing intensity he has whenever I've given him money. I hesitate. How would this end? When would I in good conscience be able to stop caring for him once I got started? I'm here to write about him, not save him. I withdraw my hand from my pocket without my wallet. Ghani's head sags to his chest and he turns away.

"When bad luck comes, it comes from all sides," he says after a long moment.

"What will you do?" I ask him.

"What can I do? My arm is in pain but all I can do is work."

He stands and cradles his bad arm against his stomach. Dragging his sack behind him with his other hand, he shuffles away.

In the following days, Aarash and I search for Ghani but we can't find him. Not at NATO. Not in Kart-e-Now. Not anywhere. We ask everyone we've met about him.

Jawad: "No, I've not seen this boy. I'd say he is not honest. No Afghan related to this family would leave orphaned children like this, especially with an unmarried girl of sixteen."

Mohammed Tahir: "He has not been by here since I last saw him with you. Such a mess. He might not be an orphan. Beggars are trained. They make fake tears to get to your heart. If that is the case, he got to mine."

Hamood: "I don't know where he is. Sometimes when these beggar boys say they have no parents, they do this to protect their mother, because their father is dead and they don't want men to bother her."

Enit: "No family would leave him alone in a condition like this. If the father dies, an uncle would marry the mother. They would not let a boy tell them he was responsible for the family. The children would not be abandoned."

Sanam Sadaat: "Maybe he is hiding something. Is his mother alive? Or is an elder telling him not to say much to strangers? We don't know."

Qudratullah: "I see street kids and I think my kids could be them if I am killed. How would my wife ask them to pick up cans? I don't know what happened to this boy. But unless everyone is dead—aunts, uncles, grandparents—someone would help him."

Their comments give me pause. Was Ghani an orphan? Was he caring for his older sister and two younger brothers as he said? Was no relative willing to take them in? Would the village elders have prevented us from meeting his siblings as he said? Had he used me as much as I had used him—a boy suitable for my story—and abandoned me as much as I would have abandoned him had he not already done so?

Aarash: "Ghani is gone from us. This is all we know."

III

Jawad continues to see Aarash and me in parks and on the street, wherever we catch him polishing shoes. He tells us he has called the mullah several times but no one answers. His older brother doubts his intentions.

"No one helps for free," he warned.

Without telling Jawad, Aarash and I have decided to meet a man who has connections with conservative Muslims and may know about Omar Madrassa. His name is Ali, and he and Aarash taught English together before Aarash started working as a translator and they lost touch. Then a few years ago, they ran into each other. Ali said he had been traveling between Kabul and Peshawar visiting family. I have been to Peshawar a few times. Each time I dressed in a salwar kameez and hoped to pass as Pakistani. I doubt I fooled anyone, but the area around Peshawar, and parts of the city too, were then and remain heavily Taliban, and I felt more secure not wearing Western clothing.

Walking downtown, we reach an office complex where we're to meet Ali at Tasty, a restaurant below a bank. Sunlight glints off the building and I see mud-hut-lined mountains on the outskirts of Kabul reflected against the blue-tinted windows of Tasty, giving the impression that the mountains stand underwater. Tiny figures move about the slopes, leading goats and donkeys on narrow paths far from the roads leading into Kabul and its crowded shopping centers. The post-Taliban entrepreneurial class, boosted by tens of millions of dollars of international investment and thousands of foreign troops, contractors, and aid workers with money to spend, has adopted visceral, sensory names for new Western-style eateries. Aarash had hoped we'd meet at Yummy Fast Food, a restaurant similar to McDonald's.

Dim lighting keeps much of Tasty's interior dark and impenetrable and we pause inside the door until our eyes adjust to the dark. Square glass tables are arranged in rows by the front door, and across the room, sofas and deep chairs encircle a flat-screen TV. Fans stand behind the sofas but have not been plugged in. The air feels cooler than outside but heavy and damp. A Bollywood movie plays without sound.

Aarash notices Ali sitting on one of the sofas, his back to the television. He looks up at the sound of our steps against the tile floor. Standing, he hugs Aarash. Ali is twenty-four. He wears jeans and a pink shirt buttoned to the collar. Prayer beads encircle his right hand and he rubs them with his thumb. Without the beads, Ali would pass as a member of the post-9/11 generation of young, Western-influenced Afghans.

Aarash is unmistakably Westernized. He, too, likes blue jeans and brightly colored shirts, sans the prayer beads, and he leaves buttons open to expose his chest. I have never seen him stop to worship, even when mullahs announce the call to prayer on loudspeakers heard throughout the city. He has no regard for the Taliban. A friend of his was arrested by their morality police for licking an ice cream cone in public in 1999 and was charged with suggestive behavior. He spent a night in jail. Aarash laughed at the absurdity of his arrest.

On another occasion, the morality police stopped at a school where Aarash taught English. A policeman shouted that a mullah had accused the English students of not attending their mosques. Aarash locked the front door so the police would think the school was closed and he and the students lay down away from the windows to avoid being seen. The police pounded on the door and did not leave for three hours.

Those years feel very distant inside Tasty. After Aarash introduces me, I tell Ali about Jawad and Omar Madrassa.

"I can see why he would be drawn to the madrassa," I say. "He would be taken care of, and his family too. Without a father, that's pretty attractive."

"Jawad has no father?"

"No. His father died a couple of years ago."

"I don't know Omar Madrassa," Ali says. "I do know madrassas look for students they think are already good Muslims. They recruit people we can count on."

He stops, covers his mouth.

"They, we, with my English I get my pronouns confused," he says and smiles. "I was born in Peshawar, did Aarash tell you? When I was eighteen, I moved to Kabul with my family in 2008. I still have connections in Peshawar. Sometimes at a wedding party or a funeral I meet them. Connections help me when I travel to Pakistan because the areas between Kabul and Peshawar are so insecure."

"These connections, are they Taliban?"

"Inside the Taliban there are so many people. The Taliban

can't count all the people working with them who have different ideas and answer to different philosophies. Let's just call who I know as my connections."

"And the people they do recruit, what do they want with them? Jihadists?"

"In the Holy Koran, God never forgives anyone if they take even a penny without that person's permission. If God forbids taking a penny, how can he condone taking a life?"

He pauses.

"There is a verse in the Koran: Whoever kills without reason, he will be in hell forever."

"But if they don't agree they will find another verse," Aarash says.

Ali gives Aarash a look of surprised annoyance.

"Not everyone believes the same," Ali tells him.

"Not everyone," Aarash agrees.

I try to ignore the discomfiting silence between them. A woman in the Bollywood movie dances up a flight of stairs to a balcony overlooking the sea. Her hands press against her bare stomach and she sashays in circles around a young man who reaches for her, but she remains beyond his grasp.

"Teachers with madrassas don't recruit on the street," Ali says after a long moment. "The people on the street are not reliable. They are just surviving. They have no convictions. They steal. They are not good assets for the country and not even for their family. I'd be surprised if a mullah is interested in Jawad."

"He polishes shoes at a mosque."

"Which one?"

"Wazir Mohammad Akbar Khan Mosque. On the main road."

"Yes, I know it."

"In exchange, he sweeps and mops the floors. The mullahs must like him."

"I see," Ali says. "If he helps at the mosque, then he may be recruited. He sounds like a good boy."

A waiter stops at our table and we order Cokes and he gives us a box of Kleenex to use for napkins. He calls for the Cokes and another waiter rushes over with them. Both waiters wear ill-fitting white shirts, black vests, and black pants. The first waiter offers us menus filled with misspellings: Piza. Hamurgers. Ches burgers. Chic burgers. Chic wings.

"Just Cokes," Aarash says, handing back the menus.

The waiters nod and leave.

"The people I know, some of them are with the armed side, others the political side," Ali says, inserting a straw into his Coke. "The political side is filled with well-educated people. Someone who would recruit boys would be part of the political side. They have networks or departments within the group, says the Taliban. The youth network observes schools. It confronts boys, 'Why aren't you going to school? Why are you absent?' They pressure schools to fire teachers not teaching true Islam. They see which boys have potential. When is Jawad at the mosque?"

"Afternoons. After school."

Ali nods, sips his Coke.

"From my point of view, the youth networks are taking care of boys so they don't become problems. So they don't end up on the street like Jawad. When does he attend school?"

"Mornings."

Ali glances at the dancing women on the TV and blushes. We finish our Cokes and I pay our bill. The two waiters slouch on chairs by the front door with bored expressions. They don't acknowledge us as we walk outside and squint against the bright sunlight. I shake Ali's hand and thank him for his time.

"When will you see Jawad again?"

"I don't know," I tell him. "He has a mobile phone but he doesn't have the money to pay for minutes. Aarash and I usually just drive by the mosque. Sometimes we see him. Sometimes we don't."

"He has a mobile?"

"Yes."

Ali asks for Jawad's number. Aarash taps a file on his iPhone and gives it to him.

"I'll better understand Omar Madrassa, what the man said to him, if I talk to him," Ali explains.

"It would be easier if you come with us when we go to the mosque. We'll call you. You can meet him then."

"I will try calling him," Ali says.

We shake hands again and he walks toward downtown, merging into the crowded sidewalk until he is indistinguishable. There is a boy you should meet, I imagine him telling his connections, a good boy for the youth network. Ali is getting by in his own way as much as Jawad is in his. I have an uneasy feeling that I told him too much.

On my last day in Kabul, we join Jawad at Kart-e-Now Hill Cemetery, where his father is buried. Large stone slabs shaped like arrowheads mark the graves on a barren hill overlooking a parched valley of brown mud huts. Weeds snake through the ground and plastic bags snagged on rocks flap in the wind.

We stop at a grave surrounded by an ankle-high fence. Jawad's father lies here beneath the hard, dry, uneven ground. Jawad visits every Saturday. His mother never accompanies him. A mullah told her that the dead can see all the visitors naked, and she had a dream that night in which Jawad's father told her not to come. He did not want dead men to see her body. Jawad wonders whether dead women see the naked bodies of men.

"A memory I have of my father was on a trip we made to Mazar-e-Sharif," Jawad says. "He moved his mouth as if he was chewing and made me laugh. He was always making me laugh."

Jawad prays to his father and tells him things to pass on to God. Like how he is in love with a girl beyond his reach and needs God's help to find another girl. He believes that with his father's help, God will assist him with this problem.

A convoy of military vehicles inches forward on the thin ribbon of road beneath us. One green truck has a flag I don't recognize painted on its side. European, I'm sure, but I don't know what country. NATO member, certainly. We watch it pass. I tell Jawad I have to go, type up the day's notes, and get ready to fly out in the morning. In the States, I'll speak to my editor. I called him from my hotel after Ghani disappeared. I told him I had another kid, Jawad. Not as good as the nine-year-old, he said.

Jawad, Aarash, and I leave the cemetery. The convoy rounds a curve and suddenly we can no longer see it. In less than twenty-four hours I'll be gone too. I give Jawad twenty dollars. At first he refuses to accept it but I insist and he grins and thanks me.

"Have you prayed to your father about the madrassa?" I ask him.

"No," Jawad tells me.

He assumes God knows all about madrassas and that there is no need for his father to intervene. He will call the mullah again. If he does not answer, Jawad will shine shoes. It is his life.

GRAVE DIGGER

By the time I reach the morgue on a hot August morning, Khwaja Naqib Ahmad has already finished washing the two male bodies that he and an assistant and I will drive to a cemetery to bury. He wrapped each of them in white cloth twenty-two meters long and thirty centimeters wide. A worker from the Ministry of Health helped him. He cataloged the bodies as Nos. 337 and 312.

At fifty-two, Ahmad stands a little stooped. Gray hair flecks the beard that comes to a sharp point at his chin. His tanned, lined face breaks into an easy smile when he talks. "We carry on. It's just a job," he says of his work. Yet as he speaks, his eyes have the distant look of a man who spends his time in realms of sorrow and loss, a proximity to death that he experiences alone, among maimed bodies, unidentified and unclaimed.

He does not know how 337 and 312 died. They did not die at the hands of a suicide attacker; he knows that much. They are whole, in one piece. Whole bodies are cool to the touch when he washes them. He feels the difference between life and death in their stiff, cold limbs. They appear as if nothing is wrong. He half expects them to talk.

Ahmad has no illusions of life when corpses come to him in pieces. It is complicated when the body has been destroyed by a bomb. The bodies come apart in his hands. He sees worms. He coughs, gets sick.

On October 8, 2009, Ahmad buried what remained of a suicide bomber who attacked the Indian embassy. The explosion killed seventeen Afghans and wounded sixty-three others, including Indian security personnel. The Taliban took responsibility.

I tell Ahmad that two days ago I interviewed the widow of an Afghan National Police officer who had died as a result of this attack. Ahmad says nothing. I want to know what he, as the man who buried her husband's killer, would say to her. But his silence cuts me off. Perhaps he has enough on his mind without considering the widows and orphans and others who have been left behind.

The twenty-seven-year-old widow of the dead police officer lives in a mud-brick house in west Kabul. Her name is Gulaly. On the day of my interview, she stands waiting for me at the door. I follow her into a living room filled with red carpets and colorful wall hangings. Motioning toward a couch, Gulaly waits until I sit down before she takes a chair across from me. I give her a bag of grapes to show my appreciation for her hospitality. She thanks me, gets up, and puts them in a glass bowl. Rinsing them with water from a pitcher, she sets them on a counter near photographs of her dead husband, Abdul Majeed, and her three children, a three-and-a-half-year-old boy and two girls, five and six.

Abdul is standing before a blue backdrop, unsmiling, a formal look for the camera. He has black hair and a thick black mustache. His chin juts forward with pride. I assume his stiff pose is his idea of appearing dignified. I find it almost comical, and imagine his shoulders relaxing and a smile crossing his face once the photographer finished, laughing at himself for the stern posture he assumed. But maybe he did no such thing. That is what I would have done. I am imposing my personality on his to understand him, to make him come alive for me. I tell Gulaly what I am thinking.

"I was not there when the photograph was taken but you are right in that he had a sense of humor," she says. "We never fought or argued. He was a flexible man. He behaved like a child with our children and an adult when he was around an elder. I would ask him, 'Why are you being a child with our children?' and he would say, 'With a child you have to be a child to bond with them.'"

She looks out an open window overlooking a street filled with people. I notice two vendors selling bananas and oranges, and the men and women picking through their wagons.

"When Abdul died I lost part of myself," Gulaly says without looking away from the window. A breeze ruffles her red head scarf and inflates her red pants and long-sleeved red blouse.

After a long moment, she turns to face me. She remains remote. Her mouth slants down on the left side of her face where she has lost some teeth and gives the impression of a perpetual frown. She takes her time formulating answers when I ask her questions, each pause stretching between us until at times I wonder whether she has forgotten the question. Occasionally tears fill her eyes and her face grows taut as she fights them back. I look out the window and wait until she regains her composure.

Abdul called her after the bomb exploded.

"I'm OK," he told her.

"I just saw it on the TV," she said.

"I'm OK," he insisted. "I'm in the office. There was a fight between some police and terrorists. They were hurt. I wasn't in the blast. I'm OK."

Gulaly asked when he would be home.

"I'm taking the injured to the hospital. I'm just taking care of others. If I don't come home, it is because I'm busy with them."

After three days he returned home on crutches. A plaster cast encased his right leg. Blood leaked through the cast.

"What happened?" Gulaly asked him.

"I just got a small injury," he said.

After two weeks, when the bleeding did not stop, he told Gulaly he had been severely injured. He had lost most of his right foot in the blast. Gulaly had not noticed, because the cast hid what remained of his foot. Abdul smiled as if embarrassed.

"I'm fine," he told her. "After all, I still have my left foot."

Ahmad and his assistant carry Nos. 337 and 312 out of the morgue on green cloth stretchers to a white van. The parking lot reflects the bright sunlight and they pause in the glare, squinting. A security guard shies away from them.

"When the bodies smell, you skip away from the door," Ahmad says and laughs.

They set the bodies side by side behind the front seats of the van and the three of us get in, flies trailing after us, and shut the doors. The assistant drives. Ahmad and I sit scrunched together on the passenger side. I watch Ahmad reach for a black and gray prayer shawl to cover his balding head against the sun and then, without at first understanding why, I feel frantic and push back against my seat and cover my face, shaking my head against an indescribable odor. Sharp, acidic, spoiled. The bodies. Ahmad puts mint leaves in a surgical mask and hands it to me. I press the mask against my nose and mouth and tie it behind my head and take short, quick breaths. Behind me, I hear the flies buzzing.

"After all these years I am still not used to the smell," Ahmad says as he crushes mint between his fingers and into his mask.

Ahmad works for the Municipality of Kabul and has been responsible for the burial of unclaimed bodies since 2005. He now organizes the burials of anyone brought to the municipality's attention by the police department, part of the Ministry of Interior.

According to documents, No. 337 came from Parwan Province, north of Kabul. No. 312 died in central Kabul. Ahmad does not know their ages or causes of death. Because he cleaned them and shaved their body hair, he knows that both of them are adults. No. 312 remained in the morgue for two days before the police notified the municipality about him. Parwan Province police held No. 337 for sixteen days. The drive from Parwan to Kabul would have taken about three hours. Ahmad does not know how long No. 337 lay in the heat before then. Other than Kabul, most police stations and morgues lack refrigeration.

"Even in plastic bags, they still smell," Ahmad says.

We turn onto the rutted road leading out of the morgue. The bodies bounce with each lurch of the van. The flies butt against the windows. I press the surgical mask harder against my nose. The sun beats down on us.

"Except for us, there will be no one there to cry for them today," Ahmad says.

Gulaly's husband, Abdul, continued working after his release from the hospital, but his injuries did not heal and he was in constant pain. After six months he resigned. He received sixteen hundred afghanis a month in disability, a little less than three hundred dollars. The police department sent him to specialists at Indraprastha Apollo Hospital in New Delhi. The doctors there amputated his right leg below the knee. They told Gulaly that Abdul would be fine, but his leg continued bleeding. The doctors then removed the rest of his leg. "He will be fine," they said again. Still the bleeding and pain continued.

The doctors performed three additional surgeries on the stump, all that remained of Abdul's leg. Nothing relieved the pain or the bleeding. The doctors assured the family that Abdul would recover and they returned to Afghanistan. When the pain became too great, Abdul made an appointment at Kaisha Health Care in Kabul. After an hour-long physical examination, the doctors concluded that the chemicals used in the bomb had poisoned his body. They told Gulaly he might live another year, maybe two or more, but he would never recover. She said nothing other than asking them not to tell Abdul. On her way home, he laughed and played with their children. Gulaly tried to ignore their antics; otherwise, she thought she might scream. She thought she was the one dying. She felt dead already.

On our way to the cemetery, Ahmad pulls over to help a motorcyclist stuck in the mud. He stops again to buy tea and cigarettes before he collects a pick and shovel at the Ministry of Health, as well as two stone slabs to put over the graves so that dogs don't dig up the bodies. We pass trucks carrying wood beams and shepherds urging goats and sheep along the road. Turning off onto what is little more than a dirt path furrowed by recent rains I see the plain, arrow-shaped headstones of the cemetery in the distance through lines of granular haze. Tree-less mountains rise up behind the cemetery, and a deep blue sky, intimidating by its vast emptiness, spreads above us.

"We are in Tara Khēl, a village in Deh Sabz District north-west of Kabul," Ahmad tells me. "The municipality owns the land but a warlord controls it. The warlord has guns; we have a van and shovels. How can we fight or challenge him?"

Ahmad parks by two open, narrow graves. I look into them at the clods of mud and stone strewn at the bottom and the tangled roots of some shorn plant jutting out on either side. A hot wind comes off the mountains and stirs the dirt at my feet. Emaciated dogs run ahead of Ahmad as he walks among the tombstones, all of them numbered. He points to a grave. A girl. Murdered in Bagram Village. Stabbed. She had been dead a month before Ahmad buried her fifteen days ago, her body bloated like a balloon.

Beside her lies a man from Khost Province, No. 225. Murdered, possibly kidnapped. After two months, no one claimed him. Old man, seventy-some years. Near him, the graves of three Afghan soldiers killed in Gardez. No family. A female commander in the Afghan National Army lies farther away. Murdered. No family. Not far from her lies the grave of a Nepalese man. He had been a guard at Bagram Airbase. Ahmad doesn't know why no one knows his name. Beside him, another foreigner. Ahmad can't remember the name of his native country.

Some of the dead are identified after they have been buried, Ahmad says. A family asks about a missing person, the police make an inquiry, and God willing, an identification is made. If the family has money, they will pay to have the deceased's name put on the tombstone. If they do not—and most do not—the number assigned to the dead person remains.

Ahmad walks a few feet from the foreigner's grave to what appears to be empty space within the cemetery. He stops and points at the ground. Beneath him in unmarked graves lie six men who were part of an attack on the US embassy in September 2012.

Just once in Ahmad's experience has a family asked for the body of a terrorist. A man came by Ahmad's office and said he was a victim of the June 2012 Taliban attack on the Spozhmai Hotel outside Kabul. He asked where the attackers were buried. Ahmad refused to tell him. The man came by so many times that Ahmad grew suspicious and told him to speak to officials within the Ministry of Interior. It turned out he was the father of one of the attackers.

"So many terrorists," Ahmad says. "They have family too."

Two days before Abdul died, Gulaly asked her husband whether something was wrong. "You look sad," she said. "No, I'm fine," he said. "I have a headache." He got his crutches and went out shopping with the children. Gulaly thinks now that he knew he was dying. He had grown weak, confused. He could not stand without help.

The next night, Gulaly was unable to sleep. She tried to pray but the words would not come. In the morning she fried eggs for the children. Afterward, she left the house to buy water. Her husband stayed behind sitting in their living room, his sister beside him. She had moved into the house to help with his care.

Gulaly had just reached the bazaar when her brother-in-law called her cellphone. He told her that his sister had called him and said, "Abdul is shaking and having convulsions." Gulaly almost dropped her phone. She ran back to the house, her sandals slapping on the pavement, the wind dragging at her clothes.

Abdul lay in bed, arms by his sides, eyes closed, a red comforter pulled up below his chin. His breathing was harsh and labored, his face pale and damp.

"Open your eyes," Gulaly told him. "See your children one last time before you leave us."

Abdul opened his eyes. He turned to look at his daughters and son and began to weep. His son cried. Abdul closed his eyes, took three deep breaths and died. October 28, 2012. Three years to the month after he had sustained his injuries. He was thirty-nine. At the funeral, his son asked why his father was being put in the ground; why was he being taken away? Because he is in Paradise, Gulaly told him.

"I want to be with my father," the boy said when they left the cemetery.

"He's not coming home," Gulaly replied.

"I know," the boy said.

For four months, Gulaly did not speak. She prayed and sat in the same chair in the living room day after day and rarely moved. Her family insisted she eat. "You'll get sick, and who will take care of the children?" they told her. "He's not coming back. Only you are here for them now."

Nine months elapsed before the police department completed the paperwork necessary for Gulaly to receive Abdul's death benefit of just under two hundred dollars a month. She would have received a higher stipend had he died on duty.

These days, her seventy-year-old father helps her. He takes the children to school and provides food. A brother-in-law wants to marry her. He is a rich man but she does not want to be his wife. "You are like a brother to me, not a husband," she told him. He expects her to ask for his help someday and then he thinks she will marry him. He knows as she does that her father won't live forever.

Gulaly bows her head. Her face quivers and I can see her struggling not to cry. "I'm sorry for your loss," I say. She nods, looking at the floor. I wait until she wipes her eyes. When she looks at me, I stand up.

"I should be going now," I say.

She follows me to the door and asks me how much longer I'll be in Afghanistan.

"A few more days," I tell her. "I have one more interview."

"With whom?" she asks.

"A man responsible for the burials of unidentified people," I say. "Including suicide bombers."

Gulaly gives me a sharp look. She steps in front of me and puts a hand out and stops me from opening the door.

"Your cemetery man is a good Muslim and does a good job, but they should not be buried," she says. "There is no afterlife for a suicide bomber. God will sentence them to the worst possible hell."

At the cemetery, Ahmad tugs on rubber gloves. He and his assistant carry Nos. 337 and 312 like sacks. Ahmad holds their legs; the assistant grips their shoulders. The bodies sag between them. A wet stain marks where they had lain on the stretchers. They lower the bodies into the graves. Ahmad shovels in enough dirt to cover both bodies. Then the assistant places the stone slabs over the bodies and together they shovel more dirt until they fill both graves.

Ahmad drops his shovel and writes 337 on one tombstone and 312 on another. Beneath the number he scratches, DIED,

DATE UNKNOWN. He wedges the tombstones at the head of each grave. He raises his hands, turning his palms toward the sky, and speaks a verse from the Koran: "O my servants who exceeded the limits, never despair of God's mercy. For God forgives all sins. He is the forgiver, most merciful."

Ahmad lowers his hands.

"Now we are done," he says.

The assistant gathers some twigs and starts a fire to boil water for tea in a kettle he brought from the morgue. Dogs bark somewhere far off. Ahmad brushes the dust off his pants. He washes the stretchers and the back of the van with water. He shakes his head at the lingering odor.

"Water doesn't clean everything," he says.

We sit and sip our tea. I tell Ahmad about Gulaly and the death of her husband, Abdul. I ask him whether the men who attacked the Indian embassy are buried here.

"No," he says. "They are somewhere else."

"Do you think they deserved burials?"

"We don't think about who they are, what group they belong to," Ahmad says. "Everybody is the same for us. Even suicide attackers."

He recalls a suicide attack near his office in downtown Kabul in 2012. A red van. About one hundred meters away. Ahmad stood looking at it out his window when it blew up. He felt the blast. He lay on the floor amid shards of glass. His ears rang and his head felt stuffed with cotton. The police collected the body parts of the van's occupants and delivered them to the morgue. Ahmad washed each piece, knowing full well he would have died in the blast caused by these dead men had he been outside instead of in his office. Still, he did his job. He wrapped what remained of the dead men in white cloth and buried them in unmarked graves so the organizers behind the attack would not remove them and deify them as martyrs. When he hears of a suicide attack inside Kabul or in the surrounding provinces, Ahmad always stops what he is doing. He looks out the window of his office where the van exploded and where he might have died had the circumstances been a bit different.

"Another body," he tells himself, "another body."

I shift on the hard ground, throw the dregs of my tea against a rock. Ahmad stares at the anonymous graves. I can't imagine what a family must think not knowing. Where is my husband? Where is my wife? Where is my child?

"How many people have been killed in the ongoing wars in Afghanistan since the 1979 Soviet invasion?" Ahmad wonders aloud as if he has been reading my thoughts. "So many rockets fired. So many dead. So many stories. You couldn't bury your dead then. If you tried, you'd be shot. You did everything at night so no one would see you. And now there is this war and a new weapon, the suicide bomber.

"Before the Americans came, Afghanistan did not have suicide attackers," Ahmad continues. "That means the Americans have trained these people. The Americans decide who should go on suicide attacks. They want to show that Afghans are bad people who kill one another and need America to protect them. But it won't change anything. Death is the final destination of us all."

We heat more water for tea and the sound of boiling water breaks the stillness around us. The wind has settled and the vacant sky hovers motionless. I turn to Ahmad. He stares straight ahead through the pickets of tombstones. He buries in good conscience whomever he is assigned to bury, the suicide attackers and their victims, beside those who have died in other violent ways. They are all human. They are all grieved. They are all his duty.

FIRE IN THE HOLE

The convoy stops and the LT lowers his binoculars and opens his door and points at four Afghan men standing on a ridge beside a red telephone tower. They look little more than dots against the horizon. Boulders lie strewn across the slope of the mountainside and some have tumbled down to the pitted dirt road. The LT gets out. He picks six men and a translator. The four Afghan men watch as the soldiers trek uphill toward them, walking first to their left and then to their right, weaving back and forth, back and forth, in continuous motion to lessen the strain of the steep ascent.

"I hate it here," one soldier says.

"Some people look at you weird," another soldier says. "Kind of a glare. They're just backward. They're not used to hammer and wood. Not to the point of building walls and standing them up. They're used to rocks and mud huts. They're just trying to survive. I get that."

"Fuck," the first soldier says. "I hate it here. They can't read their own language. You tell them not to do something so you can do what you have to do and they do it anyway."

The second soldier offers him a cigarette and they keep climbing until they stand with the LT, the translator, and the rest of the soldiers beside the four Afghans. The Afghans smile and ask whether they want tea. They point at a pot and a small fire made from charcoal and twigs. They extend their hands and the soldiers shake them, except for one soldier who served in Iraq. He stands apart and stares across the ridge and then turns and faces into the wind.

The LT moves toward the telephone tower. Beside it in the rubble of what had been another telephone tower, he sees an unexploded IED. The Afghans walk up behind him and the LT spins around sharply and the Afghans stop.

"Put your hands on your heads," the LT says.

An interpreter speaks to them in Pashto. The Afghans put their hands on their heads. They continue smiling but look confused. One of the Afghans tells the interpreter that they work for Roshan, a telephone company. They had discovered the IED moments before the convoy stopped.

"Do they have weapons?" the LT asks the interpreter.

He shakes his head no.

The LT stares at the IED. He lives in St. Louis and joined the army after September 11th, so he could say he did something for his country. He might go back to his job at Budweiser. Stocking supervisor. But the economy back home sucks. Some European company now owns Budweiser. He doesn't know whether he wants to work for an American company owned by foreigners. He looks at the Afghans. Hands on their heads, still smiling at him. When he arrived here in Khost Province, a drill sergeant told him to be prepared for lots of contact. Nearly six months later and halfway through his tour, he hasn't seen a firefight yet.

"They want to keep it," the interpreter tells him.

"Keep it?"

"The IED. So they can use it against the guys who put it here."

"They know them?"

"They think a relative one of them has been feuding with put it here."

"What are they feuding about?"

"The relative works for another phone company, AWC."

"Jesus," the LT says.

He looks up at clouds ballooning across the sky. He faces the interpreter.

"We'll detain them. Tell them to sit down. If they have cell phones, tell them to put them on the ground."

The interpreter translates. The Afghans place their phones on a rock and sit calmly on the ground with their hands behind their backs. One of them tells the interpreter that his brother is an interpreter at Bagram Airbase. The interpreter says nothing. He remembers the Russian retreat from Afghanistan and the civil war that followed, his father's death by heart attack, and the emergence of the Taliban. He fled to Pakistan and then Australia. Now he lives in New York. He signed on with the army as an interpreter for the money and to be a part of history. To be able to tell his kids, "I was part of this." He doesn't like Afghan president Hamid Karzai. Karzai is like the Mafia. He controls everything and is very corrupt. The interpreter doesn't know how this war will end.

"I found AKs," the Iraq War soldier says. He collects three guns beneath some rocks and carries them to the LT. One of the Afghans starts talking.

"They hid the guns when they saw an army helicopter," the interpreter says. "They say they need the guns to protect the remaining tower. They knew we'd take their guns if they told us they had them. They are sorry for this. They want to know if they can keep the IED and show it to their employer."

"What the fuck kind of question is that?" the LT says. "No they fucking can't keep it."

One of the Afghans complains that the ground is too hard to sit on. He stands.

"Sit the fuck down," the Iraq War soldier says. "Get the fuck away from me."

He shoves the Afghan back down to the ground by the shoulders. The soldier lost a friend to a roadside bomb in Iraq. He was walking behind him when his friend stepped on it. The explosion damaged the soldier's hearing. He did two tours in Iraq. Now he's in Afghanistan. He hates the slow pace, the lack of contact. He wished he had fought in Vietnam. No fucking rules of engagement in Vietnam. You did what had to be done. You wasted motherfuckers in Vietnam.

One of the Afghans' cell phones rings. At the third ring, the LT tells the interpreter to answer it.

"Are you Khalid?" a voice on the other end asks.

"Yes," the interpreter says. "Who is this?"

The caller hangs up. The interpreter looks at the LT, shrugs, and puts down the phone. Some birds fly above the remaining tower and the wind picks up. The LT radios in for an explosive-ordnance disposal team. After they blow up the IED, he will transport the four Afghans to Fort Salerno for questioning. Their names and fingerprints will be taken and run through a computer. If they're not listed as "persons of interest" or wanted for terrorism, they will be released. Maybe they'll be recruited as informers. Maybe not. The LT will never know. He feels sure he won't see them again.

When the EOD team arrives, the LT and his men crouch behind some boulders.

"Fire in the hole!" the EOD team leader shouts, followed by a second man's yell, "Fire in the hole!" The explosion rips the very fabric of the air, spewing dirt and rock over the soldiers. The ground quakes and the LT lets out a long whoop. He stands and shouts again and his men join him, screaming at the sky and pumping their arms.

They all laugh, feel the mountain shake until it no longer does. A weighty stillness follows. The LT looks toward the road. So much time in front of them. He starts walking. The four Afghan prisoners and the interpreter and the Iraq War soldier and the other soldiers follow him downhill weaving back and forth, back and forth, toward the waiting convoy.

IN THOSE DAYS

I reached Kandahar at night and checked into my hotel, Bamiyan Guest House, a series of red-brick rooms with a wide courtyard encircled by a wall. Vines stitched across the wall and trees consumed the noise of traffic. Every so often, as I tried to sleep, deafening explosions reached across the city and swept through my open windows in blasts that thrust my curtains aside and would have, I'm sure, blown out my windows had they been shut. A *Washington Post* reporter at the guesthouse explained that US forces were detonating Taliban arms caches. I was surprised to see him. Most reporters I knew, anticipating war in Iraq, had left Afghanistan for Baghdad.

I woke before sunrise the next day, the air already warming. In those days, February 2003, almost two years after 9/11, the weather in Afghanistan turned from winter to summer just like that, and an intense heat lacquered the sky a pale white, and all day long the unrelenting intensity of the sun would parch my skin.

A journalist I knew set me up with a translator and fixer named Maqsood. He was twenty-three. A lip of curly black hair hooked over his forehead; he brushed it back constantly but to no avail. He had arranged interviews with commanders of the new Afghan National Army for the next day. For now, he insisted on showing me around the city.

As we drove, Maqsood spoke in a rapid-fire manner about his life. He had been studying to be a doctor, an eye specialist, when the coalition invaded. After the collapse of the Taliban, he realized he could make more money as a translator. Recently, he applied for a US visa but was rejected. He thought a comment he made after a 2002 attempt on the life of Hamid Karzai, Afghanistan's interim leader, may have been the reason. He told a friend that he thought the would-be assassin was a lazy Taliban fighter. Instead of carrying a machine gun, he should have used a pistol. A machine gun was too cumbersome—with a pistol he could have gotten much closer to the car carrying Karzai. The Talib, he concluded, wasn't thinking. He thought his friend may have told a government official what he'd said.

It would have been a great loss for Afghanistan if Karzai had died, Maqsood told me. I didn't say I wanted him dead.

He stopped talking and we passed rows of mud-brick shops with flat roofs made of lumber. Faded movie posters of *Rambo III*, in which Sylvester Stallone rescues his commander from Soviet soldiers in Afghanistan, have peeled off walls. Donkeys trundled past, heads bowed, hauling loaded wagons through a particulate haze, and we entered a roundabout where a sort of evolution of locomotion unfolded in a confusion of men on horseback and other men on bicycles and still other men in black Hummers.

Do you know John Rambo? Maqsood asks me.

I saw the movie.

It was good.

Not so good.

Maqsood disagreed. The movie was good, he said, because Rambo defeated the Soviet troops. Maqsood hated Russians. He was a small boy when the Soviet Union left Afghanistan in 1989, but he remembered them. They were very alert, he recalled, fingers always on the trigger of their guns. They misbehaved—stopped innocent people and killed them on the street like crazed dogs. Every Afghan, north and south, east and west, became their enemy.

One day, when he was with his father in his tailor shop, Russian troops came down the road. They looked at Maqsood and his father, pointed their guns, and stopped. Shoving their way into the shop, they arrested a man who repaired radios for Maqsood's father. Maqsood never saw him again.

Titanic, Maqsood interrupted himself, his mind returning to the subject of movies. Did you see it?

I did.

Good?

Good.

The girl was very beautiful.

Yes.

What was the name of the boy?

Leonardo.

He was very beautiful too. I once changed my hair to look like his.

How'd you see it with the Taliban here?

Black-market DVDs.

Maqsood pointed out his window at a sprawling mosque with a red dome. The dome had been green until the Taliban changed it, he said. Once known as the Omar Mosque, it was now the Red Mosque.

Do you have a girlfriend?

Yes, I answered.

How many?

Just one.

Married?

No.

Why not?

Just not, I said.

I have two wives and a girlfriend. I don't know if she loves me. She won't marry me. Why, I don't know.

Maybe because you have two wives. Two's company, three's a crowd.

Maqsood laughed.

Two's company, three's a crowd. I love American expressions.

He turned a corner onto a narrow street and men with thick black beards and black turbans walking on the road threw us sidelong glances. I wondered whether these men were Taliban, or Taliban sympathizers.

Probably, Maqsood said with indifference when I asked. You have nothing to fear. They are not strong now. They will be strong again when America gets tired of Afghanistan, but not now.

We inched forward in the slowing traffic.

Like the Russians, the Taliban treated Afghans harshly, Maqsood said. He hated them. People who adapted to their strict ways got along with them, but those who didn't suffered. Now, under Karzai, life was easier, but everyone knew Karzai had no power. His strength came from the Americans. If the Americans were to leave, no one would listen to him. And the Americans would leave. They were not Afghan. Why would they stay? The Taliban won't go, because they are Afghan. Right now, Afghanistan was in the middle of a storm. Everything was calm today, but soon the winds would start blowing again.

Maqsood continued driving. We didn't speak. Then he broke the silence and asked me whether I wanted to see a Taliban graveyard. I turned to him but did not answer. I wondered about my safety.

You have nothing to fear, he said, as if he read my thoughts.

The cemetery stood in an isolated corner of the city far from the tumult of shops and traffic. Small stone slabs marked the pebbled graves. Torn plastic bags snagged by thorny twigs flapped against the cracked ground. One grave had an inscription commemorating six Taliban fighters: six stars of the Taliban were killed in the battle against the enemy. We ask God to forgive their sins and put them in heaven. A few men in black turbans moved about the cemetery. I stayed close to Maqsood. He looked at me and smiled. He was in charge. He enjoyed my unease. I assumed he was testing me, sizing me up. I tried my best to keep a straight face and not reveal my nerves as an elderly man approached us.

He considered me with a blank stare. His clothes were sweat-soaked and his gray beard grew unevenly around his face. He seemed more curious than threatening; I asked Maqsood to introduce us. The old man placed his right hand over his heart and bowed. His name was Abdul Zahir. He lived in Helmand Province, not far from Kandahar, and had stopped at the cemetery to pay his respects. He was a merchant and had no family here. Gesturing at the graves, he said some of the dead men had been captured, taken to Kabul, and executed. He pointed to one grave of a mullah he had known. The mullah died in a bombing raid by coalition forces.

We have good people here, Abdul said.

His older brother had been taken prisoner by coalition forces in Herat fifteen months earlier, he continued. Abdul had appealed to the government for information, but a bureaucrat in Karzai's office demanded nearly six thousand dollars in response. Abdul had seven hundred. His brother was thirty-five, married, the father of five children.

I am angry about this, Abdul said, and will resist all Western forces until I get my brother back.

Other men and some boys approached us with the same hollow stare as Abdul; they were war-weary and uncertain, I presumed, of what to make of me. Abdul pointed to one fifteen-year-old whose father, he explained, had worked for the UN but had been arrested in Herat.

It was a misunderstanding but they did not release him and he died, he said.

Another man asserted that his father fought with the Taliban under the mullah Mojan. He died in a battle with coalition forces.

I look like my father, the man said.

I considered his face: his blue eyes, full beard, the black turban. His neck banded with dirt. His silence revealed nothing more about him than a fatigued endurance that I had little doubt would outlast my visit.

A graveyard for Arab fighters, thought to be members of Osama bin Laden's al-Qaeda network, stood off a path a short drive away. Nearly one hundred Arab and foreign fighters and members of their families were buried here, Maqsood said, killed in combat with the international military coalition.

Six men clad entirely in black walked among the graves. I

knelt to examine one tombstone encrusted with weeds. Then it grew dark and I assumed a cloud had blocked the sun, but when I looked up, I saw I was surrounded by the six men. They stared down at me in a tight huddle, Maqsood among them, his face taut with tension.

Infidel, one man said. Non-Muslim.

This is a place for martyrs, another said.

Get up, Maqsood told me.

I stood slowly. The men pressed against me. Maqsood took me by an arm and the men parted enough for us to walk back to our car. We had not gone far when the first stone hit me in the back. More fell around us and we started running and I heard the men following us, and more rocks struck me until we got in the car and sped off.

That evening, I sat in the guesthouse courtyard, the chirping of cicadas interrupted only by the explosions of weapons caches. Some housekeepers moved in and out of shadows, giving me sidelong glances. In Kabul, hotel staff would exchange greetings with me. They bowed and hurried to meet my every need as if I was a demanding colonial administrator. Amid all the traffic and new high-rises and glass banks and garish mansions of government ministers, and mingled with the self-involved teams of dozens of NGOs debating reconstruction strategies—How will I spend fifty thousand dollars? an American with an aid organization asked me one day. I have fifty thousand dollars left in my budget and I have to spend it or my budget will be cut next year. Maybe buy a Jeep?—the war seemed to have wrapped up just as a new one in Iraq was coalescing.

But it did not feel the same in Kandahar. No matter how much I tried to speak to the housekeepers in my limited Pashto, they would only nod or not respond at all. Always polite, yes, but they avoided me. It wasn't as personal as what I'd experienced in the Arab cemetery. Still, the message was clear: I did not belong among them.

Maqsood picked me up the next morning to meet with Abdullah Lali, the Afghan National Army commander in Kandahar. A boy ushered us into a square concrete building and we walked up two flights of broken stairs to Abdullah's office, where he sat behind an expansive desk stacked with papers that he leafed through without apparent interest. Grimy windows filtered the afternoon sun and the light slanted across birdcages suspended from the ceiling above a green carpet mottled with holes. Maqsood and I sat on a red couch, dust rising as we sank into fat, pale cushions. Abdullah folded his hands and began speaking without waiting for me to ask a question.

Kandahar, he said, was peaceful, but the rural areas outside the city were not. The reason was simple: he had the budget to fund police in the city, whereas he had nothing for the villages. The new government in Kabul was not thinking, he complained. Cities like Kandahar were becoming isolated. The government seemed surprised that more than a year after the collapse of the Taliban, the resistance had not been quelled.

The reason, Abdullah thought, was simple: their enemy was fighting a guerilla war. They attacked in small groups, created problems, and then escaped. They did this with the support of villagers resentful of Western soldiers in Afghanistan.

Now, he lamented, the US would soon attack Iraq. It cannot keep both countries under control. Busy in Iraq, the US will have its eyes closed to Afghanistan. Abdullah had eight brothers, but only he held a job. He worried about them and other Afghans who had no work and had suffered in the fighting. They had expected a better life for themselves after the US invaded. If he were a young man, he said, gesturing to Maqsood, he would be disappointed. Disappointment fed the resistance.

Abdullah leaned back and stared at one of the birdcages. The bird inside perched on a stick, looking one way and then another, but it made no sound.

The central government did not seem to care the Taliban was regrouping, Abdullah continued, breaking from his reverie. All the reconstruction funds went through Kabul and all the ministers—warlords, many of them with their own militias—wanted to get their hands on the money. Consequently, Abdullah had nothing to pay his officers.

If he could have one big battle with the enemy, things would be better, but these small skirmishes only exhausted his troops. The enemy attacked in Kandahar, escaped, and then attacked again outside his jurisdiction—another general confronted the same problem. Like a fly too fast for him to kill, this kind of fighting left Abdullah feeling frustrated and helpless.

How do you fight a bomb explosion? he asked me. You don't. You only clean it up. For the moment, the government has influence in every part of the country because the coalition is with it. But if the US leaves, it won't have control of Afghanistan. Only of Kabul, and not even that for long.

Maqsood and I departed Abdullah's office for lunch. On our way to a restaurant that Maqsood liked because it showed Indian and Iranian movies, I asked him what he thought about what Abdullah had said.

We have been fighting since 1979 when the Russians came, he

answered. I've stopped caring. Afghans have stopped caring. I am enjoying this time while I can. Tomorrow will be a different day.

And with that, living for the moment, he changed topics and talked about his wives.

My first marriage was arranged.

Did you love her?

No. I was seven years old when we were engaged. She's my cousin. My uncle arranged it. I could meet with her then, but I could not sleep with her.

Seven? I said.

It's the way of my family.

Jesus Christ.

Maqsood laughed.

Jesus Christ. I love American expressions. You insult your prophet and don't care. Muslims would never insult the prophet Mohammad.

We parked outside a two-story building with a balcony. Walking inside, we bounded up steps to a room with long tables similar to a cafeteria. We sat beside some men who got up and moved to another table.

Untroubled by their reaction, Maqsood watched a Bollywood movie on a TV above the door. A woman shimmied around a clearly lustful young man who sang to her. She joined him in a high-pitched voice, and they leaned into each other, thrusting their abdomens and hips in a provocative dance. The men who had left our table watched Maqsood with disapproving scowls as he stared at the TV.

She has long breasts, Maqsood said.

Large, I corrected him.

I love Indian movies.

He turned and called to a waiter for tea.

I would like to meet a woman like her, he said of the Bollywood actress. My first wife is infertile and my mother wanted grandchildren, so I married my second wife and she gave me two daughters, and my first wife watches over them. I am with one wife one night and the other wife the next. But the second wife sees her only purpose as to give me children. I don't think she loves me. If I marry a third time, it will be for love. I would want that wife to live in another house. I'd spend three nights with her and the other nights with my other wives. All my life, my best friends have been girls. Now I have two wives and want a third. It's a problem. What do you think?

I think you're going through the motions of what your family expects of you and you're not finding whatever it is you think you're looking for.

Maqsood made a face. Then he burst out laughing.

Going through the motions. I love American expressions.

After lunch, we met with the acting governor of Kandahar Province, Khan Mohammad. His office, like Abdullah's, had dust-covered couches and a desk so big it came up to his chest, diminishing him. He wore a green military uniform and his beard and hair were dyed deep black. He nibbled nuts and raisins from a tray. He told a boy to bring us tea.

Khan had no doubt the Taliban was regrouping. Three nights earlier, he captured a man with explosives and arrested another man who carried a letter warning Americans and the Karzai government that a jihad was imminent.

I am very concerned, Khan said. Kandahar is surrounded by Taliban. In the south, Helmand Province is all Taliban. In the east, Qalat Province is all Taliban. The enemy was defeated, but it was not destroyed.

He had ordered his security people to search houses and detain any suspicious persons. The big problem, he lamented, was the lack of a budget. Just the day before, he used his own money to pay Afghan soldiers to patrol the streets.

It is the responsibility of the government to fight the enemy, he said.

The letters mentioned by Khan were posted at night all over Kandahar, Maqsood told me. There was one at the Red Mosque. I asked him to show it to me. We maneuvered through the busy streets until we reached the mosque. Maqsood read aloud from a peeling piece of paper attached to the door:

In the name of a kind God, Islamic Jihad of Afghanistan. Dear Muslims, we all know what God created us for. You know the jihad will remain until judgment day, whether we are in trouble or comfortable. Dear Muslims, you know that through the help of a kind God, when the Russians invaded our Holy Land, we defeated them. And now the infidels of the whole world with their dirty thoughts want to see their ways imposed on our land. Look at the responsibilities God has given to us. Where did the hopes of our Mujahideen brothers go? How can we defeat the heathen if we don't do jihad? Dear Muslims, this is not the time to hide the voices of the Holy Koran from you. Afghans, we will continue our jihad. Please help the Mujahideen. And if you don't help the Mujahideen, please don't help the non-Muslims. And don't let the younger generation work for the non-Muslims. We have started our jihad against the non-Muslims. We demand your help. If you interrupt the work of the Mujahideen, if you stop the Mujahideen from doing their work, your punishment will be the same as that of Americans and the men who work for them. You will die and never see Paradise.

When he finished, Maqsood looked at me.

What do you think?

Not good, I said.

He shrugged and walked back to the car without another word. I hurried after him.

How old is Arnold? he asked me, referring to Arnold Schwarzenegger.

What?

You know, Arnold? I'll be back. Him. How old is he?

It was more than a little disconcerting to have just read that flyer and then be asked about a Hollywood action star. However, as I thought about it, I understood. Maqsood grew up in chaos. His interests and desires existed parallel to war. With no idea of what the future held, he bounced from one impulsive thought to the next in a way I found hard to follow, but made a skewed kind of sense given the circumstances.

Sixty, I said after a moment. I think Arnold is sixty.

Two days later, I caught a UN flight back to Kabul. That night, I wrote about the situation in the south: *With the United States preoccupied by Iraq, government officials in Kandahar are warning that insurgents are threatening the security of Afghanistan*, my nut graf read. The story, however, was held. Little space existed for anything other than Iraq. An auguring of things to come, I think now, but not then. Like every other reporter I knew, I wanted to be in Baghdad.

Maqsood called from time to time. Among other things, he told me someone had attempted to assassinate a Kandahar official near the Pakistan border. The assailant used a pistol. Then, in that split-screen attention span of his and without transition, Maqsood complained his girlfriend still would not marry him.

However, she had agreed to lunch.

WEIGHT OF THE WORLD

Last night, Emran's uncle punched his father, and a cousin called the police. They had been arguing about whether NATO forces should stay in Afghanistan or withdraw in 2014 as planned.

"If they leave, the economy will collapse," Emran's uncle said. "If they leave it will be like a disease and destroy everything."

Emran's father disagreed.

"The Americans destroyed Iraq," he said. "It is the same here. Since they have been here, I've lost my way. I have two kids. They were in good schools but they are jobless. Since the Americans came, other people with government connections get the good positions. The problem is not Karzai, but the Americans. They are making the rules."

The discussion grew heated, each man unyielding in his point of view, until it became personal; they stood up, raising their voices, and began shoving each other until Emran's father dragged the uncle outside. Neighbors tried to stop the fight before Emran's cousin called the police. The police arrested both men but released them a few hours later. His father returned to the house in west Kabul, his face bruised, and in the morning he left to drive his taxi without saying a word. Emran followed him outside carrying a bathroom scale.

An Afghan National Army soldier stops by Emran and steps on the scale. One hundred forty pounds. He gives Emran twenty-five afghanis, or fifty cents. The soldier, Rafiullah, is twenty and on leave. He stares at Emran with heavy-lidded, bloodshot eyes and asks him his age.

"Fifteen," Emran says.

"Join the army," Rafiullah says. "You'll make money."

Rafiullah has been a soldier for almost two years. He thinks the Afghan National Army is a good army but worries that if NATO leaves, the fighting and dying of the last twelve years will have been wasted. The work will get harder without NATO. The places Afghan soldiers can't reach, NATO coalition forces bomb. Without NATO, the army won't get help like that.

As a university student, Rafiullah had been studying economics at night and working during the day in a paint shop. But then the shop closed and he could no longer afford school, so he joined the army. The hardest thing was the drills. He had to march and run every morning and then do push-ups and sit-ups. Six o'clock to eleven o'clock, and then again from three to seven with a prayer break at five. Sometimes American commanders watched them train. They yelled a lot and seemed scared. Rafiullah laughed at them. Afghans had been at war for more than forty years. He thought of killing as a game; he had nothing to fear.

Today he no longer endures drills, and he carries his weapon to fight, not to march. He remembers his first battle near Ali-hell, a village outside Jalalabad. The mayor had been shot and killed

by Taliban fighters. The next morning, three army battalions—
two hundred eighty soldiers, including Rafiullah—confronted
about the same number of Taliban. When he saw a soldier shot,
Rafiullah fell and began shaking. Other soldiers carried him to
a hospital where he saw more injured soldiers and dead bodies,
and he began shaking again. When the fighting stopped, he left
the hospital and returned to his battalion. He says he'll never
go near that hospital again. He doesn't worry about his life anymore. Bullets come from the Taliban side and he shoots back
without thinking. He no longer considers fighting a game. He
doesn't know what he thinks of it—he tries not to think. He
smokes hashish before and after a fight. In his dreams, he sees
people bleeding, dying.

Emran bought the scale three, maybe four years ago when
his father told him to work and help support the family. He
starts at seven in the morning. He walks from his home in west
Kabul through the courtyards and crisscrossed laundry lines of
the Mikrorayon, gray apartment blocks built for Soviet admin-
istrators and the Afghan elite in the 1980s that stand amid
the central districts of Kabul, and wends his way to Masood
Square, past compounds ringed with barbed wire and the busy
markets that surround them to Wazir Park, holding the scale
under an arm and stopping now and again to weigh people.
A street boy seen so often, a boy in a sea of street boys, eager
and despondent both—Emran is no more remarkable than
Kabul's summer heat, than its mix of glass, castle-sized malls,
and polio-afflicted beggars, although some people do recognize
him and shout, "Hey, weight guy!"

More Afghans ask to use Emran's scale than foreigners. One
Afghan man weighed three hundred fifty-two pounds and

broke his scale. He was a normal guy but fat. He wore a West-ern-style suit and tie and wiped sweat off his face.

"Look at you. You have nothing," the man said. "Are you going to weigh people for the rest of your life?"

Emran said he didn't know. The man told him he worked for a bank and suggested that Emran stop weighing people and attend school and one day he could work for a bank too. Go to school now, he cautioned, because soon Afghanistan will not be worth living in.

"Everyone who can is escaping," the man said. "Worse days are coming. NATO is leaving, the economy is going down, unemployment is up."

Emran thought the man sounded like his father. He looked up at him, the man's face blurred by sunlight, and said nothing.

"Save your money," the man said.

He stared long and hard at Emran and then gave him ten dollars.

"Buy a new scale, or save it and everything else you earn, and escape."

Emran sits cross-legged on the sidewalk, his baggy clothes deflated around his thin body, his face knee-high to the frac-tured flurry of legs stepping around him as he squints against the stirred dust and hot air dragged by cars, trucks, and buses that shroud him in a granulated fog, turning his black hair to gray. He presses a hand against his nose to block the stench rising from a dumpster. A boy sits not far from him, a palm held out to anyone who passes.

"Hello," he says.

"Hello," Emran says and turns away and tosses a pebble.

He was three years old when the Twin Towers fell. He does

not remember that day. His father has told him that security under the Taliban was much better than it is today.

"Before NATO, there were no suicide attacks," his father said. "That means NATO has trained these people. NATO decides who should go on a suicide attack. It does this to show that Afghans are bad people and that NATO is here to take care of them."

Far above Emran, sunlight splayed across billboards promoting UK Life Style Gym (Our membership has dropped. Everyone is saving their money to leave Kabul after NATO), New Kabul Bank (Every day, people come to withdraw money. They say they are leaving for Dubai), Saifi Global Advertising (Our clients are looking to take their business outside Afghanistan).

Young men and women, not much older than Emran, hurry past him staring at Facebook on their cell phones and texting friends. The girls wear head scarves and tight designer jeans and the boys unbutton their shirts to expose their chests, flipping scarves over their shoulders as if nothing matters. Discussions of NATO's withdrawal plans weary them and bring out a dismissive cynicism that feigns worldly experience and what they might imagine to be the air of an existential Western hipster. Among their comments:

"The future is never certain. Who stays in Afghanistan?"

"I am twenty-six and still I've not seen a safe and secure Afghanistan."

"Why do people make weapons? To find and get more power. It means wars will never end."

"I am going on as I have. I don't know what will happen."

"War means there is no God. I am a pagan."

The fathers of these young people have told them stories of past wars: the Soviet occupation, the civil wars, September 11th and what followed. Those times sound like this time with no end in sight. They move around Emran, focused on their phones. He is small, they say, as if, like the casualties of the wars they know only through their father's stories, he does not exist.

Haji Shir Mohammad steps aside for the clot of young people to pass him and then asks Emran if he may use his scale. The numbers tremble. Almost one hundred eighty pounds. Emran's eyes widen and he looks at Mohammad, at his heavy black beard, gray turban, and thick body, and Mohammad laughs and folds his hands over his stomach. He can't remember whether he has noticed Emran before on those afternoons, like this one, when he prays at the Wazir Aberhan Mosque, not more than a block from the park.

He sees many children like Emran and always notices the filthiness of their clothes, the dust begrimed into the thin fabric. They could just as easily be his sons if he were to die and it became necessary for them to earn money. On the street, their future is destroyed. If one boy is good, more than a handful will be bad.

"What is your name?"

"Emran."

"Do you attend school?"

"Yes."

"How do you spell your name?"

Emran doesn't know.

Mohammad has fathered ten children: five boys, four girls, and one dead son, Raz, the eldest, a former police officer in Ghazni. He died in March, at just twenty-three. Days earlier, Raz had requested leave to be with his wife in Kabul when she gave birth to their first child, a boy. A week later, dressed as civilians, he and three friends rented a van to return to Ghazni. Just before they reached the city, the Taliban stopped them. They got out of the van while the Taliban searched it and their bags. Raz had hidden his police uniform and identification in a side panel. Finding nothing, the Taliban released them. As they got back into the van, NATO jets bombed the area. Raz and two of his friends died instantly. The driver suffered shrapnel wounds.

Mohammad had been looking at the electric bill for his house when the driver called him.

"There has been fighting," he said. "Your son is injured."

"How badly?" Mohammad asked.

"Just come to Ghazni Hospital," the driver told him.

Mohammad did not tell his wife about the call, instead saying he needed to visit a sick cousin. When he arrived at the hospital the next day, he saw no one who resembled his son or the driver. He was told some of the injured had been taken to the Emergency Surgical Center for War Victims in Kabul and he hurried there. Doctors told him to file an email request to visit his son. Three days later, he was allowed into the surgical ward and introduced to a patient with the same name as his son, but the man was not Raz.

Mohammad returned to Ghazni with a photograph of Raz. He wandered through the city showing the photograph to one person after another until a man said he recognized Raz. "I took this person from the front seat of the car," the man said. "His left leg and left hand had been severed."

Dizziness overwhelmed Mohammad and for a moment he had trouble standing. The man said he had collected the body parts and buried Raz by the side of the road where he had died.

"Show me where," Mohammad said.

A small mound of dry dirt marked the grave and a green flag flew above it to indicate Raz had died in the fighting.

"Do you want to take him out to be buried in Kabul?"

"No. Leave him. He is buried already."

As a Muslim, Mohammad is proud of Raz for serving his country, but as a father he can't bear the loss of his son. He keeps his feelings to himself and cries inside. He has high blood pressure but despite his medication, his heart races and his chest aches especially when his wife and widowed daughter-in-law hear news of a fight between government forces and the Taliban and scream throughout the house as if Raz has died again.

Mohammad feels hatred only toward those NATO soldiers who killed his son. They have cameras. They should have distinguished the normal people from the Taliban. He has seen on television so many homes destroyed by NATO just to kill one or two Taliban. Why not use their technology to spare innocent people?

Clicking through his cell phone, Mohammad searches for a photograph the driver sent him. He stops at one photo of a crumpled white van charred black, the hood riddled with holes. Another photo shows Raz, a thin young man holding his sleeping infant son. Raz looked the same at that age, only a little heavier.

Mohammad shuts off his phone and gives Emran fifty afghanis, about one dollar. He knows that when NATO leaves next year, no one will be held accountable for his son. When he was a boy, Afghans spoke to one another without guns. He hopes the fighting will stop. Perhaps there will only be small fights between warlords and those people will be arrested. Perhaps not. Raz is dead. Anything else is speculation.

When he gets bored, Emran stands to be noticed and feels the afternoon bear down on him. He believes people respect him for not begging and sifting through garbage like other boys, something he has never done. He earns four, six, seven dollars a day. Sometimes he works with his younger brother, Raziah, and a friend, Abdullah. They meet and spread out. Raziah will push Abdullah and then say he didn't do it, but they fight anyway. Raziah also keeps half the money he collects.

"Why do you give me so little?" his father asks him.

"That is all I earned, Father," Raziah says.

"Thank you, my son," his father says.

After dinner, in the silence of their bedroom, Emran stares at the ceiling and tells Raziah that when NATO leaves, the Taliban will cut out his tongue for lying.

At seven in the evening, Emran folds his scale under an arm and walks home. He hears the call to prayer and takes advantage of the empty sidewalks. Sunset bleeds the sky. Emran has no thoughts about Rafiullah and Mohammad. They told sad stories about things he doesn't understand. He considers the bank man and wonders how many people like him will escape Afghanistan. If he were one of them, where would he go? He stops walking. The thought perplexes him.

Where would he go?

He searches for an answer. Unable to fathom one, he thinks about tomorrow. Rather than stopping at Wazir Park, he will walk to the teeming downtown bazaar and sit with his scale on the uneven sidewalks in the broken shade of a vendor's stall. He smiles. It is a good plan and somewhere to go.

MOST DANGEROUS, MOST UNMERCIFUL

You know how it is.

You can't run off to every bombing, even with a presidential election just days away.

When I started here in 2001, I could chase them down, because traffic didn't exist and there wasn't a police force to seal off an area. I could walk through debris and bodies without question and watch other reporters pose in the shattered remains of cars as colleagues snapped their pictures.

Now, in August 2009, Kabul is a chaotic city of three million mostly impoverished people, but it has only enough housing and roads for half that number. With so much congestion, what was once a thirty-minute drive can take as long as two hours. By the time you arrive, the fledgling Afghan police force, US military, and international security forces will have sealed off the area so tightly that all you will see is yellow tape, maybe a charred car, and some dazed people who don't know much other than one minute they were walking and the next the air heaved and tore at their bodies and then threw them to the ground.

No, the place to go is Akbar Khan Hospital, where the injured are taken. There, in an effort to rally international support against the Taliban insurgency, doctors will allow you to walk among the maimed and injured and snap photos and take notes and then leave. The people you see will be one more example of a tottering government that can no longer provide security as it engages in a presidential election that is just so much background noise to the real noise of bombs detonating. In time, all this won't bother you. No shock, no despair, nothing. Only fear. Sometimes fear can lift the coma.

So I am sitting this morning in the lobby of the Mustafa Hotel drinking lukewarm Nescafé with a Dutch news photographer and watching the BBC when another bomb explodes. I feel it more than hear it. That little ripple beneath our feet, the air vibrating as the walls absorb the wave of a far-off blast that somehow has reached us. We both stand and look out a window but see nothing other than a few frantic policemen pointing and shouting in opposite directions and looking into the sky. We sit back down. By now, we know the drill. I check my watch. In an hour, I'll call my colleague, Bahar, and we'll head to the hospital. The photographer nods in agreement.

"You know what, mate?" he says. "If we don't care, nobody cares."

Mohammad Heider stands outside Akbar Khan Hospital with both his calves and both his hands wrapped in bandages, and small scratches scarring his bearded face. Beside him on the cracked steps, a man sits in a wheelchair, his left foot wrapped in a cast and thrust straight out into the air like a thick tree limb. Blood drips off the heel of his foot onto the damp pavement. Women wail at the bottom of the steps leading into the hospital. On blankets, men sip tea and wait for word of a family member injured in the bombing.

A taxi pulls up and three men struggle to lift the man from his wheelchair into the back seat. Once they get him inside, the women seat themselves in the open trunk while the three men squeeze into what little space remains inside the cab. Mohammad watches them leave and waits for his own family to pick him up. Just this morning, he was walking by the headquarters of the International Security Assistance Force when a shock wave tossed him toward the sky. He landed on his left side and thought, I can't move. Splinters of glass rained noisily on the pavement and his ears buzzed. When he opened his eyes, men and women, chiseled with cuts, lay all around him. His feet bled as he crawled over glass to a doorway. The explosion still roared in his ears. A man picked him up and carried him to a car where three other bleeding people sat slumped to one side in the back seat. Mohammad sprawled against them. All the roads were blocked and, despite his bleeding passengers, the driver had to show his identification to dozens of nervous police officers to pass through the checkpoints.

At the hospital, the doctor worked quickly. He washed Mohammad's legs and hands, bandaged them, and told him to return in three days to have shrapnel removed. Mohammad left and borrowed another patient's mobile phone to call his son. Three hours after the explosion he stands here still waiting for his ride. He feels better, but the pain in his feet racks his body with tremors. He looks at his hands, blood already staining the fresh bandages. The doctor told him to change the dressings daily. He wonders where he will get the money for new bandages.

Until now, he had not decided whether he would vote in the presidential election. Now he knows: he will not. It will hurt too much to walk to the polling station near his home. Why put himself through that for corrupt men? If you don't take a bribe as a government official, President Hamid Karzai won't give you anything. You must be dishonest. No matter who wins. That's how it is. Nothing changes in Afghanistan, he says—except his life will never be the same after today.

Driving back to the hotel, Bahar shouts through his open window and jokes with other Afghans stuck in traffic about the campaign billboards scattered throughout Kabul. They compose slogans to go with the candidates.

For Karzai, the favored candidate, shaking his fist: Vote for Me, or I Will Box You.

For smiling Abdullah Abdullah: Vote for Me, My Taliban Brothers, and You Can Keep the South.

For bald Ashraf Ghani, running a distant third: Vote for Me, So I Can Afford a Hat to Cover My Head.

Karzai is the butt of the most jokes. Bahar especially enjoys the one about tribal leaders in a rural province who were tired of all the corruption. A small group of them journeyed to Kabul and requested a meeting with Karzai. He gave them five minutes.

"Mr. President," the lead elder pleaded, "you must stop all the corruption in our province."

"I will be happy to," Karzai told them. "But first, how much will you pay me?"

The young man sitting across the table from me at the Mustafa Hotel introduces himself as nineteen-year-old Shakib Ayubi. He says he had worked for eighteen months as an interpreter with the US army in Kandahar but quit two weeks ago because his mother was ill. He had asked for an emergency leave but was told that it would be impossible, so he resigned. Now he will reapply. The army needs translators and he needs money. Most jobs in Kabul don't pay as well. Banks maybe, but what does he know of accounting? Nothing. But he can speak English and translate.

"I fear going back but I have to feed my family."

Shakib dismisses the election as a waste of time. It won't help the country. Afghanistan cannot be peaceful. Especially in Kandahar—the most dangerous, most unmerciful area of the country. Always bomb blasts—morning, noon, and night. Some districts are getting worse. Especially farther out from the city. The people in Kandahar City can vote, but where? Outside? No. Too many areas are not controlled by the government. The Taliban would not allow it.

"Have you been there?"

"In 2003," I tell him.

He waves his hand, swatting my words from the air as if they were flies. Six years ago. Too long. Much has changed there.

"Listen," he says, leaning forward. "Women, even men, won't take part and vote. They will be threatened. They'll be seen as part of the government and then killed."

He talks earnestly and does not blink but stares intently at me. His fingers dance against his teacup. A waiter at a nearby table tells a guest that dinner will be kabab and rice, but the cook is asleep so who knows when he may eat. Shakib looks at me, oblivious to the rising anger of the hungry guest.

"Once we were in a convoy," he says. "Eight roadside bombs exploded. Five Americans were injured and one Afghan with the National Army. They used a clever procedure when they planted the IEDs. They lurked nearby, hiding. The IEDs exploded and they opened fire so no one could get out of their vehicle. They cooked inside like kabab."

Shakib turns and faces a window. A hospital has been built across the street where vendor stalls and kabab shops once stood. That was also in 2003, when a new hospital was not needed and you could go out alone at night unafraid. He recalls how scared he felt in his first firefight, a fear so paralyzing that he has trouble describing it. He told his commander that he was quitting. "Not now," the commander said above the gunfire. "When we're back at the base you can quit." Dust clouded his vision. Explosions reverberated against his chest and his ears filled with angry sounds; gunfire popped everywhere. That night Shakib slept fitfully. In his dreams, he decided to remain with the army. For the money—six hundred dollars a month. His dreams included military strategizing. He concluded that without aircraft it would be impossible to beat the Taliban. In the mountains they could not be found with mortars. He awoke exhausted, defeated.

"Now I am used to IEDs. My parents tell me, 'Don't go back.' But it's my job. I have to do it. If I don't go back I can't feel peace. I'll have no work."

He finishes his tea and the waiter offers more, but Shakib decides to leave, and the waiter nods. He is very solicitous. You come to a place like Kabul often enough, you start to seek out small comforts, trappings of the familiar. I like the Mustafa, and the waiter remembers me from previous trips. He flatters anyone with me. I know he's hoping for a big tip—and you can't blame him—but, interrupted, Shakib can't muster the energy to continue talking.

"No more tea, thank you," he says, and stands.

"Will you vote?" I ask him.

He studies me for a moment, as if I haven't heard a thing he has told me. But if you come to Kabul days before the election, you're expected to ask stupid questions.

"There are Afghan people who think they are still fighting the Russians," he says with a sigh. "They stay in their villages, never come to the cities, and don't know time is passing. One day, on patrol, I heard a soldier's radio pick up a Talib saying, 'Red guys coming in force.' Red like communists, you see? They don't let us explain we are not Russians. They open fire. There's no opportunity to understand one another. How can you vote in a country like that?"

Maggie Cook with the United Nations Development Programme has no time for Shakib's concerns about the election. "This time," she says with confidence, "the election is being run by Afghans."

The UN has sunk one hundred million dollars into voter registration and will spend an additional two hundred twenty-five million dollars to cover all costs of the election, including a runoff if none of the candidates receive fifty percent of the vote.

"The criteria should be tougher, some people say, to reduce the number of eligible candidates," Maggie tells me. "But without political parties, a country tends to have many independent candidates. If politics here were more of a party-based system, there'd be fewer. Will come in time."

She sits behind a desk with a computer in a second-floor room of a three-story house. Another large office stands across the carpeted hall. Men move back and forth holding stacks of papers on the election process. The air-conditioning makes Maggie's bare feet cold and she adjusts the thermostat.

"No one denies bad things are happening," she continues.

"It's a new process. Afghanistan has been bedeviled by war for thirty years. This remains a culture where women can't participate in anything as easily as men can. I know this."

The problems, however, extend beyond the ongoing plight of Afghan women. The Free and Fair Election Foundation of Afghanistan found instances of underage voter registration, negligence of Afghan electoral staff, and insufficient security to protect polling stations, especially in the south, to name but a few irregularities documented in a fifty-page report.

Maggie remains upbeat.

"The voter registration process is on its way to being viable—but not this year, I know. Procedures are in place to ensure people only vote once."

She raises her hands to show her fingernails stained with the indelible ink voters will have to dip a finger into when they vote to prevent them from voting twice. Weeks, she said, were spent devising the right ink. She leans backward and squints, examining her hands as if they were pieces of fine art.

"Are there areas of the country where people won't be able to participate and may never be able to participate because they are under Taliban control? Yes. No surprises in this. The process is Afghan-led."

In the morning, several hotel guests and I have to vacate our rooms. Karzai is going to make a campaign stop at the new hospital and all facing rooms must be searched. His security detail breaks the locks on doors, feels the beds, checks the chests of drawers. They stand in the middle of someone else's life, surrounded by open luggage, not sure what else to do other than tear it apart. Once satisfied, they stand in the halls with their guns to keep anyone from returning, order tea, and wait for Karzai.

I sit with a burly US army contractor in the TV room. He had been a commercial fisherman in Puget Sound, but then a buddy in Kuwait suggested he come over and make some real money. He sells air-conditioning units to the military and calls everyone "dude"—even a woman from Montana, who says she is in Kabul to teach American kids about Afghanistan via the internet. He has so influenced all the guests (journos, contractors, and aid workers alike) that we call him "dude" too.

Behind us a Zimbabwean gunsmith plays pool. He calls himself the best gunsmith in Afghanistan but complains that he can't find work in a country that has been at war for thirty years.

"Hey, dude," the gunsmith says.

"What's going on, dude?" the contractor responds.

An explosion interrupts them. East of the Mustafa this time, from the sound of it. I can't see smoke or any evidence. Too far away. But some newbie photographers run outside to chase it. They'll learn. I check my watch. Give it an hour, then back to the hospital.

"What were you saying, dude?" the contractor says.

A former minister of planning, a member of parliament, and a scholar of law and political science, Ramazan Bashardost is one of the forty-one candidates running for president. He lives in a tent across from the parliament building and lags far behind the front-runners but is not discouraged.

"I am of the people," he says from his office behind the tent, a bare concrete room equipped with a desk as well as a generator and fan plugged into wires that hang from the ceiling. "As minister of planning, I gave back my salary. The people say of me, 'He can live in a tent and give back his salary because he is not corrupt.' I am accessible and can speak directly to them."

Although the sun has barely risen, people have begun gathering in his tent. They walk across the bare ground in sandals, wrapped in prayer shawls. Dogs hover in the distance watching vendors setting up their stalls.

"I want to be president because it is a good life," Bashardost says and then laughs. He holds two fingers to his lips as if he has a cigarette and sighs—a gesture of mock opulence. "Seriously, I want Afghan politics to be clean. I fought corruption when I was minister. I want the next president to believe in the values of human rights and to have the support of all ethnic people. I have the support of the nation."

Just the opposite is true. He runs about fifth in national polls. Yet his tent has garnered attention, and attention has fed his visions of greatness.

"Karzai does not believe in good governance, in human rights. His philosophy is a tribal vision. He never decided to fight corruption. For him corruption is part of life, part of a tribal vision. Your brother kills an innocent man, you support your brother, your tribe. It is a Mafia system. I will make a clean state without warlords. We cannot have peace and govern with criminals. We need an independent president."

He stands, brushes dust off his clothes. It is time for him to hold court in his tent.

"Unlike Karzai, I never receive threats. I go into all areas without bodyguards, even Kandahar. All the people say I am welcome."

Not everyone agrees.

"He is twenty percent lying," a vendor tells me as he arranges soft drinks and snacks in his stall. He watches Bashardost speak to his supporters. "He can go without bodyguards because people are not interested. They know he won't be president. If he had forty percent support, he would have bodyguards. How does he travel if he gives his money back to the government? His campaign posters must cost at least one dollar each. That is not just from donations. He is taking money from the government. So, no, he is lying at least thirty percent."

Remember this: a trip to Kandahar, the birthplace of the Taliban, must be planned carefully. Only one guesthouse is safe for Westerners. It is, of course, watched by the Taliban. As a Westerner, you must change your schedule daily while you are there. Avoid routine. Stay three, four days at most.

A translator and fixer will ask for one hundred fifty dollars apiece or more per day. If neither has a car, you will have to pay for that as well. You don't bargain down the price. They will keep you safe, alive. Don't go cheap. Now make the call.

"Yes, yes," a translator says over the phone from Kandahar. "I can work for you."

He has been recommended to me by a *Wall Street Journal* reporter.

"How will I know you?" I ask.

"I will know you."

He hangs up. I call back.

"It is not safe to plan on the phone," he says and hangs up again.

I stand alone on the balcony of the Mustafa. If a man approaches me in the Kandahar airport and says he was the voice on the phone, do I believe him? The other day I took a taxi, though the hotel manager had warned me only to ride in private cabs, but I was in a hurry. The driver sang to himself. As he drove, I realized I didn't know Kabul well enough to understand whether he was taking me to the address I gave him. The driver kept singing. His yellow cab was old and dented, no company insignia. What kind of prize would I be for a poor man? What kind of ransom would you command? I looked out the window. I knew the area but nothing looked familiar. Who would pay for me if I were kidnapped? Who would pay for you? My heart raced and I told him to stop. Stop! He looked at me, confused. I slapped a wad of afghanis into his hands and got out and walked back to the Mustafa through the crowded bazaar. I shouldn't have been on the street either. I felt the stares of everyone.

"Hey, dude, you want some melon?"

The army contractor has joined me on the hotel balcony. He holds out a plate of sliced watermelon. I glance at my cell phone.

"In a minute."

I dial the man in Kandahar again. It rings a long time. No one answers.

Would you be scared? Would you still board your flight?

Remember: you're a reporter. You should fly to Kandahar and report on the campaign from there—but would you? Or would you stay in Kabul and eat melon, tasting your fear and shame with each bite?

Michelle Bayat Secondary School in south Kabul serves fifty to sixty children who have lost parents to war since the US-led invasion in 2001. None of the presidential candidates has visited the school. Campaign posters hang from lampposts outside the long, tree-lined drive that leads to the main building. Water gurgles in streams and birds sing in the shade. A great photo op. What American politician would pass it up? But still the candidates don't come.

The children are not happy, explains the general director of the school, Ali Mohammad. Their mothers were pregnant during the war. When they were born, they saw shelling, rockets—and now they never smile. "Even my daughter," he says. "Her first word was 'bomb.'"

A teacher beside him objects.

"I am like the students' mother, like their father. I never let them think about the war. I keep them so happy."

The teacher's voice fades beneath the noise of a Chinook helicopter flying low overhead. When it passes—the echo of its rotors still chuff, chuff, chuff through the air—Ali continues where he left off, raising a hand to silence the teacher.

"Westerners train animals for the circus," he says. "Because of good food, land, and teachers, they have the time even to teach animals. From the beginning of life here, our children are very sad. They can't forget all the things that happened before."

He pauses, opens the door to his office, and ushers in some children. You will see this from time to time as a reporter: a well-orchestrated show, put on especially for your benefit.

Eight-year-old Maryam: "My father is dead. I was very young. I don't know how he died. I was told he died during a bombing in 2005 on the other side of Kabul. No, I don't know where. I remember him as thin. He would take me to the bazaar and buy gum. Balloons. Sometimes I think of him. When I dream, I see my father and I am happy. I wake up sad. He takes me to the bazaar in my dreams."

Nine-year-old Habib Ullah: "I lost my father during the Taliban time in Logar. There was fighting between the government and Talib. My father was taking me to the bazaar. He was shot and the bullet hit my left foot. My mother and sister carried me to the house. My father died in the bazaar. He would play soccer with me. He liked to buy fruit too. Stocky. I don't remember anything else. I forgot. It's been too long for me to remember him more."

Ten-year-old Ahmad Martin: "My father was killed in 2001. I was two years old. He was a farmer. He was in a field and a bomb hit him. I don't know whether it was from the Americans or the Taliban. He had a big beard. I try to forget about his death."

What can you say? Ahmad holds a wrinkled color photo of a heavyset, bearded man with two children on his lap. A studio photo. The man wears a brown jacket and a red vest and sits stiffly before a backdrop of a painted forest. He appears very solemn but the children are smiling and he grips them with his big arms as if he will never let them go.

"He died," Ahmad says. "He just died."

You could spend all day at preselected interviews, news conferences, and carefully choreographed bits of political theater. The major campaigns—Karzai, Abdullah, and Ghani—all call to inform you of their events.

Women announcing their support for Karzai at two p.m.

Abdullah to speak at the Intercontinental Hotel at eight a.m.

Ghani to make an announcement at his campaign headquarters at five p.m.

Most of these are mere photo ops. Advertising posing as news. Nothing will be said that hasn't been said before. How many Americans will really care about this? Your editor will want to know.

The aides to the presidential candidates call and call and tell you again and again about a particular event.

"I know, you already called me," I tell them.

Still they call and keep calling.

"It means no one has shown up," Bahar explains.

The doctors at the Kabul-based International Committee of the Red Cross orthopedic center see at least two patients a day who have lost a leg to IEDs. It takes about five to seven days for a client to get accustomed to a prosthetic limb if the amputation is below the knee. Above the knee, one week. Most days, men and some women with missing limbs fill the center's compound waiting for a doctor, their stumps tapping the air impatiently.

In an exercise room, a teenager stands between parallel bars balancing on his right leg while a physical therapist adjusts the prosthetic limb on his left. He lost his leg when he stepped on a mine walking home from school in Nangarhar Province.

"Feels tight," he says.

"Now?" asks Sayed Musa, the physical therapist.

"A little pain."

"Let's try it again."

Sayed's own left leg was blown off in Kandahar in 1988. He was a soldier on patrol near a Chinese-run hospital. November. The weather not too cold. He stepped on a mine with his left foot. Shrapnel ripped his right leg into strips. He felt a blast, his body smoked. A soldier carried him into a tank and used a cloth as a tourniquet on his left leg. Blood, a deepening river. Doctors at the hospital held him down and cut off his leg with bolt cutters. No anesthetic. No time. Too many wounded and not enough anesthetic for everyone. The last sound Sayed heard was the echo of his own screams. When he awoke, his leg was gone. He thought he had lost everything and he prayed to God, Take my life.

"I don't believe I will walk again like you," the boy tells Sayed.

"You have to trust. The prosthetic is new now. You will become like me, if God is willing. Put pressure on it."

"It hurts."

"Be brave. You don't see me handicapped. You are handicapped only if you give up. Keep in mind everything I show you. I won't always be with you."

Three months after his leg was amputated, Sayed started using a prosthetic leg. With it, he was strong. He had not told his family he had lost his leg. Wearing his prosthesis, he visited his mother in Kabul. She did not notice anything different about him. "Mother," he said, "touch my leg." She raised his pant leg and started crying. "Don't worry," he told her. "It's my destiny."

"When I walk it hurts," the teenager says.

"Rest now," Sayed says.

The teenager sits on a bench. Sayed removes the prosthetic leg and rubs the boy's stump with talcum powder. The center will be closed Election Day to allow the workers to vote, but Sayed will not go. The government doesn't care about his patients. How many months has the center needed money? Doctors fund it by begging on the street. None of the candidates talk about this. None of them talk about amputees.

"How's that?" Sayed asks the teenager as he adjusts the prosthetic leg over his stump again.

"Loose."

Sayed still dreams of his leg. He is outside, running. Then he wakes, that sense of himself, whole, fading.

This evening an Indian businessman tells me he has construction contracts with the US military. He lives in Kabul but plans to leave. Already he has moved his family to New York. "Too much corruption here," he says. "You have to pay off the Karzai family. You can't do anything without them." He will oversee his business from New York. He sighs. It will be very difficult.

"They say everything will be better after the election," he continues. "The security, the corruption. I don't believe it. I don't. Karzai will be elected by a foreign country. The election will be decided by Washington, D.C. For this reason, there is no point to the election."

I decide to take a walk even though I know it isn't safe to wander alone at night. But you can only be cooped up for so long. On Chicken Street, fires burn in bakeries where boys pound flour into pancakes and then lift them into ovens and watch them rise into bread. Campaign workers plaster walls with posters of their candidates. They do this work at night so the glue dries while their opponents sleep and the posters will be harder to scrape off in the morning. Their shadows stretch and shrink in the bright orange glow of the bakery fires. I think of the refugee camp I saw this afternoon with its smell of smoldering wood fires mixed with the dried blood of a slaughtered goat.

Most of the thousand Pakistani people in the camp had recently fled fighting in South Waziristan, the tribal region separating Afghanistan from Pakistan. The camp is so new it has no name. They call it Kabul Refugee Camp. The adults sit in circles on the rocky ground and hold registration papers from the United Nations written in English they can't read. They cling to the incomprehensible documents as if the mere act of holding them will eventually translate into some sort of assistance.

Zal Mohammad left the Chitral District of South Waziristan with his wife and ten children. He decided to get out before the fighting came into his village. He has been in Kabul for six weeks and no one has helped him.

"We stay in Kabul until the government helps us. Who knows how long that will be?"

Another man left Helmand Province for South Waziristan

because of the fighting in southern Afghanistan. Then eighteen months ago, the Pakistani army went into South Waziristan with rocket-propelled grenades and Kalashnikovs and he fled for Kabul.

"What do we do with these papers?" he wants to know.

I ask whether he has posed his questions to any of the presidential candidates.

"What? No candidate has come here. We're not even Afghan. Why would they come?"

Thirty-year-old Shahzada Khan has been clearing mines near Bagram Airbase since 2005. He works for Halo Trust, an international demining organization. Since 1988, Halo Trust teams have cleared more than twenty-six thousand acres in Afghanistan—removing nearly seven hundred thousand mines, nine million items of large-caliber ammunition, and more than forty-five million rounds of conventional ammo.

The sappers like Khan work on their hands and knees, moving inches at a time with metal detectors and trowels. When the metal detector squawks, he ropes off the area. Then he digs with his trowel. Slowly, slowly, until he taps something. If it is just a piece of metal or shrapnel, he will put it in a box. If it's a mine, he will call his section leader. Everyone steps back about a hundred yards and the section leader explodes it.

It is impossible to say when all the mines will be cleared, if ever. In three weeks, Shahzada found one hundred fifty mines near Bagram. He no longer feels fear when he finds one. Maybe a little bit nervous but not scared. If he discovers one mine but misses another he might step on it. Yes, a little bit nervous. But the pay is good. He earns one hundred eighty-five dollars a month. It is one of the better-paying jobs.

Shahzada has seen sappers injured. Recently, a team walked into the garden of a house. They thought the area had been cleared. He heard the explosion, saw the black smoke rising. The sapper lost a leg and an eye. A medic and a doctor went to his aid while everyone else returned to work. Shahzada has not seen him since.

Halo Trust gave the demining teams two weeks off so they could follow the election and vote, but Shahzada will stay home. What's the use? If he voted, who would hear him?

August 20, Election Day, seven o'clock in the morning. The reason I came here. The day all the bombs were about. All the posters. All the phone calls from the campaigns about rallies and news conferences.

Yet the streets are empty. Some day laborers are out, hoping someone will stop and offer them work. Bored-looking police stand at vacant intersections. Fears of suicide bombers and distrust of the process have kept the majority of people inside. I stop at one polling station. The wind tosses a loose poster encouraging people to vote. A few families linger outside. The booths should have opened an hour ago but officials have not finished sorting ballots and arranging tables.

"I will vote," a woman named Raza tells me. "I'm very poor and live in a tent. I came to vote for the future. I don't want to be top man or rich. I hope my candidate will help all the poor."

A boy insists he will vote for Karzai so the next five years will be better than the last five. I ask his age. Sixteen, he tells me— too young to vote. He explains that his village elder called a meeting and announced his support for Karzai. All the people should vote for him too, he said. Then he contacted the staff of the voting commission and asked them to come to the village and register everyone. The village elder told the commissioners that all the village teenagers were eighteen.

Another sixteen-year-old boy says he registered to vote in Kabul and gave his correct age. The registrar told him he had to be eighteen and marked his registration card accordingly before handing it back to him.

"I found the long list of candidates confusing," the boy admits, "and didn't vote."

What can you say? Do you want to ask them how they ever expect democracy to work if they are already subverting it?

"Whether they are old enough to vote or not, it doesn't mean anything," Bahar tells me. "It makes no difference who wins. The outcome is the same. Corruption remains."

He looks at me to see whether I understand. He has grown tired of translating my questions and getting the same answers.

"Democracy in Afghanistan?" he scoffs. "Never."

SHERPUR CEMETERY

Rahimullah Habibullah slouches in a chair by the gate of Sherpur Cemetery, watches the British couple by the grave. They stand with their hands at their waists for ten, fifteen minutes. Then the woman moves near a tree behind the tombstone and asks the man to snap a photograph. He takes several pictures. When he's done, they walk down a stone-rutted path toward Rahimullah, past broken tombstones and unmarked graves, and tip him two dollars and leave.

More than one hundred people, mostly Europeans, lie buried in this decaying Kabul cemetery. No Afghans. Only foreigners. Germans, Swiss, some Americans. Rahimullah doesn't know why foreigners have a separate cemetery. They just do. Perhaps because they are infidels. He shrugs. This cemetery in Kabul has always been the place where foreigners are buried.

In 1987, a Russian general stopped at Rahimullah's tire shop just outside the cemetery gates, gave him a paper, and told him he was the new caretaker of Sherpur. He didn't ask questions— and now, at fifty-eight, having survived the Taliban and the Americans, he still doesn't.

Looking at his watch, he notices the time. Three in the afternoon. Only the British couple so far. He was busier under the Taliban. Relatives of the dead always visited then and tipped well. Times are different. The Taliban left but the radio warns against traveling. Bandits on the road, terrorists. He knows that people forget the dead when they are scared for their own lives.

He stands, shuffles to a grave visited by the British couple. A breeze catches his white beard, lifting it off his chest. He tugs his tattered coat around his chest, eyes crinkled against the dust-filled wind. His bare feet look hard as bark. He stares at the ground where a tombstone lies strewn with brush.

Germain Tanguay
Quebec - Canada
1944 – 1972

After the 1989 withdrawal of Soviet troops from Afghanistan, the new government built a mud-brick wall around the cemetery. An Italian priest would read from a book over certain graves. Rahimullah didn't understand the words.

Most of the foreigners buried in the cemetery died in Kabul. Only five people have been laid to rest here since Rahimullah became caretaker. The last one was a German doctor in 1992. His burial was hasty because of fighting between opposing Afghan militias. A man told Rahimullah that the doctor's wife would bring a tombstone but she never did.

Sometimes as he watched a casket being lowered into the ground, Rahimullah would fixate on his own mortality. The thought depressed him and he would return to his seat by the gate and leave the grieving family alone.

Mark Aurel Stein
Born in Budapest 26 November 1862
He died in Kabul 26 October 1943
A man greatly loved

Every morning, Rahimullah sweeps the graves and tries to water the spare trees that stand like half-starved sentries along the footpaths, but he doesn't have a water pump, and the nearest well is far—the buckets of water get too heavy, so the trees will die. Summers, Rahimullah picks flowers wherever he finds them in the city and scatters them over the graves. When they wither and die, he collects more. Flowers are lighter than buckets of water.

A Northern Alliance soldier holding a machine gun watches Rahimullah from the second floor of a bullet-scarred house that overlooks the cemetery. Rahimullah ignores him and feels a mounting resentment. Soldiers have ruined the cemetery. When factional fighting broke out between Afghan militias in the early 1990s, the cemetery turned into a battleground. Many stone and marble tombstones were shattered from exploding rocket shells and hand grenades. Huge chunks of the wall fragmented into dust. In all the years since, only two people offered to help repair the damage. A woman brought buckets of mud to patch the wall and a doctor donated forty trees that Rahimullah could not water, but no one offered to mend the graves.

Six members of Rahimullah's family were killed by a grenade during that sorrowful time and were buried in a cemetery for Afghan people on a hill above Sherpur Cemetery. Green flags flew over their graves to show they had died in the fighting.

Frederick Newgard
American engineer
Born 7 February 1908
Seattle
Died 31 July 1946
Kandahar

When the Taliban ruled, officials in the Ministry of Virtue and Vice would come to the cemetery two and three times a month to question Rahimullah.

"Why do you keep this place?" they demanded. "You keep foreigners' graves. Why?"

"I'm an old man," Rahimullah replied. "I can't do any other kind of work. If foreign or Afghan, graves are no problem. If you tell me not to work, I won't work."

The Taliban let him stay. Each time they left, Rahimullah would sit in his chair by the gate consoled by the silence of the cemetery.

In loving memory of
Ron Henley—Age 30 years
Carol Henley—Age 28 years
Motor accident on the Salang Pass
On 30th June 1964

A grave with a cross-shaped marble tombstone intrigues Rahimullah because the deceased was married to an Afghan. The memorial inscribed on the tombstone explains that Eva Sharif was from Holland and died in 1988. Her husband was born in 1939 in the Panjshir Valley north of Kabul. Rahimullah wonders how they met and whether the husband is dead and whether he is buried in an Afghan cemetery or in another country.

At four o'clock Rahimullah locks the gate for the day, walks to the tire shop he once owned all those years ago, and sits on a bench. Crossing his legs, he asks a passerby for a cigarette. A very slow day. Only the one couple. There was a time when so many families came to the cemetery that Rahimullah would earn ten, twenty dollars a day in tips. He draws deeply on the cigarette. Tomorrow, he will sweep the graves and wait and see who might stop by.

He tries not to think of dying. When he dies, everyone in his family will stand by his grave and recite verses from the Holy Koran. They will bury him and leave and visit once a week. Rahimullah has been fortunate. He was not killed in the decades of war. If the fighting stops he may never get killed and have a green flag fly over his grave.

FARMER BY DAY

I'm sitting next to this guy on a flight from Kabul to Dubai when he says he likes my pants, all the pockets.

L. L. Bean brand?

No, Columbia.

You are?

A journalist.

I'm on my way home from an embed with the army's 82nd Airborne Division in Kandahar. Three months earlier, I had flown into Kabul from Dubai. My colleague Bahar met me at the airport. We stopped at a restaurant before Bahar would drop me off at the American military base in Bagram Village. From there I'd catch an army transport plane to Kandahar.

In the restaurant, customers watched Bahar and me sit on a rug and order Kabuli pulao. Just a month before my arrival, leaflets distributed around the neighborhood where Bahar lived urged people to kill the Western invaders. He showed me one of the fliers, a dirt-smeared piece of paper filled with words I didn't understand. Many of us would die, Bahar said, reading from it, but we would at least get some of them. Outside the open restaurant door, I watched men hose down the street to settle dust. Water splashed against a dove of peace painted across a blast wall. Bahar folded the leaflet and put it in his pocket. Everyone continued to watch us. I did not feel threatened so much as I felt their resentment, as if I were not allowing them even this small amount of time free from the presence of foreigners. We waited a long while to be served.

On our way to Bagram, Bahar told me he had canceled his oldest daughter's engagement to a young man who planned to move to Holland, where his father owned a jewelry store. She had agreed to leave, but Bahar told her it was not her decision to make; he would not tolerate one of his children resettling in a non-Islamic country. He had arranged the marriage and he would end it and find her another husband, and I realized that Bahar, like the men in the restaurant, saw the West as a threat—an intrusive entity that would take his daughter and turn her into someone else, someone in violation of his beliefs, and on a certain level, I, and others like me, made tangible that something, made us the faces of the threat by virtue of who we were. I liked Bahar and trusted him to arrange interviews and provide translations, and I believed he liked me, but this was not about how we felt toward each other. This went deeper, beyond our working relationship and beyond my understanding. I knew he would not want me harmed, but I also accepted that we were not friends.

When I arrived in Kandahar that evening, a public affairs specialist, Corporal Keith Klue, met me at the airfield. I was his charge. In the coming days, I learned that no matter how I greeted him, Good morning, or, How're you doing, no matter the day or the time, he'd always respond, It's just another fucking day in Afghanistan. The other thing I picked up on was that Klue and all the other soldiers I met said fuck about every other word until its constant use achieved a kind of absurd, syncopated beat that soon became part of my vocabulary too.

Klue, a cop from Florida, believed in the war, was very gung ho. He had drunk the Kool-Aid and spoke in the cliché syntax of a bumper sticker. His favorite expression: power comes through a gun. That's what made America the biggest kid on the block in Afghanistan. He joined the Army Reserve out of old-fashioned values: honor and service. He believed in the US and what it stood for. There was a fear factor when he went out on an operation, he admitted, because he never knew what would happen. So far nothing had. From Klue's perspective, that sucked. Like blue balls—all hyped up and nothing happens. What good was he if he wasn't killing the enemy?

The army had intel but nothing's perfect, he explained. The fucking hajis keep getting away. Every time he was deployed, as he got closer to the start of an operation, he felt less and less for his wife and family and more for his fellow soldiers, all of them bound together by their desire to use their weapons and kill the enemy.

And what were you doing in Kandahar? the guy on the plane asks me.

Writing about American soldiers.

Ah, yes, American soldiers.

He's Afghan, the man tells me. He was born in Kabul but moved to the States as a kid. Lives on Long Island, married to a woman from Uzbekistan. Both of them speak about nine languages. They have two children. Everything was fine until the 2007 recession hit and he was forced to shut down the convenience store he operated. A short time later, he signed with the US army as a translator and now earns about two hundred thousand dollars a year. Gets three weeks off every six months and returns to Long Island to see his wife and children. Now he's leaving Afghanistan after another six-month stint.

Where will you stay in Dubai? he asks.

Majestic Hotel.

He suggests I try another hotel where Russian women will sit on your lap in the bar until you arrange something more intimate. Book a room first—it's cheaper than asking for a room without a reservation.

He considers me for a moment and then asks whether I used protective military gear.

No, I tell him.

He shakes his head, says he wears a Kevlar vest when he's on the army base near Pul-e-Charkhi, not far from Kabul, where young Afghan men train to be soldiers. American soldiers and their Afghan translators get very nervous when the trainees load their weapons. Snipers peer down, ready to take out anyone who has a sudden urge for jihad. When he leaves the base, the translator never tells the trainees where he's going.

My handler, Klue, was also surprised I didn't carry a weapon. Can't as a journalist, I explained. Not part of my job description. Fuck that, he told me. One morning, he and I hooked up with an LT in charge of a medical mission. He gave brief instructions to his squad: they were to escort the medics to some village whose name he couldn't pronounce. Stay fifty meters apart so the fucking enemy can't take out a bunch of us at once; in case of an ambush, lay down repressive fire, and start a fucking flanking maneuver; if we hit a fucking mine, an armored security vehicle would push the damaged vehicle the fuck out of the way. If they experienced fucking sniper fire and they didn't know where it came from, they were to get out of the goddamn line of fire without lighting up the fucking countryside; and finally, if there was enemy contact in the village, the medics would be removed first and then the rest of them would pull the fuck out.

Return fire and aim fucking well, the LT added before he walked off to consult with his CO. Klue and a private shot the shit and waited.

Hurry up but don't go anywhere. That's the army way, Klue said.

Where's the fucking caterer? the private asked.

I don't know, Klue said. I told them I wanted a fucking king-size bed, not a queen. And an Asian chick, not some round-eyed bitch.

I just want to go to a fucking Outback and get me a raw, raw steak and those mashed potatoes with skin.

I want a fucking ice-cold Slurpee from 7-Eleven.

I just want to kill, the private said.

An hour later, the LT reappeared. Move out, he said. We piled into Humvees and put on goggles to protect our eyes from the dust. The flat barrenness of the sand-covered land pocked by thorny scrub consumed time and dimension, and I had no idea how long we'd been driving before I saw the mud huts of the unpronounceable village and panicked women covering their faces and fleeing our arrival, barefoot children chasing after them. Sullen men waited as the LT approached, and he explained through an interpreter the purpose of our visit. The men's expressions did not change. They offered green tea that the medics declined but the men insisted, and a boy brought a tray with glass cups and tea and a thermos of hot water and a sugar bowl. The medics thanked them and ignored the boy as he poured the tea, and the villagers watched the medics unfold a long, collapsible table and then they formed a line, the expression on the faces unchanged, and they accepted what help the medics offered: eye drops, Band-Aids, and tablets of Advil mostly, without hope of anything more.

American soldiers no older than twenty-five took up positions, their weapons pointed at the line of men waiting to be seen, and they assumed the hard pose of what they thought men ready to kill would look like until the line dwindled to the last patient and the medics packed up while the male villagers stood staring at us, and their wives, mothers, and daughters peered through windows and doors.

Ya think any of these guys are fucking bad guys?

Farmer by day, Taliban at night, dude.

That means I can fucking kill them?

Laughter.

I had trouble getting the fuck up this morning.

I fucking worked out.

I just didn't want to get the fuck up.

How late were you playing fucking cards?

Not that fucking late.

Where the fuck're we going next?

Other side of the fucking wadi.

To do fucking what?

Find fucking bad guys.

The next morning at 0700, Klue and I sat beside Specialist Scott Eberlein in a Chinook bound for Helmand Province to flush out Taliban fighters.

All that sound, Klue shouted at me above the noise of Chinook's twin rotors, tells the Taliban we're coming to fucking kill them!

Eberlein's face notably paled at Klue's warrior pose. He told me he had been an actor and had bit parts in the television shows *The X-Files*, *Nash Bridges*, and *Martial Law*. He joined the army the day after 9/11. His acting friends thought he was fucking crazy.

He was scared, he admitted, but when the Chinook landed, he'd focus on his memories of the Twin Towers falling. He shook my hand and wished us both luck and then he said goodbye in case he didn't make it. For the first time, I thought I might die too. I didn't feel fear so much as loneliness, surrounded by young men with guns, strangers, without my family or anyone I knew. I couldn't fathom getting shot, however—it didn't feel real, although of course I knew it could happen. My inability to comprehend getting shot or getting blown up or whatever else might kill me eased my fear, but the loneliness lingered.

The Chinook landed and we all ran down a ramp and dove on the ground. Nothing happened. We had no contact with the enemy. Not a shot fired. Helmand was a bust.

They climb mountains like fucking goats and we can't fucking catch them, Klue bitched. Fucking Chinooks, they heard us a mile away.

That night back in Kandahar, Eberlein talked about *The X-Files*. He had played a hit man who kidnapped a psychic. The psychic led him to an alien and the alien threw him against a wall and killed him. All the guys thought it was pretty cool he'd been on TV, although they would rather have talked about all the bad guys they'd shot to hell in Helmand, but that didn't happen, and they were still all hyped up. Just hours earlier they thought they'd take enemy fire; they thought they might die in the vague way that something like that can be imagined, while still being vivid enough that their hearts raced and the palms of their hands got clammy. But still death, the permanent darkness of endless sleep, was impossible to comprehend. Restless, they made their way to "the whack room," a latrine stuffed with *Playboy* magazines, and jerked off. After they took care of business, the soldiers came back and asked Eberlein what it was like to be on *Nash Bridges*.

I glance out the plane window at the mountains spread out below us and imagine trying to find anyone in the nooks and crannies of those bare peaks. Small, square patches of land mark where farmers till soil in narrow valleys at the base of the mountains. The translator looks out the window too.

Did you meet Afghan soldiers? he asks me.

No.

They don't like discipline. They don't remember what they've been taught and quit at a moment's notice. The army will spend a year and a half training one guy and then he goes home for a month, and by the time he returns to base he has forgotten everything.

He blames this on their lack of education: Most Afghans can't read or write their own language. They are doing it only for the money.

Unlike you.

The translator smiles.

You are very clever.

The plane carries us over a military base in the foothills of some of the mountains. The translator points at a group of square, brown buildings.

There, that's where I was, he says.

He hiked around the mountains for five hours just the day before. Afterward, he caught a ride into Kabul and stayed at the

Intercontinental Hotel. Great barbecue. He recommends I try it the next time I come out.

You'll think you're back home.

I doubt that, I say.

Will you be back?

I don't know.

It's not close to being over, you know. The Taliban has belief. You can't beat belief.

I didn't see any Taliban.

You don't see belief, my friend, the translator said.

My days in Kandahar revealed nothing but flat deserts and poor families eking out a subsistence living off the parched land. They seemed oblivious of the war, oblivious of what we considered to be their impoverished state, as they had lived simply like this for generations— undisturbed, it seemed, despite the Soviet invasion, the civil war that followed the Russian retreat, the rise of the Taliban, 9/11 and the American-led invasion—but Klue would have none of it. He shook a finger in my face and warned me of the deceitful nature of Afghans. We could be here ten fucking years and never find all the fucking weapon caches. He didn't know what he'd say back home if someone asked, What was it like? He hadn't used his weapon, just handed out food and medicine to the enemy, that's what it was like. That would always be between them, what he hadn't done, and what they assumed he'd done. He wished he could tell them something profound. What was it like? He'd repeat the question and then answer, Just another fucking day in Afghanistan.

The translator and I don't speak again for the rest of the hour-and-a-half flight. When we land at Dubai International Airport, I get out of my seat and step back in the aisle to give him room to stand. He hefts a large backpack out of the luggage hold above our heads. We shake hands and I follow him off the plane and search for a place to buy coffee. I have a twelve-hour wait before my flight to D.C. At home, I assume I won't sleep, because of jet lag. I'll lie awake and think of an empty, morose expanse, its weighty silence and unsettling monotony. Fucking Afghanistan, I hear Klue curse.

After a few days, I'll be OK.

A MERCY KILLING

The restaurant opens to the street and the jumble of Kabul's downtown bazaar.

Stray dogs move in uneven packs past vendors whose listing burlap stalls lean into a quicksand of low-lying fog. Police flatten the tires of illegally parked cars and the cars sink into the mud and potholes of the ruined road wheezing air in an odd sort of gasping unison while their irate owners shout obscenities at the police. In the sky above this splintered section of city, a plane's white contrail cuts lazy curls that vanish almost as fast.

Inside the restaurant, wood tables full of bearded men wrapped in shawls crowd the uneven floor, the air heavy, the room seeming to swell and pulse against the smudged walls with the odor of sweat and unwashed bodies and the heat from burning charcoal. I see no place to sit. Then a man waves to me and points at a space open beside him.

I wash my hands in a sink by the door. Frigid water trickles from the faucet. A cook stands nearby in clothes blackened with grease; behind him hangs the carcass of a lamb, its fur a bundle at his feet, a bloody knife entangled in the matted hair. He hacks off chunks of meat and throws them into a pan popping with oil; then, as it browns, he cracks an egg over the meat. The yolk slides off and dances in the hissing, popping oil until it floats white and bubbly. I shake my wet hands, and the cook throws me a grimed washcloth to dry them. I hand it back to him and make my way through the crowd toward the table where the man who had waved me over waits.

He tells me his name, Ghul Rahman. Deep lines river out from around his eyes and mouth. Beside him sits a gaunt man who stares at me as do the rest of the men seated at the table, a singular contained attention focused entirely on me. Westerners don't often go downtown by themselves for fear of being kidnapped or targeted in some other way. A drive-by shooting perhaps, or a bomb, or a rogue Afghan policeman emptying his gun into the chest of a Western contractor. But I get more than a little stir-crazy remaining behind the walls of my hotel when I am not working, until I get hit with the feeling that I must leave, go somewhere. However, as an American in Afghanistan, I remain caged no matter what I do. There is a quality of "whites only" when I leave my hotel for some other place—a restaurant usually—considered safe for Westerners. Afghans are not allowed in these places and armed guards stand at every entrance.

So today, I've decided to venture out on my own away from the sanctum of my hotel, restaurants, and other safe retreats. With so many eyes on me, however, I wonder, with the growing unease of a child who cavalierly entered a dark room on a dare, only to imagine the sounds of ghosts, whether I've made a terrible mistake.

"United States," I tell him. "Journalist. Where did you learn English?"

"The university. Do you need a translator?"

"No. I have one."

He taps his fingers against the rough boards of the table. He has long, stained nails. His lank, thinning hair hangs down past his ears. His crooked teeth are stained, as is his graying beard, and his bony shoulders resemble small rocks jutting beneath his shirt.

"Hello, how are you mister?" the man besides Rahman shouts. Before I can answer, he says, "Thank you, mister."

Rahman raises a hand for him to be quiet. A waiter brings me a dented tin plate with an egg and a paddy of fried lamb. The man beside Rahman watches me with wide brown eyes that seem too big for his narrow face.

"I need a job," Rahman says, tearing at a chunk of bread and sopping up the mashed egg on his plate. "I have to answer to a man for his mercy. You see, my cousin in Kabul City hired a man to kill my father. My father owed my cousin money, but refused to pay, because he said he had already paid him. He called my cousin a liar. There was bad blood between my cousin's family and ours. They are Pashtun. We are Tajik. I bought a gun from a friend. I killed the man my cousin hired to kill my father for insulting him."

I nod, shift on the wobbling bench. When I first began working in Afghanistan, I knew nothing about its tribes and their rivalries. Over the years, I have learned that the country is a loosely knit conglomeration of competing ethnic groups. Chief among them are Pashtuns, Tajiks, Uzbeks, and Hazaras. Strong animosity exists between the Pashtuns and Tajiks. The Taliban emerged from the mostly Pashtun region of southern Afghanistan. The Tajiks made up the bulk of the Northern Alliance and fiercely resisted the Taliban. Then the Taliban gov-

ernment collapsed in the wake of the American-led invasion
following the September 11th attacks. The Northern Alliance dominated the new government led by Hamid Karzai, a
Pashtun. But many Pashtuns felt Karzai served only as a figure-
head to appease international demands for a multiethnic unity
government. He held little power by himself. It was the Tajiks
who ruled. Instead of unity, people retreated to their tribal affil-
iations and mutually held antagonism, and prepared to resume
age-old conflicts as soon as Western military forces quit the
country.

"In Afghanistan, if we kill somebody and the family of that
person says, 'No, we give mercy,' then you will not go to the
jail," Rahman says. "The father of the man I killed is very poor.
He is Hazara. The Taliban killed many Hazara people. Thousands and thousands of Hazara people. I said to this man, why
would your son kill for a Pashtun? He said his son did not have
a job. This man told the police to release me, but now I have to
answer to him. I have to pay him for his mercy."

"How much?"

"He will not tell me. He says he will let me know when I
have paid him enough. But you see, I don't have a job to pay
him anything. You are sure you don't need a translator?"

"I'm sure."

"Do you know someone who does?"

"No."

Rahman shrugs. He dabs at his mouth with his fingers and
drags them through his beard.

"The Americans will leave Afghanistan soon, yes?"

"I think so. Most of them anyway."

"Then I will only pay him a little every month. Soon it won't
matter what I owe. There will be fighting when the Americans

leave. He will be on one side and I on the other. He will expect no money when we are shooting at each other."

The cook brings a pot of tea to the table. Rahman motions at my plate and tells me to eat. Blood from the meat mingles with the eggs. I dab at it with some bread. Rahman watches.

"Hello, how are you mister?" the man beside him says again.

"I'm good," I say.

"Thank you, mister."

"Those are the only English phrases he knows," Rahman says. "'Hello,' 'how are you,' and 'thank you, mister.' He won't learn more, because he hates the United States."

"Why?"

"Americans are not Afghan. They don't belong here. Are you alone?"

"No," I lie. "My driver is waiting for me outside."

Distorted Indian music screeches from a radio the cook has turned on. He tosses more meat into the pan and an explosion of hissing rises from it and a plume of gray smoke clouds the open kitchen and I can't see anything of the cook other than the suggestion of a form and then the movement of his arms tossing meat.

"Hello, how are you, mister?"

"Quiet," Rahman tells the man beside him. He pours me more tea.

"Fifteen days ago, I saw the guy my cousin hired to kill my father. He was in a garden in Farza Village outside Kabul. I was carrying a gun and I was walking down the street and I shot him and I killed him. A friend had offered me two, three guns to kill the guy but I only needed one."

I finish my tea and wave the cook away when he offers me more bread. I let Rahman take my plate and finish what I've left.

"Hello, how are you, mister?" the man beside him says yet again. He nudges Rahman and laughs like some sort of manic sidekick gleefully waiting for I don't know what. I stand up.

"Are you sure your driver is outside?" Rahman says.

"Yes."

I point at a car where a man leans against the hood.

"There," I say.

"Let me walk with you."

"I'm good, thank you."

Rahman looks down at the table. The man beside him gives me a long compassionless stare, but says nothing. I move to leave. Rahman grabs my hand.

"I will be staying in Kabul to watch my cousin," he says. "He is my enemy. If you need a translator, you know where to find me."

BOOK LADY

She walks without hurry, somewhat stiffly, sore, a diminutive woman unnoticed, burdened, using her chin to clamp down on a column of books she holds against her chest. Thin paperbacks most of them, a few hardcovers. All written by her husband. The books appear as worn as she does. Her tired eyes, lined face; a forehead wrinkled into streams. Maybe from long, nightly exposure to the humid, sooty air, the white smoke rising from kabob grills wafting around and powdering her with ash. Maybe from seventeen years of selling her homebound husband's work. She does not know, does not really consider her fatigue any more than she reflects on how she sees and breathes. Block by block she maneuvers through the teeming sidewalks of Kabul's Shar-e-Naw shopping district until she enters Ice-Milk Restaurant, and stops at a table of young men.

"Would you like to buy a book?" she asks them.

The twenty-somethings talk to one another while staring at their iPhones, oblivious of her. Outside, more young people gather, dressed in tight blue jeans and dazzling, multicolored shirts with wide collars. They talk loudly, with an air of "we are special," laughing, hurrying past storefronts promoting Mastercard Premium, Marco Polo garments, Alfalah Visa, United Bank, Body Building Fitness Gym, New Fashions Kabul shop. Their shadows converge and fade into the glow of so many green and blue and red blinking lights that dangle from the shop awnings above advertisements for pizza and club sandwiches and chicken fingers, and those same shadows cross a boy leaning on crutches in the middle of the sidewalk, his left leg gone, his right hand out for money, and the young people swerve around him as if he were standing in the center of a traffic roundabout, and amid this confusion the book lady leaves Ice-Milk Restaurant without having sold one book and stops at the next restaurant, Fast Food Pizza and Burger.

The West's influence can be seen throughout Shar-e-Naw in the kaleidoscopic displays of consumerism and high prices that momentarily render the decades of ongoing war here as obsolete as the donkey-drawn carts next to the black Hummers stalled in traffic. But the sight of a begging child—injured, she presumes, by a mine—reminds her that beneath the sequined mannequins and the suggested affluence and the rush to catch up with the twenty-first century, Shar-e-Naw is still Afghanistan.

"Shar-e-Naw is a lie," she told her husband one night when she came home, the unsold books weighty in her hands, her mood dark from the long hours of being on her feet in threadbare sandals and walking from one restaurant to the next. "A fairy tale of success," she continued, "concealing the fear people feel."

Her outburst, she remembers now, prompted him to write an essay about self-delusion. Neither her expression—mouth downturned, but not quite a pout—nor her slow, shuffling gait changes as she stops at a table in Fast Food Pizza and Burger. She exudes a kind of passive, stalwart acceptance, almost anticipating rejection; sometimes it even prevents her from asking, Would you like to buy a book? Instead, she considers the people seated at the table, their arms sticking to the red plastic tablecloth, a few returning her look with blank expressions, and, without another word, she walks to the next table, an empty one. She sets the books down, sits, rests her hands and arms in her lap, and orders tea. The books get so heavy and she feels pain in her back. Perspiration dampens her cream-colored hijab. Sometimes she stuffs the books in a small pack, shifting the pack from one shoulder to the other through the night. The strategy does nothing to alleviate the pain, but simply moves it around. Her back still hurts, her feet still ache, and she supposes the young people around her, if they reflect on her at all, see her as no different from the begging child outside. A poor woman trying in vain to make money selling books. How surprised would they be if they knew she was married to a man of ideas?

Her name is Dijon, her husband, Mohammad Rasoul Jahanbin. He has written and self-published twenty books, books that cover a range of topics. Family matters. The right way to raise children. Politics. His book *The President Is Like a Squash*, a farcical commentary on the incompetence and corruption of the Afghan government, sold better than the rest. He avoids no subject—women stoned to death in Badakhshan; government soldiers killed fighting the Taliban. He makes people laugh and cry.

Around Dijon, the tables crowded with young people buzz with conversation, conversation about the insecurity of the country. The increasing strength of the insurgency in the north. NATO's withdrawal. The throngs of families leaving the country for Europe. How they, too, want to go. One young man complains of how backward Afghanistan is. He says that one day a guy at his job asked him, Do you have a rug to pray on? The young man said no. Why not? The young man said his prayers didn't need a rug, his praying didn't need a precise time or number. The guy threatened to kill him for not being devout. Dijon repeats this story to herself until she knows she will remember it and tell it to Mohammad. He would appreciate its potential, she thinks, use his sardonic sense of humor to adapt the story and mock those who would use Islam as cudgel. She rubs her face, sighs, and stretches her legs beneath the table. Her frayed, leather sandals slip off her soiled feet. A man pauses to glance at her books and she turns to him, but he says nothing and neither does she, and she watches him continue toward the back of the restaurant.

Dijon starts selling books at four in the afternoon, once her youngest daughter comes home from school. If Mohammad feels ill, as he often does, she won't go out at all. His health deteriorated during Afghanistan's civil war in the 1990s. So many bombs fell on Kabul then. One night he went to sleep and when he woke up in the morning, he could not see.

"What is in front of my eyes?" he said. "Everything is red."

Dijon saw nothing wrong and wondered whether he had become mentally distracted. A doctor told them he had internal bleeding in his eyes from chemicals released in the bombing. He gave him eyedrops and his vision cleared only slightly.

One week before the Taliban entered Kabul in 1996—before her son and daughter were born—she and Mohammad fled to Mazar-e-Sharif in the north. They knew no one there, had no relationship with people who had influence, had no work. But Dijon was a good cook. They opened a one-room restaurant in the garage of the house they rented. University students and teachers came by, sat, and talked, creating a relaxed academic environment—more like a gathering of friends than a business.

Two years later, the Pashtun-dominant Taliban overran Mazar. Mohammad was arrested and put in jail for associating with the Hazara, a people from the central highland region of Afghanistan engaged in a decades-long feud with the Pashtuns. At Dijon's urging, he had allowed two homeless Hazaras to stay in their house. She had told him, "We know what it is like to be alone. We should help other people who are alone."

The Taliban released Mohammad two days later, his body bruised and swollen from beatings. A friend told them, "You will be OK now. You have been arrested once. They won't bother you again."

But Dijon and Mohammad thought, No, we should leave for Pakistan. They took books, clothes, and some family photos wrapped in rugs so the Taliban would not destroy them. The Taliban criminalized the taking of pictures as a violation of the Holy Koran. How different it is today, with young people using their phones as cameras, she thinks. She watches a group of boys lean into one another for a selfie. One young man heavily perspires. He talks fast, complaining of the lack of jobs. He says the Taliban controls many Afghan provinces because the people there don't care. They don't have jobs so they have no loyalty to the government. If the Taliban offers them work, they will support the Taliban. If the government offers them work, they will support the government. He would do the same if the Taliban offered him employment. A friend gives him a napkin to wipe his damp forehead.

Dijon knows from listening to her own children that young people often make comments they don't mean. No one in their right mind, especially someone as Westernized as this young man, could ever contemplate joining the Taliban. Frustration makes you say nonsensical things. That would be a good subject for Mohammad. She lodges the thought in her mind.

What is he doing now? she asks herself. Writing. He writes every day, despite his eyes and two heart operations that have left him weak and, on some days, confined to his bed. How many doctors has he seen? Too many. The best doctors were in Pakistan. His eyes improved there, but their lives did not. They were seen only as Afghan refugees. No one offered them work. Dijon cooked and catered food again. But one day Mohammad said, "No. There'll be no more restaurant. We have done that once already. We are in a different country and have to think in new ways."

He decided they would survive by using the academic skills he had acquired as a university professor teaching Afghan literature. They would start a magazine. They called it *Takahnak*, or Shock. He wrote the stories—funny, absurd tales of refugee life. Stories of collecting cans to earn a little money, of police shaking refugees down for cash, of living on top of other families and overhearing the most intimate things. He wanted to make people laugh.

"Being Afghans won't make us happy," he told Dijon. "We have to make ourselves happy."

They published seven issues of *Takahnak*, until it ran out of money and Dijon returned to cooking. She and Mohammad returned to Kabul after the Taliban fell in the wake of 9/11.

A young woman behind Dijon interrupts her thoughts. She complains that everyone has forgotten Farkhunda Malikzada. This year? Last year? The young woman stammers self-consciously. So many deaths. She can't recall the exact date. Her friends laugh, point their fingers at her.

"You have forgotten her too!" they shout.

"It happens to all of us," she says. "People think only of themselves, not others. That is what war does. You leave for work, you don't know what will happen. You don't have a chance here. Farkhunda was a martyr but we're too preoccupied to think of her."

"I am planning to leave," a boy beside her says. "The legal way, by applying for school in Germany. If that doesn't work, I will leave with smugglers."

Dijon shakes her head. He has no idea what he is talking about. With a smuggler, he would walk for days and sleep outside with no guarantee of reaching his destination. She and Mohammad walked five days to Pakistan through steep, wooded mountain passes to avoid the Taliban. With a newborn, no less. No, this boy cannot imagine. Dijon has more sympathy for the young woman's point of view. People would not have treated a dog as they did Farkhunda. Dijon was home when she died, and heard about her murder on the news. She told Mohammad, "I will tell you how I feel about Farkhunda. I was like a bird when I heard about it. I wanted to fly away from this country. If I were God, I would have killed all the people who killed her. Now you can see how I feel."

"We don't have good leaders in Afghanistan," Mohammad responded. "We have business owners, politicians, but we don't have good leaders. Farkhunda made a mistake. She didn't know she was living in a country with no leaders, no laws. She didn't know this country is one where the only power is with a gun not with the tongue. She spoke out but it was a waste of time. Without a gun, her tongue was powerless."

After Farkhunda's death, Mohammad wrote a book, *Who Is the Good Leader?*, in which he railed against a government unconcerned with human rights. Dijon prefers Mohammad's less political books. Like *About Myself: Broken Wishes*, in which he describes goals he did not achieve. Before he studied education and became a teacher, he wanted to be a television anchor. He was actually hired by a TV station during the time of the Russians. But then he had a motorcycle accident and could not work and lost his job. Another time, he wanted to be an actor. He auditioned for a play and got a part. But acting did not pay enough to earn a living, so he did not pursue it. Still, he had followed his ambitions and eventually found something he loved: teaching. *About Myself: Broken Wishes* is a book you can't just agree or disagree with, as you can with politics, Dijon tells herself. It makes you examine the choices you have made in your own life.

She has had her own broken wishes. She wanted to attend a university, but her mother and father did not encourage her to go to school. The Holy Koran says, It is the duty of every Muslim man or woman to seek knowledge, she told her parents. The holy book also says, And abide in your houses and do not display yourself, they countered.

Looking around at the full tables, her neck stiff, Dijon believes it would be a tragedy if all these young people abandoned Afghanistan, if their naive yet curious, groping minds were gone from here forever for countries that don't need them as much as Afghanistan does. She can understand why they would go, of course. She and Mohammad left too, when they were young and the country was imploding. They knew who to run from then. Now, with suicide bombers, she has no idea whom to fear other than everyone. They came back, but who can say they would not leave again? Where would they go? Mohammad finds his stories here. The market for his books, such as it is, is here. She does not want to go and see him experience another broken wish.

Dijon stands to leave. Seven o'clock. She won't return home

before ten, when the crowds in Shar-e-Naw begin to thin. She looks out the open door at the beggar boy, still there, leaning on his crutches, one hand extended in a silent plea for money. Begging children disturb her more than the threat of a suicide bomber. With an explosion, life ends. With begging, life ends too, but not for a long time, and for children the end comes at the beginning of their lives. They will learn to have no hope, to settle for the begging life, which is no life. Sometimes she talks to the older children and asks to meet their families. She tells their mothers and fathers that it would be better for them to beg than to ask their children to do so.

Children are like plants, she says. Bend them and they will grow in one direction or another. You are bending your children the wrong way. Better that you work, even if it is something simple like selling gum and candy for pennies, than to send your children out begging. You will earn the same and your children won't develop bad habits. Better they have an education.

But people, Dijon knows, want only money. They don't seek knowledge. Still, she tries not to judge too harshly. Knowledge does not fill an empty stomach. She has lived a privileged life. Her son, a computer programmer, supports them. Mohammad is free to write and she is equally free to sell his books. They put aside what she brings home, saving for six months, twelve months, however long it takes until enough money has accumulated to print more books.

The ache in her feet returns and runs up her ankles. Pain settles in the small of her back. She mulls over the strands of conversation she has overheard, running them through her mind once more as if studying for an exam. After a moment, satisfied she will remember them, she lifts the books against her chest, pressing her chin against the uppermost one, and turns toward the door and the beggar boy beyond it, his face a mosaic of color from the chimera of lights illuminating Shar-e-Naw.

MAYBE ONE DAY

Afghan police officer Said Amir doesn't know how long he'll guard Farkhunda Malikzada's home. After her murder, her family received death threats. They were accused of being atheists, and fled Kabul. Amir heard about Farkhunda's death from his younger brother. It upset him that this happened in Afghanistan—a young woman beaten to death, dragged, and burned. He couldn't look at the photos of her that appeared on Facebook after she had been assaulted by a mob. Her bleeding face, her palpable fear. He could not believe something like this could happen. She was a good girl. She wanted to be a teacher. He believes her death is a metaphor for the insecurity that has taken over Afghanistan. What happened to Farkhunda could happen to anybody. Get out with your family, his friends tell him. The threat is great.

September 2015. The editors at *The Progressive* and the *National Catholic Reporter* ask me to write about families leaving Afghanistan because of the rise in violence. Indiscriminate bombings and shootings have resulted in the deaths of hundreds of civilians. Taliban fighters control wide swaths of the country and

US officials admit that mounting casualties among Afghan National Army soldiers are unsustainable. As a result of insurgent gains, more than forty thousand Afghans have sought sanctuary in Europe, the third-largest refugee group entering the continent, behind only Syrians and Eritreans.

The killing of Farkhunda Malikzada on March 19, 2015, also galvanized many Afghans to leave for the sake of their children, especially daughters. She had been falsely accused of burning pages from the Koran in a shrine near downtown. The accusation was enough to set off the mob that killed her. I never saw the videos of Farkhunda's death posted on Facebook, but I did see photographs of her battered face as she pleaded for her life. She was just twenty-seven but looked much younger. Her hijab had been torn off her head and her hair hung limp and askew over her face. Police officers stepped in and fired warning shots, and some people in the crowd tried to stop her assailants. The police pulled and pushed Farkhunda onto the corrugated metal roof of a nearby building in a failed effort to get her to safety but Farkhunda fell, or was shoved, back into the crowd and the police backed off. After she died, her killers dragged her body behind a Toyota hatchback, dumped the corpse in a dry patch of the Kabul River, and set it on fire.

I accept the assignment and call my colleague Aarash in Kabul. He knows many people who are intent on leaving Afghanistan. Together we make a list of potential interviews. Then I book my flight.

Now, three weeks later, Aarash picks me up at Kabul International Airport. As we drive to my hotel, the Park Palace Guest House near the city center, I roll down my window, and the dust from the street and the shouts of vendors, along with the heavy, trudging sound of donkeys pulling carts past storefronts made from mud bricks and the noise of cars and belching trucks and slow-moving traffic, rush upon me, combining with the intense heat, and I think: I'm back in Kabul, as if I'd never left and my life in the US a mere twenty-four hours earlier seems to have been conjured from some other time. Aarash laughs when I tell him how I feel. He reminds me that I can enter and leave Afghanistan as I please. He, however, cannot. He tried to leave once, and failed.

It had been a simple plan: In November 2014, Aarash's wife, Sharjeela, was pregnant with their son. They knew a smuggler with contacts in Italy and he got Sharjeela a counterfeit passport. Sharjeela would request time off from her job at the Ministry of Interior, where she translated documents for US officials, leave for Rome, and have the baby there, making him an Italian citizen. Then she would send for Aarash. Borrowing money from family and friends, they paid the smuggler six thousand dollars.

Aarash drove Sharjeela to Hamid Karzai International Airport the morning of her departure. They tried to stay calm so no one would suspect what they were up to. Don't cry, Aarash told Sharjeela, or security will know. He watched her board a plane to Dubai without mishap. From there, after a long layover, she'd fly to Italy. Aarash returned home and waited for her call. When she did, Sharjeela was crying. He thought she just missed her family, but it was much worse than that. Airport security in Dubai had detained her. She was about to board the plane to Rome when a guard pulled her aside, took her passport, and walked her into a room with only a table and two chairs. Who made this? Where did you get it? the guard demanded, waving the passport. He spoke Italian and then English. Sharjeela insisted the passport was legitimate. The guard kept her in the room for hours before he put her on a flight back to Kabul. He never told her what he had found suspicious about the passport.

Don't ever try this again, he warned her.

Aarash called the smuggler.

You have to do something, he said.

I have connections. Don't worry.

I don't want her taken off the plane in handcuffs.

Don't panic, the smuggler said.

Aarash remained worried. He had seen people arrested for drugs on TV, shackled from head to foot, and he feared Sharjeela would be removed from the plane like a criminal. He felt as if he had lost everything. He had expected to meet Sharjeela in Rome. Now, she was returning twenty-four hours after she had left.

The smuggler picked her up at the airport. He paid off the necessary people so he could take her directly from the plane rather than walk through the airport with the police. When they got outside, he called Aarash.

I'm here. I have your wife.

After Aarash finishes his story he wipes tears from his eyes. Lately he has been receiving threatening phone calls. He does not know how these people got his number. They ask, Why do you work with foreigners? Join the jihad. He asks them, Will the jihad pay as well as the foreigners? He told Sharjeela that should anyone ask where she works, she should say she is a nurse or a teacher. To tell anyone about her job at the Ministry of Interior would only create problems—a woman doing a man's job for the Americans. Aarash sees no good reason to mention it. Nothing may happen or something might. In Afghanistan, no one can predict the future.

A red light flashes behind us and Aarash glances in the rear-view mirror and curses. A policeman is waving us over. We stop and Aarash reaches for his registration in the glove compartment. The officer gets out of his car and walks to my window. Ignoring Aarash, he asks for my passport. I give it to him. He thumbs through a few pages before he drops it back in my lap and gestures for us to go.

Why do you come here, he shouts at me as we start to pull away, when everyone else is leaving?

Noor Mangal, a cousin of Aarash's father, lives near the Park Palace and we stop by his house on the way to the hotel. He doesn't meet us at the door but instead stands at the top of a flight of stairs and waves for us to come up. He suffers from intense back pain and wears a brace. Afghans always experience some kind of physical pain, he believes, as a result of stress. Hurt your back and a man feels ancient. He does not appear as old as he sounds. His black hair and beard carry only the slightest hints of gray and despite his pain, he stands erect, but his lined face and the sadness in his eyes suggest a troubled, restless mind.

His back did not hurt in Russia or later in Germany. Those countries presented challenges, of course, but not stress. At least not the stress he knows today. A moment does not go by when he doesn't think of his life in Moscow and outside Berlin. He had left Afghanistan in the Taliban era when he was much younger and willing to take chances, and there were as many problems in Afghanistan then as there are today. The vice police with their questions: Why don't you have a beard? Why don't you cut your hair? Why do you have TV and videos? He'd had enough of this nonsense and the endless days of sitting in tea shops because he had no work. He thought of living in

Pakistan or Iran, but everyone there was as poor as they were in Kabul. Russia, he'd heard, had many opportunities, and he felt the country owed Afghanistan after it invaded and then left ten years later, abandoning Afghans to fight among themselves. Had they not left, there would not have been a civil war and the Taliban would not have risen to power.

Noor packed a few clothes, some water and bread, and spare shoes. The first leg of his journey took him to Iran and then Turkmenistan. From there, he had just enough money to catch a train to Moscow. He worked twelve-hour days in restaurants, shops, anywhere he could find work. Shopkeepers asked him, What can you do? Whatever you give me, Noor answered. He never had money for anything but food. For an apartment, he rented a storage container. It was damn cold in winter but cheap. In the bazaars, he met an Afghan who told him he was leaving Moscow for Europe. How are you going? Noor wanted to know. How much will it cost? Twenty-five hundred dollars, the man told him. Noor didn't have that kind of money, but he asked to be introduced to the man's smuggler so he'd have a contact for the future. The Afghan introduced him to one man who turned him over to another man who turned him over to another man and then another and another. He met more than a dozen intermediaries who suspected he might be an undercover policeman. After he allayed their suspicions, yet another man drove him to a shed miles outside Moscow and introduced him to the smuggler. The smuggler, wrongly assuming Noor had already paid, told him to join a group of migrants standing behind him.

They left for Germany in June 1998 on foot and walked west through woods and mountains. The smuggler gave them nothing to eat. Noor heard the calls of animals and was afraid.

He squeezed water from grass and plants and licked it off his fingers. Men and women who fell behind had to fend for themselves. It grew cold and six people froze to death. Somewhere between Ukraine and Czech Republic, the migrants sank in snow up to their waists. An infant died and her mother buried her beneath rocks. The woman was ready to abandon her two other small boys before Noor offered to help. He carried one of her boys on his shoulders and took the other one by the hand. The woman had no husband. Widow? Did she leave her husband? Noor didn't know and didn't ask. He was afraid that with one wrong question, one wrong move, she'd lose her mind entirely. One morning, he woke up and learned she had gone into the woods with her children.

The migrants continued without her. Noor walked bent over, almost crawling, his feet were so sore. At the Czech border, they rested for three days. Then they crossed and walked along a road, running and hiding in ditches when they saw headlights. The smuggler took them to a house where they changed into fresh clothes and shoes and then they resumed walking. Their trek led them through woods to a river where they boarded a raft and rowed for one hour before they reached the opposite shore. Noor asked questions—What's the name of this river? Where are we?—but the smuggler said nothing. They hiked through more woods until they crossed into Germany.

You're on your own now, the smuggler told the group.

He turned and left the way they had come. Noor collapsed with exhaustion and other migrants fell around him. Those who remained standing staggered like zombies. When a police officer approached them, they no longer had the energy to run. We're Afghans, the migrants told the officer, and he radioed for help. More police came and they carried some of the migrants on stretchers to ambulances and a few of the exhausted men and women opened their eyes and asked whether they were alive.

Noor lived in a detention camp for six years and shared a room with four other Afghans. A camp volunteer taught German. When Noor walked past shops, he asked, Do you need help? just as he had in Russia. Do you speak German? Yes, he lied, a little bit. What can you do? Whatever you give me. OK, come wash dishes. The jobs paid poorly, but Noor did not complain.

Germany left him speechless. He could not help but compare it to Afghanistan. The roads were paved, the buildings sturdy and not made of mud. Traffic flowed. The police did not ask him about the length of his beard. Germans struck him as very relaxed. The country had many laws—speed limits, no littering, small things that produced an order he had not known in Afghanistan.

Noor shows me a photo. In the picture, he stands in a mall, mirror balls suspended from the ceiling. The bright lights cast a gold sheen across the tile floor and glass counters of a jewelry display. He wears a jean jacket, sunglasses, a shirt unbuttoned to his chest, and tight blue jeans. At that time, he worked at a large hotel in Munich cleaning rooms. The hotel had thirty-five floors. He had just been promoted to supervisor of maintenance. It was always very busy, especially during soccer matches, when many tourists checked into the hotel to attend the games. He remembers a flower shop and nearby café. Stone paths led to seating in a garden. Guests gathered under umbrellas and ordered salads, wraps, pizzas, and Mexican food.

He wired money to his wife but she grew impatient. She wanted him to send for her. When he didn't, she showed his photo to the German embassy in Kabul. He has escaped Afghanistan, she told an official, and left me. Noor was in the process of getting his citizenship when the German police arrested him in 2006.

On the flight back to Kabul, Noor thought he would go crazy. At home he wept and punched the walls. He fought with his wife. I was saving money to send for you! he yelled at her. You have ruined our lives! He sank into a depression and slept alone. He woke every morning impatient for the day to end so he could go back to sleep and dream of Germany.

After the mob killed Farkhunda, he thought, What the hell is going on? Who will die next? Although he no longer speaks to his wife, he worries about her. If she goes to the market and someone accuses her of something, what will happen? Will she, too, be beaten to death? Will they come for him?

He has to get out. Return to Germany or somewhere else where he can live in peace, but he has no job. Every plan, no matter how simple, requires money. He'll see what he can save. He can't stay in Kabul.

Aarash and I leave Noor's home for the Park Palace Guest House. We inch through a shopping district in bumper-to-bumper traffic before we turn down a dirt alley and stop outside the heavy metal door of the guesthouse. I get out with my duffle bag and ring a bell and a guard carrying an AK-47 assault rifle lets us in. We raise our arms and he pats us down and then shows us to the courtyard where the landlord sits by himself at a table. He smiles when he sees me, stands, and gives me a hug. I've rented a room here every year since 2004. The landlord attended the University of Kansas as an exchange student in the 1970s and speaks excellent English.

Aarash and I sit at his table, our plastic chairs listing on the uneven ground.

What brings you back to Afghanistan? the landlord asks.

Another story, I say.

You journalists. It's always another story.

I smile, shrug.

It is your life, he says.

I smile again.

How have you been? I ask.

This is Afghanistan. There are good days and bad.

Inshallah, I'll have more good days than bad, I say.

Inshallah.

How much are you charging for rooms?

The landlord rocks in his chair and says nothing. I let him consider my question. He's in a bind. Four months earlier in May, a Taliban gunman shot up the guesthouse and killed five Afghans and nine foreigners, including an American woman, four Indians, two Pakistanis, an Italian, and a Kazakhstani, before police killed him. Not too many people want to stay in a guesthouse that has been attacked by terrorists. I figure I can cut a deal.

I rub my eyes against the heat, see rainbow colors flare behind the pressure of my palms. Water splashes over the sides of a fountain absorbed almost instantly by the parched ground. Flies hover over the dry grass. I stare at unoccupied tables. Above me on the second-floor balcony, a frenzy of dead leaves spins from a blast of dry wind and when the wind subsides the leaves fall, gathering in clumps by doors of vacant rooms. Across from me in the main building, I see the windows of the dining hall where guests would eat when the delirium of mosquitoes outside became too much, and I consider the chipped plaster walls scarred by bullet holes.

How about fifty US dollars a night including breakfast and dinner? the landlord suggests.

Aarash pulls his chair beside mine, whispers, You can do better.

Earlier in the day, we had looked at another guesthouse. It cost forty dollars a night, meals not included. A good rate—however, I'd rather stay at the Park. It's near downtown. People in the area know me.

You'll have guards? Better than the ones you had in May? Aarash asks.

Of course, the landlord says. I have to protect my property. I had hired a company to manage the guesthouse but they had poor security. I've canceled their contract. I have a good guard now.

So, what happened here? I ask.

It was not as the media said.

What did the media say?

That it was more than one man, the landlord replies. It was just one man and no more. I was in a room when the shooting started. I ran outside through a side door. The American woman had walked in just as the shooting started. She lay on the ground bleeding and lived a long time and asked for help, but no one wanted to risk their lives for her. She was taken to an Afghan hospital and then a Western one and died.

I had planned to come here in May, I say.

It's good you didn't, he says. Did you fly direct?

No, I had a twenty-four-hour layover in Dubai.

While I was in Dubai, I stopped in a restaurant designed like a British pub and sat beside a very drunk man as he participated in a quiz. A waitress asked questions and patrons wrote their answers on sheets of paper and another waitress collected them. I had no idea what the prize was. The drunk man said he worked for the International Red Cross. His name was Derrick and he had just been in Afghanistan and was now traveling to Islamabad, but his flight did not leave for six hours. I told him I was leaving for Kabul in the morning.

Where will you stay?

The Park Palace Guest House.

The one that got shot up?

Yes.

Is it open?

Yes.

Derrick said he knew the American woman who had been shot, Paula Kantor, the former director of the Afghanistan Research and Evaluation Unit, an Afghan organization that conducts studies aimed at improving Afghan life. She had returned to Kabul for a few weeks on a short-term consulting contract. Derrick was friends with a man she knew. Nice lady. Shame what happened. How was it a man could book a room and then kill fourteen people in the dining room? Before he left Kabul, Derrick had had dinner with Abdullah Abdullah, the chief executive of the Afghan government, essentially co-president with Ashraf Ghani, whom he had opposed. Derrick said Abdullah was planning to leave Afghanistan when it imploded. Corruption was killing the country. A resurgent Taliban had regained territory. Let them. No one, Derrick slurred, has been able to conquer Afghanistan, even its own people. That's why nothing will stop it from unraveling.

Derrick kept talking but I no longer understood his intoxicated speech except when he shouted an answer to the quiz.

Thinking of him now, I mention his name to the landlord.

He knew the American woman, I tell him.

I don't know a Derrick, the landlord says. Did he say he was here that night?

No.

There was a party in the dining hall for people from India. I think the shooter had something against Indians. They were celebrating. He walked in and started firing his gun. Then the police came and shot out all the windows before they shot him.

We looked at another guesthouse. Just forty US a night, Aarash said.

Did it have a fountain like here?

No.

Did it have a courtyard?

No, Aarash admitted.

You want breakfast and dinner included? the landlord says.

Yes.

Forty US.

Thirty, I say.

Thirty-five.

Thirty.

The landlord wipes his forehead.

It's very hot.

Yes, I agree.

OK, the landlord says. Thirty.

We shake hands. Aarash looks annoyed.

If you had let me talk to him for a little longer, he would have agreed to twenty-five, he says.

After I check in to my room, Aarash and I eat lunch at a nearby kabob stall. A young woman crosses in front of us wearing flesh-colored pants that at first glance give the impression she has nothing on.

What the hell! Aarash shouts.

The woman looks at us. She wears lipstick and makeup. She smiles and continues walking.

Amazing, Aarash says. Is this how they dress in the United States?

When the Soviet Union controlled Afghanistan in the 1980s, Aarash tells me, women wore miniskirts and loose blouses that exposed their breasts when they leaned forward. He recalls fairs with stalls and clowns and singers and women with their children, everyone wearing Western clothes, especially blue jeans. When he was in the fourth grade, he attended a community center for boys and girls. The gray slab of a building had been built by the Soviets and despite its dour design it bustled with activities. Soviet-trained teachers taught painting and music and coached sports. In those days, Aarash didn't see anyone carrying a gun. Even the police didn't have guns. Their authority alone had value.

Afghanistan started to dissolve after the Soviets left, Aarash has concluded. One day there were Russian uniforms, the next day civil war, and the day after that the black turbans of the Taliban. Then American bombs rocked Kabul. Aarash's family put blankets in front of their windows to protect the glass from flying debris. Barbers opened their shops and men lined up to have their beards shaved to celebrate the defeat of the Taliban. Boys collected bullet casings that littered the ground and people cheered in the streets.

Aarash never suspected that the US would abandon Afghanistan. Now, he thinks he should have known, but at the time he had seen so much war that he wanted to be happy for a moment and not think of the future. When he considers the decades of fighting, Aarash concludes that Afghanistan was

better off under the Taliban than at any other time. It had
security. No freedom, but it was safe. You could leave your car
without locking it and no one would dare touch it, because
they knew they'd be punished.

Aarash thought the US would leave something behind when
it began removing troops. Russia left good roads. Aarash still
uses a drinking glass made by a Russian shopkeeper. The Taliban left moral discipline. What has America left? The roads are
shit now. There is no security. People don't have work.

Do you know what today's date is? he asks me.

No.

The eleventh. September 11th.

I've got jet lag.

No one in Afghanistan remembers either, Aarash says. It no
longer matters. Nothing here does.

After lunch, Aarash drops me off at the Park and we agree
to meet at eight o'clock the next morning. I sit alone in my
second-floor room, a desk lamp providing the only light. Feral
cats call from the roof. I hear music from a radio carried by
the guard. When he shuts it off I feel the quiet of the empty
rooms around me. The sun sets, darkening the balcony. I feel
bad about the people who died here, Paula Kantor and the
others, and how I used their misfortune to bargain for a cheap
room. I saw an opportunity and I took it, but I wonder what
this says about me and my work that I have come here so often
I would assess a tragedy only in how I might benefit from it. I
google Kantor's name. Photos show a woman with short, gray
hair and glasses. The website of an NGO says Kantor wanted
to improve the lives of women and girls in countries affected by
war and terrorism. She was forty-six.

I'm sorry, I say aloud to no one.

A young man the landlord hired brings me beef kabob for dinner but I've had enough kabob for one day. When he leaves, I break up the meat and toss it outside my door for the cats. Soon they come running and I watch them snarl, scrambling for food, oblivious of me until I move and then they scatter, but their fear is temporary and they return. When the food is gone they attempt to enter my room. I close my door, shut off the light, and get into bed. The cats yowl. I listen to them fight as I try to sleep.

The shopkeepers of Timor Shahe near downtown Kabul still talk about Farkhunda. Their small businesses surround the yellow two-story mosque on Andarabi Road where the mob attacked her. The Kabul River, less a river than a wide sewer where women wash clothes and refuse lies in fetid piles for opium addicts to pick at, steams in the heat now as it did that day.

The doors of Dunja Optics open to the crowded sidewalk. A slow day, the sun blinking off the dusty counters where the owner, Abdul Whaham, displays an assortment of glasses. He had just opened when a mob assaulted Farkhunda. He heard yelling and hurried outside to see what the commotion was about. A group of men moved toward him and he stepped back inside. More people rushed over from across the street. He closed the doors to his shop and watched the crowd shouting and shoving, and he saw a woman's face covered with blood, her clothes torn, and then she disappeared. Men tied her to the back of a car and dragged her on the street, people striking her with sticks and kicking her as the car raced forward, and other men with cell phones filmed her body bouncing on the road.

Kill her! Kill her! men shouted.

They threw her body beside the river, covered her with sticks, and started a fire. Abdul can't say how long it took for the police and ambulance to arrive. Their cars could barely move through the crowd, with so many people converging on the river while others leaned over the guardrails and watched men striking Farkhunda's burning body with sticks. So much blood. Abdul got sick and hurried back to his shop. He heard men yelling that she had blasphemed Islam. That she was an atheist. That she was a Christian. Come hit her and get your reward in Paradise. Abdul saw black smoke rising from her body as it burned. The next day he returned to work as if nothing had happened. Everything seemed the same, but it was all different, a shared secret no one wanted to discuss. Abdul felt involved somehow, though all he had done was watch. Still, he could not escape a sense of his complicity. He washed his hands but felt dirty. He doesn't understand. Afghans take care of girls more than they do boys. They care for girls as if they were precious stones.

This morning, as I wait for Aarash in the courtyard of the Park Palace, I recall sitting here just twelve months earlier, chatting it up with expats from Britain, Germany, and India. Most of them were contractors of one sort or another. They occupied a majority of the hotel's one hundred rooms. I'd listen to them shout at waiters, insisting on more coffee, more kabob, more of something, while feral cats fed off scraps they tossed on the ground. The cats ate hurriedly, scattering as waiters rushed forward in the rumpled white shirts and black slacks that they often wore to bed so they would be available 24-7, leaping up from mattresses in the small rooms they shared in the main building, Yes, sir, yes, sir, how may I help you? Erect and alert and subservient, standing almost at attention at the now empty and dust-covered tables around me.

Good morning, brother! Aarash shouts above the noise of army helicopters flying low overhead. Because of recent bombings, Kabul government officials travel by air rather than by car. The chuff, chuff of rotor blades has become a constant and overwhelming irritant. After the helicopters pass, Aarash tells me about a friend—Jamshid—who left Kabul for Russia but returned. He suggests he'd be a good interview, and I agree. Taking out his cell phone, Aarash makes arrangements to pick him up. Then he gets on Facebook. Months earlier he started an account, Afghanistan Security, to record news and social media reports about the latest insurgent attacks. He posts information from notes scrawled on a scrap of paper:

Kabul, September 8 at two fifteen p.m.: A magnetic bomb exploded and injured one Police Officer and destroyed a few vehicles in the area. It was attached to a car.

Kabul, September 11 at five fifteen p.m.: An explosion took place in Airport Residential Apartments.

Ghazni Province, September 14 at ten a.m.: A group of armed men attacked Ghazni's prison and almost four hundred prisoners have escaped the jail.

What's a magnet bomb? I ask, reading over his shoulder.

It's an explosive insurgents attach to trucks and cars.

We should check your car.

With you here, I will every day, Aarash assures me.

Before we leave, he gives me a paper he calls his threat statement. He has decided to apply for a special US immigration visa. The visas are available only to those Afghans who worked as translators, interpreters, or other professionals employed by or on behalf of the United States government for a minimum of two years. Aarash was employed by a private American contractor in the early 2000s and he believes that his job qualifies him for the visa. I disagree. What he did for the contractor is not the same as being employed by the US military, I tell him, but he won't listen and insists I evaluate his statement.

I begin reading, writing in all caps and bracketing my comments: *Beginning in* [NAME A YEAR] *I started work with DynCorp International, a US-based aviation firm; I was with the division of DynCorp that trained the Afghan National Police.* [SAY WHAT YEARS YOU WORKED THERE.] *During this time I was under threat from insurgents. Consequently, I moved around to other DynCorp locations for my own safety, never working in one location too long. As a language assistant, I worked with Dyn-Corp, an American global service provider in their Kabul office.* [WHAT YEAR OR YEARS? CAN YOU SAY IF D.C. WAS CONNECTED TO THE U.S. MILITARY?] *Now, I cannot go to my home in Laghman* [SAY HOW FAR THAT IS FROM KABUL] *because of my work. Many times the local village people have told me to quit my job with the US company, otherwise they will never allow me to enter the province. After quitting DynCorp I went to work for Afghan companies, but the suspicion that I had been a spy for the Americans stuck to me and people still thought of me as working for Westerners. One time, I drove to Jalalabad and a group of armed insurgents tried to stop us in the middle of a road, but we did not stop; we escaped and they shot at us.* [THIS DOES NOT SHOW THEY WENT AFTER YOU BECAUSE YOU ONCE WORKED FOR DYNCORP. FIND ANOTHER/ BETTER EXAMPLE.]

I feel like a composition teacher correcting Aarash's grammar, tightening his sentences, raising questions to better develop his argument, but I'm not hopeful my efforts will help him.

I was thinking of reporting some of these issues [REPEAT THE ISSUES, I.E., THE THREATS ON YOUR LIFE BECAUSE OF YOUR WORK WITH U.S. CONTRACTORS] *to the government in order for it to protect me but I came to the conclusion that the government is too weak and therefore I don't feel it's secure to report or live in this country. My wife and I can't go to her village in Logar Province* [LOGAR IS AN HOUR OUTSIDE KABUL. SAY THAT TO SHOW THE THREAT IS CLOSE BY] *as the people there call us both mazdor kofar, servants of pagans.*

When I finish, I put my pen in my shirt pocket and give the paper back to him.

What do you think? Aarash asks.

This just tells me you've been threatened. You have anecdotes but no proof and no connection to the American military.

Aarash folds the paper and from the defeated look in his eyes, I think he might crumple it up and throw it away.

I'm sorry.

I am too, brother, but you can leave.

We pick up Jamshid and drive an hour to Qargha Lake. It's Friday, the equivalent of Sunday in the United States. No stores or tea shops will be open. The lake will be as good a place as any to spend the morning.

Parking near the shore, we get out and gaze at the placid water. On a nearby road, cars lurch through valleys of ruined pavement toward a distant hilltop destination. Brown mountains flecked with snow pierce a hazy horizon. Thin shadows cast by leafless trees point toward pitted dirt paths, one of which we follow. Vendors sell fruit, flies swarming the discarded rinds, and we settle in a sliver of shade near a family whose children run toward the water and scream delightedly when waves lap their bare toes. One boy hurries to us and demands that we pay him for our spot. Jamshid waves him away.

The poor will try to make money any way they can, he says.

The sun shines and the lake sparkles, the light leaping off the water in glittering patterns, and a man fishes from a boat amid the dancing light as if a cluster of fairies has burst upon him. Jamshid opens a cracker tin and we pass it between us.

This is the only place for sightseeing in Kabul, Jamshid comments, sipping from a can of Red Bull. We have this lake and the zoo. We don't have anything else to do in Kabul besides these two things and avoiding dying in a bomb blast.

A young couple sitting on a plastic mat not far from us discreetly kiss and then glance in our direction. They must have concluded that we're watching them, because they get up, take their mat, and give us a resentful look before they walk to a more inconspicuous spot. Jamshid rolls his eyes.

Afghanistan is so backward, he complains. Everyone is worried about being watched. And we are watched. Farkhunda is a perfect example of that. Do you know about her?

Yes, I say.

Those guys who killed her, they're brainwashed.

Jamshid had been checking his Facebook messages when Farkhunda was murdered. He read posts about it but didn't know whether to believe it. Maybe it was just a rumor. Then he saw the photos of her beating. Oh my God, he thought, and wept. For what reason did they do this? Those men were like the Taliban. Worse. Even though they are young. Even though they wear blue jeans as he does. They accept the conservative beliefs of their parents, and they are angry because they have no jobs, no money. They behave without thinking. Like saying prayers. They don't know why. They just pray. Pray in Arabic and they don't even understand what they're saying. There is no end to the fighting. Why do people make weapons, sell guns? Because they don't want to end the insecurity. They want to fight and get more power.

He stops talking when he sees Aarash point his phone at him. He taps out a smoke from a pack of Esse Black cigarettes and strikes a pose, showing Aarash his profile, unsmiling, chin jutting toward the lake, the lean, chic cigarette raised to his lips. Aarash takes a few snaps. Then they huddle together and upload the pics to Facebook. Jamshid posts them immediately and shows them to me. The expression on his face, imitation sultry male model, makes me swallow a laugh.

I'm impressed how, in just a few minutes, we've gone from the tragedy of Farkhunda to selfies and Facebook. Like the men he criticizes, Jamshid, too, acts without thinking. Yes, he was disgusted by Farkhunda's death, but not so much that Facebook hadn't diverted his attention. And yet, the posting of his photo provides only a temporary distraction from the tragedy that is Afghanistan. At twenty-eight, Jamshid has never known peace. He remembers the Taliban but the memories do not weigh on him, because he was just a boy. The present worries him however; the rising instability and lack of jobs make him fear the future. He's married. He wants to raise a family but not in Afghanistan.

Did Aarash tell you I left for Russia?

Yes.

He pauses and stares at the lake. Clouds drift in, darkening the water with a patchwork of shade, and he lights another smoke and begins talking without taking his eyes off the water.

Jamshid left Kabul through the most conventional of means: a travel agency. A sign in the window advertised visa applications for Turkey, Iran, Russia, and Pakistan. In Afghanistan such promotions provide cover for some travel agents to link customers with smugglers. An agent told Jamshid he knew a smuggler in Moscow. He'll sponsor you, the man told him.

Jamshid paid the agent fifteen hundred dollars for the connection, and the Moscow smuggler three thousand dollars. He asked Aarash to join him but Aarash didn't have money to pay the smuggler. Over a period of months, the smuggler filed the forms necessary to claim Jamshid as a cousin to ease his entry into Russia. Jamshid then applied for a visa. He also bought a round-trip ticket to avoid arousing suspicion, and flew to Moscow in November 2014. He spent his first night in Russia with the smuggler. He called friends in Afghanistan and apologized for not saying goodbye, because, he explained, he would have started crying.

On his second day in Moscow, the smuggler introduced him to another smuggler who, he said, could get him into Europe. This smuggler told Jamshid he would have to wait six months until the snow cleared. They spoke in the smuggler's electronics shop, surrounded by oscillating fans, power cords, and coils of wire. The trip would take four or five days and cost eighty-five hundred dollars. Jamshid would be one of many migrants the smuggler would take by van into Austria and he'd have to bring his own food and water. Once in Austria, they would walk until they reached the German border. Winter made the trip more dangerous because of the cold, and they'd be making their way not on roads but through woods. The trees would be bare and the risk of being seen would be great. Better to wait until spring, the smuggler advised, when the woods would be dense with foliage. Do I wait or leave? Jamshid wondered.

After one week in Moscow, the first smuggler told Jamshid he could no longer stay with him and the second smuggler said he had no room. Where will I stay? Jamshid asked. The smuggler shrugged. Jamshid's problems were not his. With no good options, Jamshid returned to Kabul with the intention of leaving again as soon as he raised more money.

Everyone here thinks of their own life and how to make it better, he complains. Nobody pays attention to other people. The war makes people think only of themselves, of surviving. No one knows how long they will be alive. They leave for work; they don't know what will happen. You don't have a chance here. Either you're not working or you're working but you could get killed in a bomb explosion. I want to feel free and walk free and not be afraid. I want to be happy. That would mean a lot to me.

We finish our crackers and walk to the car. Aarash drives us back onto the highway, blasts of foul-smelling diesel exhaust from passing trucks replacing the cool lake air. Shuttered vendor stalls stand like the vacant buildings of a ghost town, and dogs jog down the sidewalks, pausing to rummage through garbage floating in gutters, competing with scavenging boys.

We've not gone far when a policeman waves for us to stop. Jogging to the driver's side, the officer asks Aarash to take him to a bus station. The police earn little and often stop cars and request rides when they're off duty. Turn them down, you pay a fine. We're not in a hurry and we certainly don't need the hassle of upsetting a cop.

Get in, Aarash tells him.

The policeman climbs in the back seat and introduces himself. His name is Naim, and like many Afghans, he has just one name. He's starting five days of leave. He got a ride into Kabul from the police station in Sarobi, in eastern Afghanistan, about a five-hour drive, and now needs to catch a bus to his home in Bagram, more than sixty miles away.

Naim feels he really earned his leave. One week earlier, he

and other members of the police, the army, and the American special forces participated in a firefight in Uzben, a village near the Tora Bora mountains close to the Pakistan border. Coalition forces lost Osama bin Laden there in 2001.

By the time Naim reached Uzben, insurgents had set fire to a patch of trees. American soldiers looked through binoculars but could see nothing beyond the burning woods. It's safe, they concluded. Then Taliban fighters swept down from three different directions through the smoke. Naim fled. He saw police officers and some Americans gunned down as he hid in the woods until dark, the heat from the fire searing his face.

At ten, maybe eleven at night, Naim crept out of his hiding place behind a tree and made his way to the police station in Sarobi, just outside Uzben. The dispatcher on duty nearly fainted. I thought you were dead, he told Naim. I'm not, Naim said. We've told your family you're dead, the dispatcher said. I'm sorry for this. Naim punched him in the face. Now it is my turn to apologize, he said.

He stayed at the station for two nights and called his family, but his wife thought he was someone pretending to be Naim, because the Naim she knew was dead. By the third day, Naim no longer cared about the Taliban, and told his commander he had to see his family. The commander gave him two bodyguards and he drove home to Bagram. When his wife opened the door, she screamed, You're a ghost! Naim insisted he was not and walked toward her and she began to cry and wail and sank to the ground. He looked around his house. Flowers filled the tables and a coffin took up the center of the living room. Everything had been prepared for his funeral. He started to weep. For two days, he stayed with a friend, until his wife decided that he was indeed her husband, Naim. After two weeks, he returned to Sarobi and resumed his duties.

Have you thought of leaving Afghanistan? Aarash asks.

No, Naim says. If I don't have money to get to a bus, how will I have money to reach Europe?

Good point, Jamshid agrees.

I had the money one year but still I could not get out, Aarash says.

At the downtown bus station, Aarash parks beside a table where three men sit drinking tea beneath a restaurant awning. Two yellow buses blemished with rust stand at the curb, low to the pavement on nearly deflated tires. A few feet away a bearded man shouts, Why don't you accept Islam? Do you not want to go to Paradise? Why do you dress like Westerners? Are you not Afghan? Are you not Muslim? The Holy Koran is the ultimate book of Allah. It's the one true book. Like technology, the Holy Koran is the final update to everything that preceded it. Do you believe the other books are irrelevant now? Whoever does not believe in the Holy Koran is not following Mohammad and will not go to Paradise. The day of doom is for everyone. God will judge us all. I am telling you this because on the day of judgment I will be asked by God if I told the people about the holy book. So now I have tried. People will be divided between heaven and hell. I will be rewarded with good things.

The bus drivers listen to him rant. They notice Naim, Aarash, Jamshid, and me watching him. Lunatic, a driver named Mukhtar mutters. He gestures for us to sit and offers us tea. After he fills our cups, he looks at his watch. Slow day. It may pick up because many people are escaping Afghanistan. He's had passengers, including other bus drivers, who have sold everything they have to buy a ticket to Iran. He knows of two drivers who just reached Europe. Many return. They spend all their money and then they get caught, deported. Iran, he's heard, is not kind to refugees but some people never give up. They collect money and go again. Mostly couples or single men. He rarely sees single women leaving. He gets only good girls on his bus, girls who travel with their husbands. He feels sorry for them when they don't make it. His brother, Mohammad, sitting across from us, tried to get out but got caught in Turkey and deported. He wants to try again.

You're crazy, Mukhtar tells him.

You're crazy to stay, Mohammad responds.

Mohammad left Kabul in 2014 after he graduated from Bakh University in Mazar-e-Sharif, a city north of Kabul. He had grown tired of living day by day, and by chance. The chance of being struck by a bullet. The chance of being killed in a bomb blast. He survived a bombing in May in Mazar that killed a small boy. Someone had placed an explosive in front of a pharmacy. The bomb went off beside a boy pushing a cart. In that moment, Mohammad decided to leave Afghanistan. He knew English. He did not have a wife or other obligations. He had no reason to stay. He hired a smuggler and the smuggler put him in a group of sixty-five Afghans fleeing to Europe. He knew some of them. They took a bus to Herat and then walked four hours through the mountains to cross into Iran. A falling boulder mangled one man's foot and he was left behind. Another man fell but got up and kept walking. They carried bread and fruit and little more. Some of them threw away their food to lighten their loads. A driver the smuggler hired met them in Iran. Sixteen people squeezed into a car so tightly that their faces turned red. Six others, including Mohammad, piled into the trunk where, although there were some holes for air, it was impossible to breathe well and it grew very hot. When Mukhtar asked him what it was like, Mohammad told him, If you want to know more, try it yourself. Twelve other people got in a second car. The rest shouldered their way into two other cars. The smuggler said it would take three days to reach Tehran. When they noticed a checkpoint, everyone scrambled out of the cars, spread out, and crept forward on foot, waiting for the smuggler to get past the police. They scrambled back into the cars—the smuggler shouting, Hurry, hurry!—and drove on until the next checkpoint where they got out again. A few people lost their way each time they stopped and stayed behind.

Iranian police caught the Afghans in Yazd, a small town outside Tehran. They had passed the main checkpoint, but police were patrolling the road and intercepted them as they tried to reunite with the smuggler. The police treated them worse than a farmer treats a mule. They cursed and hit them and the Afghans cried but did not resist or try to escape. They had accepted all the risks and knew capture was a possibility. Inshallah, they had said when they left Kabul—God willing we will reach Europe—but God had not willed it and they were subdued in their failure. The police took them to a customs house where they were made to unload imported goods. After three days, an officer drove them to a camp for Afghan migrants near the Afghan border in the Herat region. The Iranians held migrants indefinitely without pay, and fed them once a day. Mohammad had nearly two thousand dollars. The police took it when they turned him over to Afghan authorities.

Now Mohammad wakes up in the middle of the night furious with the way the Iranians treated him. As if he were illiterate, an idiot, an animal. He is twenty-one and has a degree in economics. At night, he stares into the dark and imagines himself as an animal in the Kabul zoo, unblinking, enraged, trapped.

Mukhtar grips his shoulder as if to shake away the memories of his failed venture, and Mohammad looks away from him and down the road where the warmth of the day is giving rise to shimmering heat haze and mirages. He intends to try again. One of his neighbors sold their house to pay a smuggler. Mohammad will go with him and twenty-one members of the man's family. He has heard that Denmark is accepting refugees while Germany has begun to crack down.

You're a fool, Mukhtar says. Our family is here.

I will send for all of you later.

It's too dangerous. Many are thrown into the sea. You have seen all these things on the news.

I'm going, Mohammad says.

Naim asks Mohammad which bus goes to Bagram. Mohammad tells him and Naim stands and thanks Aarash for the ride. His light blue, sweat-stained uniform sags off his thin body and his eyes droop from sleepless nights. He looks forward to seeing his family, and forgetting the risks of his job for a while. He receives threatening phone calls from the Taliban. If he returns to Uzben they will kill him. He avoids traveling outside Sarobi.

Good luck, Aarash tells him.

Naim shakes his hand. He won't let threats deter him. When so much could go wrong, it's important to keep his life simple.

Abdul Rahman teaches Sharia law at Bebe Ayesha-E-Sedeeqa in Kabul. Farkhunda attended his class for nine months. He recalls her as very eager. She walked to school and went right home. She had a good heart and always helped other students. Now, some of the other students are talking about leaving Afghanistan. Without her, they've lost their strength.

Like a prophet, Farkhunda spoke about right and wrong but

many people didn't believe her, Abdul says. They wanted to live selfish lives. This has always been part of the history of Islam. Say the truth and people kill you. This is why Allah took her to the sky.

Following our afternoon at the lake, Aarash and I meet with his friend Gety at the Park Palace. She hopes to leave for Europe in a few weeks and Aarash suggested I talk to her. A twenty-four-year-old model, she has spent her day posing for photographers shooting the covers of several fashion magazines. I have to admit Gety is striking. She wears a sparkling blue blouse that matches the color of her eyes, and black slacks and a pale-yellow head scarf. Aarash offers her a chair and she sits with us in the courtyard and smiles shyly; embarrassed by her limited English, she breaks into a nervous giggle when I introduce myself. She and Aarash exchange small talk. When she's ready to answer my questions, she turns very serious.

Every night, Gety tells me, she prays that the next day in Kabul will be better, but it only gets worse. Everyone hopes to leave, especially young people like her. They have no jobs and security is almost nonexistent. Her parents want Gety to go, but of course they feel sorrow at the idea of losing their daughter, and they worry about what would happen to her alone in a country not her own. Gety has no idea how she'll reach Europe. She'll pay a smuggler to get her out of Afghanistan and then hire another one and another and another, a new smuggler each step of the way, through Iran and then Turkey, until she reaches Greece. She'll have to bring her own food and water and clothes. She'll wear camo pants, a blouse, a hijab, and a jacket, and she'll use Facebook to keep in touch with her family. Friends have told her that it takes thirty minutes to reach Greece by water from Istanbul. She's heard migrants live in detention centers in Athens. They're asked where they want to go, Austria or Germany, and then they're told how to get there. Gety doesn't know where Austria and Germany are in Europe. She presumes she'll learn the language, get educated, and find a job. She'll bring makeup but use it only when she's settled and looking for work.

Up until now Gety has lived a fortunate life. After high school, she worked at TV stations, but a colleague who shot commercials encouraged her to model. You're a good-looking lady, he said. You'll get a lot of work. At first, she felt very nervous posing before a camera. When she started, maybe ten people knew who she was. Now, many do.

As a young girl, she never realized how vulnerable a woman could be. She spent her days in school and always wore a white and blue uniform and black shoes. All the girls looked alike. After school they remained dressed in their uniforms. Once she reached her teens, her parents allowed her to change into normal clothes after school. By then, the Taliban had been out of power and girls could wear blue jeans and Western-style tops. Women of her parents' age disapproved. They said, You're not in Europe. Don't wear clothes like that. Under the Taliban, her mother told her, women had to wear body-length veils just to leave the house. The Taliban would follow them to see whether their faces and feet were covered and lash them for the smallest infraction. Gety is too young to remember that time. She knows only the stories her mother tells her and the threat she herself faced just months earlier.

On a Friday night in January 2015, she caught a taxi home after work. The driver had not gone far when ten men and some boys blocked the car and began shouting at Gety. Who are you? Are you having sexual relations with this driver? Why are you traveling alone without a husband? They called her a whore and rocked the car and threw stones, breaking a passenger window; glass fell over her. The driver accelerated but heavy traffic prevented him from moving very far and the men chased after him, and although they were on foot, they kept up.

Afraid they would reach her, Gety got out and ran. She fell, and as the men closed in she got up and fled into a bakery. The mob pursuing her had grown and they lobbed rocks at the shop; the owner locked the doors and shouted at the enraged, distorted faces glaring at him through the windows until finally he called the police. An hour passed before an officer arrived. What did you do? he asked Gety. Nothing, she said. I just want to go home. That's all. The officer took her to a police station and called her parents. Her father arrived at one in the morning. A senior officer, however, told him Gety could not leave until the commanding officer ordered her release.

Hours later, the commander confronted Gety. He could not find the cab driver or anyone willing to confirm her story. He allowed her father to take her home but her home became another kind of jail: her father would not let her leave the house. Men won't blame a boy, he told her, but they'll say you're not a good girl. They'll shame you to me. After two months, Gety told her father, I'm going crazy, and he relented. I'll take you wherever you need to go, he said. He drove her to work and picked her up. If she was running late, he beat her. She lived like this for a long time, until she convinced him that she had done nothing provocative that night, and he finally let her go out alone again.

Had she not escaped the mob, Gety is convinced she would have died like Farkhunda. She has nightmares. In her dreams, men hold her against a wall and tear at her clothes. Bullets

strike her body but she does not die. She sees Farkhunda's face
and then her own. She wakes up sweating and shaking, unable
to fall back asleep.

Her father thinks Farkhunda deserved to die. She would
not have been killed had she been a good girl, he says. Gety
dismisses her father's comments. He has the old mindset, the
old point of view, and has no conception of the world as it is
today. The same is true with some boys. They don't think in the
modern way—they think like their parents and live in the past,
not in the future that Gety hopes to reach.

Aarash and I walk Gety to the street and wave down a taxi.
As we watch her leave, Aarash calls his uncle, a retired police
officer. Aarash thinks he might know someone familiar with
Gety's case. His uncle suggests we meet with an instructor at
the Kabul Police Academy, Lieutenant General Habibullah
Ranzour.

At the academy, a cadet leads us through a maze of dark halls
to a corner office with a desk and two brown couches. A bare
bulb hangs from the ceiling. Through a cobwebbed window
above one of the sofas, I can see cadets in heavy green uniforms performing drills in a field, and as I watch them march,
Ranzour comes in and sits behind the desk, shuffling through
papers as if Aarash and I aren't here. He stacks the papers in one
corner. Then he looks at us for the first time, taking us in with
his deep-set brown eyes. His clothes cling to his body, sweat
stains forming rings beneath his arms. He strokes his gray
beard and shouts for someone to bring us tea. Motioning to
one wall where the Afghan flag hangs, he points to framed photographs of police cadets, thirty of whom died in a bomb blast
at the academy weeks before my arrival, and just days before

their graduation. Ranzour was home when the bomb exploded and rushed to the academy. Seeing his students in pieces—he has no words. He and other officers collected the bodies and sent them to a hospital, but the hospital had no refrigeration system, so the remains were transported to another hospital, where they stayed until funeral arrangements were made.

Ranzour does not know Gety or her case, but what happened to her does not surprise him, not after Farkhunda. Unfortunately, Afghanistan has been at war for almost forty years, he explains. That much fighting turns people into monsters. They pick on those they believe are weak. As a woman, Farkhunda was seen as weak. He's glad Gety escaped and sad for Farkhunda, but not as sad as he was and still is for the dead cadets—because he knew them, unlike Farkhunda. He believes that after each dark day, God's light shines, and that belief gives him the strength to do his duty and not dwell on bad thoughts. Some police, he knows, take money from drug dealers. Other officers with no skill get promoted because they have a relative in government. Injustice exists everywhere. The police officers who did not help Farkhunda chose not to involve themselves in a religious matter. People don't have the right to kill a woman, but they have a right to their beliefs. When they killed Farkhunda, they were practicing their beliefs. It's not what Ranzour believes, but he was not there, so he won't judge. If Farkhunda was a good girl, then she is in Paradise and her family should be happy for her. If she was not, God will punish her as much as he will the terrorists.

Ranzour leans back in his chair and recalls a 2008 bombing in Kabul that killed a man from Denmark. He met the dead man's mother and told her that whoever killed her son was the enemy of all Afghans now. They have kept in touch and she's helping him get a Danish visa. He will never leave Afghanistan, but should he change his mind, he will live with her in Denmark.

Everyone, Ranzour believes, has the same destiny: One day they will meet God and answer to him. God oversees everything. Afghanistan is a poor country that has been fighting for too long. War no longer affects Ranzour. There will be another bombing. There will be another Farkhunda. He lives each day waiting for his moment before God. When he and other officers come to work, they kneel and pray and tell God they look forward to dying and living in Paradise. They are willing to die, and will therefore never withdraw from confronting the enemy. For those officers who did nothing for Farkhunda, for those officers who accept bribes, for those officers who have their positions through patronage, God will bring them together in the fight for Afghanistan or condemn them to an eternal death. God will hold them to account.

Khawaja Atiquallah, vice chancellor of Ayeshe Dorany, a high school for girls in Kabul, remembers Farkhunda as a simple girl who was also very curious and had a good sense of humor. She wanted to be famous and show off her knowledge of the Holy Koran, but she was just an average student in all her courses besides religion. In religion, she excelled. She always mentioned Islam in her conversations and seemed to be searching for a deeper truth, but about what, Khawaja does not know. Perhaps about women and their role in society. In Afghanistan, many people are Muslim in name only. Farkhunda practiced her faith and searched for the meaning of being a Muslim. Farkhunda was a very logical young woman who always engaged in debates without anger.

Her murder weighs heavily on Khawaja. To accuse her of

defaming Islam was a lie. She hated NATO and the Americans. She would ask, Why are they here? Why have they conquered us? Maybe that is the reason she died. Khawaja thinks the Americans might have done something to her. They would have known she was against foreigners. Any reasonable person would be opposed to people coming in and taking over their country.

As we leave Ranzour's office, Aarash receives a call from a friend, Naseer Ahmad. Naseer has just been approved for a US visa because of his work as a translator for the US military. We meet him in a barber shop, a small storefront where two chairs stand across from a rectangular mirror. Shampoo, talcum powder, razors, scissors, and toppled bottles of hair dye occupy a rack of shelves and irritate the air with their sharp odors, and magazine photos of posturing young men with stern looks and dark hair pompadoured in the latest fashions—quiff, duck-tail, Mohawk—fill the walls. Naseer sits on a bench reading Facebook posts on his cell phone and he and Aarash fist bump before Aarash sits next to him. I recognize the barber instantly. Uresh Jawid.

Malcolm! he shouts and hugs me.

We'd last seen each other the summer I rescued the cat, Whistle. Uresh had been unemployed then. After I left, he tells me now, he apprenticed for a friend of his family, a barber. He slept beneath a table in the man's shop after closing; he named the cockroaches that scuttled by his face. He spent all his days and nights there. He watched YouTube videos to learn about modern haircuts that the barber refused to teach him, because he was a conservative man and disapproved of Western fashion. He provided Uresh with a small allowance with which he bought food for his family. After he completed his three-month apprenticeship, he and another student started their own hair-styling business. Uresh thought he worked harder than his partner and soon grew tired of splitting the profits with a lazy man. One year later, they sold the shop and Uresh opened this one after a customer offered him the space. He has been here for twelve months and earns from ten to one hundred dollars a day. His mother gets angry with him for not wearing a salwar kameez to work. He tells her he can't—he must look modern for his customers.

What do you think?

You've done very well, I tell him. Congratulations.

His father, he thinks, would be proud of him. He had been a lieutenant in the Mujahideen and died in the civil wars of the 1990s. Men who served under him are now commanders in the Afghan National Army and, in Uresh's opinion, have grabbed everything of value for themselves. They drive armored cars, live in gated communities. They are happy. They can leave Afghanistan when they want. None of them came to Uresh's house when his father died. None of them offered to help his family. It was left to him to take on the responsibilities of his father.

Afghanistan was good in 2003, Uresh says. Security, the economy, it was fine. He had hope. But then 2014 came and the announcement of the NATO withdrawal was like a bullet to the head. Every Afghan has made plans to leave. The country has gone backward.

He reaches for a can of Red Bull and peels back the tab. Tipping back his head, he downs it in several gulps and wipes his mouth with the back of his hand, tossing the can in the trash. He considers me. He decides I look about the same as I did in 2013, only thinner and with less hair. He dislikes my bushy beard.

You look like the Taliban, he scolds.

Naseer was here before me, I say.

No problem, my friend, Naseer says. I'm in no hurry.

Uresh gestures toward a chair and I sit down and he wraps a white cloth around my neck and drapes a black sheet over my chest. Taking an electric razor, he adjusts the blade before he lifts my chin. I close my eyes and listen to the hum of the razor and to Aarash and Naseer's conversation. For my benefit, they speak in English. Every so often I interject a question.

As a boy, Naseer watched Hollywood movies starring Tom Cruise, Arnold Schwarzenegger, and Sylvester Stallone, and he waited tables at Bella Italia, an Italian restaurant in Kabul frequented by Westerners, where he could practice the English he had learned from action films. He began picking up side jobs that included translating for the US military in 2005. He regrets his work for the Americans because now he must leave. People know he worked as a translator. He doesn't know how they know, but they do. Total strangers confront him and ask, Why did you help the Americans? You're an atheist. He has to be careful. Not just in Kabul but all around. He can't drive outside the city without security. If people suspect he was a translator, they will kill him. How would they find out? It doesn't matter. They would. Right now, he's parked on the street and that makes him nervous. He wonders whether someone will attach a magnet bomb to his car. He's sick of being careful, weighing everything he does with the question: Will this put me at risk of being killed? If I go to the store, if I walk with my wife, if I go outside, what will happen? It's like living in prison.

A few weeks ago in Jalalabad, he saw a policeman die as he

was inspecting gutters for remote-controlled devices. The gutters were clean, so he began searching through garbage on the road and a mine exploded. The Americans interrogated the suspected bomber in Pulacharki prison; Naseer translated.

How do you work with the US government? the prisoner asked him. Do you not believe in God?

How do you guys kill civilians? Naseer countered.

The US is doing the same thing, the suspect shot back.

Naseer sighs. Everyone has a position. Everyone is a partisan. He's not going to kill someone if they disagree with him, but a terrorist will. He hears there are psychos in America. They walk into churches and kill people, the same as terrorists. Maybe it's that way all over the world. He thinks he understands. If he had no work, he'd join the Taliban. Instead of dying a partial person he'd die a whole person, as an insurgent, because at least he'd have had a job. He has friends—lawyers and engineers, well-educated people—who are leaving. They don't have money and can't find work.

Aarash asks him about getting a Special Immigrant Visa but Naseer has nothing reassuring to tell him. He has a visa, yes, but now he needs a passport. He's walked to the passport office several times, but the situation there is hopeless. The office opens at eight o'clock in the morning, but people begin lining up at four. One time, Naseer waited four hours and still didn't get in. A passport costs one hundred dollars and takes forty-five days to process. He has a wife and child. They would need passports too. That's three hundred dollars. If Naseer had nine hundred dollars, he could get passports for himself and his family in twenty-four hours, but Naseer doesn't have three hundred dollars, let alone nine hundred. He has sought help from the US embassy but was turned away. The embassy doesn't trust Afghans. Don't be scared of me, he says, but he knows it's too late for that.

Bad luck for you, Aarash says.

Naseer sighs. Like other Afghans, he doesn't have goals. Not exact goals anyway. These days, he must not focus on any one thing but be flexible and earn money any way he can to stay alive.

Uresh shuts off the razor and flicks a brush over my face, removing stray hair. Looking in the mirror, I see that my once unruly beard has been cut close to the skin. Uresh steps back appraising his work. At twenty-five, he's a young man proud of his achievements, but tired from his own hard-won accomplishments and the hopelessness of his country. When he takes a bus home, he asks himself: Will someone shoot me, stab me, blow me up? People guess his age to be much older than twenty-five. I'm not even thirty, he tells them, but they don't believe him. His mother has told him that each wrinkle in his face shows a year of his life.

If that is true, he responded, then I must be ninety.

He hopes to leave Afghanistan for another country where he'll feel safe, someplace he could call a new homeland, but he remains because of his mother, he explains as he applies finishing touches to my beard. He has not told her he has a girlfriend, because she would want them to marry—then they'd have children and it would be that much harder for him to escape to Europe. He has tried to persuade her to find him a wife outside the country. He would marry that girl and become a citizen of her country—Sweden, Germany, somewhere. He could live there legally and send for his mother. But she refuses, and he can't leave without her permission, because she depends on him. If he knew someone to look after her, he would take a bus and go to Iran as others have done, and from there travel to Turkey and then Europe. Risky, yes, but it would be a chance at a better life. However, Uresh's mother wants him to stay and marry a local girl. Not a bad girl like Farkhunda, a good girl. Did I know about her, Farkhunda? It was her fault what happened. She should have said, I didn't do anything. Then someone would have stopped the beating. Instead, she stayed quiet. Had Uresh been there, he would have asked her, Have you done this? Have you insulted our faith? If she had said no, he'd have stood in front of her and stopped the mob attacking her. This is Afghanistan. Muslims don't hurt women unless they're provoked by unbelievers. What happened is not what the media portrayed; she said something. Farkhunda wasn't a good girl. The people who beat her should not have gone to jail. Muslim men would not have beaten a good girl to death.

Do you agree?

No, I say. You don't kill someone for no reason.

There was a reason, Uresh insists.

He starts the razor again to nick rogue hairs at the bottom of my beard. I let him have the last word about Farkhunda to avoid an argument. I'm happy to see him, flattered he's being so solicitous, but I'm appalled by his opinion. My feelings are like an intense, magnified version of a teacher's—running into a student I once mentored, who is doing well, but whose life somehow falls short of what I might have hoped. What difference can any of us make, especially when you walk away?

Uresh continues talking, moving on from Farkhunda to his hope of leaving Afghanistan.

You can get up now, Uresh tells me, shutting off the razor for the final time.

He removes the sheet from my chest and I offer to pay, but he refuses. He hugs me again before I leave and tells me not to leave without seeing him again.

Hours later, Uresh closes for the night and catches a bus home. On the way he passes the home of Mohammad Qasim Karbalaye, a mender of broken bones. When he was a young man, Mohammad worked as a laborer. Short but powerful, he could do in one hour what it took other men a week to complete. He had never thought of helping people with physical ailments until he assisted a wrestler from Uzbekistan with a dislocated shoulder. He punched it back into place and the Uzbek told him he should go into business and doctor others. Mohammad opened a shop and the Uzbek would sit with him and people assumed that like the Uzbek he, too, was a wrestler, so they started calling him the Wrestler. Other than his wife and son, Mohammad does not know any other living person who knows his true name. He has been doing this kind of work for almost fifty years and has been called the Wrestler for so long he sometimes doesn't answer his wife when she calls him Mohammad.

On this evening, a woman walks in carrying a boy just twenty days old. His right elbow juts out at an odd angle. Mohammad rubs the arm with automotive grease. He tells the mother to leave the grease on the child's arm for three days to lubricate the joint. Then come back, he says, and he'll fix it.

The woman departs and an elderly man leaning on a cane enters. A thick bandage swaddles his left hand. Mohammad examines it.

Leave the bandage on for another week, he says.

The man leaves, his cane making small dents in the dirt floor. Outside, moonlight sweeps the street with a white, shivering glow and Mohammad sips tea and stares through the light at nothing. He has seen with his own eyes how much worse Afghanistan has become. Day after day nothing goes right. In Jalalabad, the wife of a man with five daughters gave birth to a son. The man fired his gun into the air with happiness. A Taliban commander said, Why are you shooting your gun? My wife finally had a son, the man explained. The commander took the two-day-old baby and crushed his head with the butt of his Kalashnikov. Then he shot the father. The father's cousin told Mohammad about this when he came in to see him for back pain. Some people didn't believe him, but Mohammad did. He knows these things happen. He doesn't need evidence. Living in Afghanistan is evidence enough. After 9/11, everything was fine and then it wasn't. Nothing is sustainable. That is why everyone skips the country. He thinks of leaving too, but how can he? Where will he go? Who will pay his expenses? He worries about these things. He'll go if someone pays his way.

Mohammad sits back and rubs his face. Another patient arrives, a young woman and her husband. The woman lifts her swollen right foot. Mohammad examines it with the tips of his fingers. He advises her to put grease on it for three days. Her ankle had become solid, he explains. Grease will loosen it.

He watches the couple walk out. If he had money, obviously he would leave Afghanistan—why not? If his patients had money, they would see a doctor and not him. For some people, there are no alternatives.

Mohammad's shop recedes in the distance as the bus carrying Uresh continues its journey, the passengers thinning with each stop until Uresh gets off and only a few remain, among them Abdul Malik Bakhytar. He lives in Logar Province, a good two-hour drive outside Kabul. When the bus stops near his house well past the hour for dinner, he gets out and pauses, listening for gunshots and the screams that often follow. On this night, hearing nothing, he hurries home, passing through the shadows cast by white stucco houses and stunted trees. During the day, he fulfills his duties as the director of publications for the Ministry of Women's Affairs. He recognizes the irony of his position: the newsletters of the Ministry of Women's Affairs being administered by a man. Men hold all the key positions in the ministry and the Taliban target them for supporting women's rights. That is Afghanistan. In the end, what does it matter? Men and women are leaving the country and would still be leaving even if a woman ran the ministry. Why would any woman or man stay? Abdul is grateful just to have an income.

In Logar, a Taliban stronghold, Abdul doesn't dare say where he works. Life here is fine except at night, when the province belongs to the Taliban. Abdul often wakes up in the middle of the night and hears shouting and fighting and terrified voices begging for mercy. Leave me alone, don't kill me! He stays in his bed, does not move. No one comes to the rescue. Everyone stays inside, prepared to defend themselves. His neighbors all have guns. No one relies on NATO or the government. At night, each family lives in fear. At night, each family is on its own.

Two weeks ago, Abdul saw a policeman return home from work. Eight o'clock at night, not that dark. The policeman lived on a street close to a stream. He used the water to grow a beautiful garden, dark green with bright flowers. Some men approached him, shot him in the head and ransacked the garden. Abdul saw the whole thing from his living room window. He doesn't know how he feels about it. Numb, not surprised. Grateful it wasn't him. Guilty for feeling grateful.

In Abdul's neighborhood, everyone is related, but outside of it he knows no one and talks to no one. On his days off, Thursdays and Fridays, he stays home. He attended a wedding the other day but he didn't participate in the reception. He does not wear Western suits but dresses traditionally in a salwar kameez. He changes into a suit at work.

A driver takes his two daughters and two sons to school. He calls home four or five times a day to check in with his wife. If he had the money, he'd fly his family out of the country. Many others in the government have sent their wives and children abroad. His friends and in-laws tell him his daughters should not attend school. If they get raped or killed, it will bring shame on all of us, they warn him. People will wonder what they did to deserve their fate. It is my right to educate my daughters, he retorts emphatically.

When he hears about boys and girls drowning on their way to Europe from Turkey, he sees the faces of his children and gets emotional. One newspaper photo showed a dead boy on a beach. He resembled his youngest son. Abdul felt ill. He quit reading and shut off the light and tried to sleep, hoping a scream in the night would not awaken him.

The next morning, Uresh catches a bus back into Kabul and calls me. A friend had telephoned him last night to say he was leaving Kabul for Germany with his pregnant wife. Uresh thinks I should talk to him and gives us his name, Shekib Younissi, and his cell number. When Aarash picks me up, I ask him to call Shekib for directions to his home. We take a narrow alley near the Park Palace to an uneven road with broken asphalt and follow it uphill; soon we have an expansive view of Kabul, and the bare, brown mountains in the distance, a grainy haze hovering above everything. The road turns and we dip downhill into a dead-end street and stop outside a two-story white house.

Twenty-six-year-old Shekib meets us at the door and we follow him inside to a room where his wife, mother, and father sit on the floor. The sun shines through a window illuminating the bare walls. I sit down and Shekib's father offers me a plate of nuts and raisins.

For two years, Shekib saved and borrowed money and eventually put aside four thousand dollars. An uncle in Germany who had left Afghanistan in the Taliban years helped with additional funds. However, Shekib still did not have enough money for all of them to leave. After a lengthy discussion, the family decided that his father, wife, and cousin would go to Iran and hire a smuggler for the long trek to Turkey and beyond into Europe; Shekib and his mother would stay behind. They hope to leave next year if Shekib raises the money. A quiet despair fills the room, the mute sadness mixed with a stoic resolve not to show it.

Shekib first thought of leaving when his wife became pregnant. Many reasons led to this decision, the welfare of his child and the lack of security being foremost. Shekib doesn't know when or where a bomb might go off, when or where a man with a gun might begin shooting. Every day Shekib meets with friends and asks, How are you? Is everyone in your family still alive? Being alive in Afghanistan is a big thing. When insurgents attach magnet bombs to cars, living one day to the next can't be taken for granted.

Shekib's wife, Yazdi, does not want to travel without him. The day she agreed to leave Kabul, she wept from morning to night. Shekib looked so sad as he explained that it was better for him to stay behind and pay back the loans and then start saving again so he and his mother could leave. He works for Kam Air, an airline headquartered in Kabul. He can save and reimburse people a little bit at a time. Yazdi told him, I know it will be hard but I tell myself I can do it.

Don't cry, Shekib tells her now. Afghans are very courageous. We don't cry.

It will be the first time I'll be apart from my family, she explains. I am seven months pregnant and I will be without my husband.

Shekib's father, Shaiq Hamid, stares out a window, eyes brimming with tears. He worries, nervously running his hands through his thinning, gray hair. He has friends stuck in Iran. They have children, and children don't run as fast as adults and they may need to run from police, border guards, and God knows who else. Like children, a pregnant woman can't run fast. The smuggler will pay the police to look the other way, but they have only so much money and there are many police. They can't pay them all.

Shekib's mother, Sham Sad, also struggles to hold back tears. She wears a black body-length veil and exposes her face only to her family. Wiping her eyes, she stares at the floor to conceal her sorrow. She knows the trip will be long and difficult for Yazdi. That is the way for Afghan women—they must suffer. Carrying a baby and clothes and food. God will be testing her. She should buy sneakers, better for walking.

Sham remembers baking bread when rockets fell around their house during the civil war years. She had to run and seek shelter with her children, only to return later to finish baking bread; otherwise, they'd have no food. As her grandchild grows, he or she will take care of her one day. That is what women hope for, the love of their children and their grandchildren.

I have to get you a mobile phone to call me, Shekib tells Yazdi.

You have to give me some of your clothes to pack.

I'll need them here.

No, I'll keep them so that I know one day you will come to me.

Farkhunda's friend, twenty-one-year-old Tuba, recalls Farkhunda as a nice girl. She had a pleasant smile and liked to joke. They took classes together. Farkhunda was the class leader. She took attendance and distributed assignments. When Farkhunda discussed Islam, she always asked questions to make things clearer. She was very knowledgeable. One time, she entered a class and pretended to be the teacher. She fooled everyone. When the teacher finally showed up and asked, What are you doing? Farkhunda ran out laughing.

Tuba was at home when Farkhunda died. At first, she did not realize that the young woman killed was Farkhunda. When she hadn't heard from her for two days, she called her cell phone and her father answered. The dead girl is the girl you knew, my daughter, Farkhunda, he told Tuba.

Of course, she is afraid. No one asked, why are you beating Farkhunda? They just beat her. What would stop them from beating other girls? When she passes the shrine where Farkhunda died, she gets nauseated and her chest hurts. She would like to leave Afghanistan but the idea of leaving her country also makes her afraid.

Tuba dreamed of Farkhunda once after her death. In the dream, she wore a black hijab and the two of them were walking together. Farkhunda didn't speak, just looked at Tuba with sad eyes. Then Tuba woke up.

Two days before I return to the States, I meet Uresh one last time at the Herat Restaurant, where I used to take him for lunch in

2003. The Herat has changed dramatically since then. The once roughhewn interior with its concrete floor and warped wooden tables has been completely remodeled. It now has white tile floors, glossy glass tables, and bright, glaring lights. Its prices have nearly quadrupled.

You see improvements like this and you think we're becoming a modern country, Uresh says, noticing my open-mouth surprise. Then a bomb explodes. Nothing is certain in Afghanistan.

We take a table and order a plate of beef kabob and two Cokes. As we wait for the food, Uresh shows me pictures of his girlfriend on his cell phone. She has a wide, open face and a generous smile. An orange head scarf covers her hair. Uresh tells me she wants to leave Afghanistan.

Let's go, she says, and then we'll marry in Europe, but he demurs. Her family, he believes, would kill him.

Why? I ask.

Before he answers, Uresh takes back the phone and deletes her pictures. If he were to lose it and her family found it with her photos, they'd shoot him, he says.

They believe she should marry within the family, Uresh says. That is the Afghan way. They don't want their daughter with a poor boy.

That makes no sense, I tell him.

He puts the phone down and faces me. The exasperated look on his face suggests I'm the one who doesn't make sense.

This is Afghanistan, he says, as if that alone explains everything.

On my last day in Kabul, I take Aarash to Yummy Fast Food for lunch. As we read a menu, he asks, after a pause, whether I would sponsor him for a US visa. His question takes me by surprise and he turns away when he sees my stunned look. Despite my shock, the thought has crossed my mind, but I've always dismissed it as unworkable. I'd have to house and support him, Sharjeela, and their son while they got settled. How long would that take? When would Aarash and Sharjeela be eligible for work permits? And what would happen if they didn't find jobs? Or, if they did, but their salary wasn't enough to pay for their own apartment and daycare? How long would I have to carry them?

He and Sharjeela should apply as foreign exchange students to a US college. Many universities have such programs. In fact, I know a number of Afghans who attended the University of Kansas in Lawrence. Why not try there? They would need to submit their school transcripts and take tests to show their proficiency in English. Aarash sees the process as too time-consuming—he wants out now. He has an uncle in North Carolina who offered him a room but nothing more. I spoke to him by phone. Listen, he told me, I left Afghanistan after the Russians came. I work three jobs now. If Aarash and Sharjeela want to stay with me for a few days, OK, but I have no time to do anything for them.

Why won't you help? Aarash asks me.

Aarash, I say, I don't have the means or the space. I rent a one-bedroom apartment. I live check to check.

He nods.

I would if I could. It's complicated. I'm sorry.

I'm sorry too, brother.

He tries to hide his disappointment with a smile. He hears the stories of families departing by bus and on foot only to return, defeated, and he knows people like Jamshid, Gety, and Naseer who, like him, are desperate to go. He wishes them well. He and Sharjeela didn't make it, but he hopes the others do. He wishes he could turn back the clock to a simpler time, before everything changed and all the joy in life vanished. But this is Afghanistan. After decades of war, he can't let fear stop him from living. After all, in Afghanistan, no one can predict the future.

ALL THAT IS YET TO COME

On June 24, 2016, while I was in Chicago visiting family, my Afghan colleague Aarash sent me a Facebook message.

Hello brother, he wrote. *Hope everything is going well with you. I'm currently in the states. Just wanted you to know.* He included his phone number and I called him.

Sharjeela's job at the Ministry of Interior had made them eligible for a Special Immigrant Visa, he told me. They and their two children arrived in the US just days before he contacted me. A resettlement agency had placed them in Seattle. For two weeks they lived with a friend they knew from Kabul, then their case manager found them an apartment. They did not like it. The pipes leaked, the carpet stunk of mildew, the lights often did not work, and stains marred the walls and floors. The importance of paying rent on time surprised Aarash. In Kabul, if he didn't have the money his landlord would tell him, OK, give it to me next month, but here finances control everything. A tenant could be evicted. The number of homeless people shocked him.

After a year and a half, Aarash moved his family into a better apartment, and he took a job delivering bread and driving for Uber, Lyft, and Amazon. Now, he and Sharjeela work for the health department of King County, which includes Seattle, as translators for Afghan and Indian immigrants.

Aarash said he could not have been happier to leave Kabul and the war, but he missed his country and all the things that once annoyed him: the crazy traffic, the dusty air, the argumentative shopkeepers and their inflated prices. He lost an uncle and two aunts in Kabul to natural causes but was unable to attend their funerals, because he did not have a green card. He longed for the companionship of his friends, like Jamshid and Gety. They hired smugglers. Gety reached Turkey but got no farther. Jamshid, his wife, and daughter made it to Germany. Aarash had not yet received his US visa when Jamshid called him from Düsseldorf. Along the way, through Turkey and Greece, other people traveling with him wandered off and became lost. He does not know what happened to them. He met the family of Shekib Younissi. They also reached Germany.

Aarash told no one outside his family that he was leaving for the US. He worried someone might try to kill him for the visa. People were scared. Anything could happen at any time. He trusted no one. He took only what would fit in one suitcase and left his books and computer hard drive with hundreds of photos behind. He feels incomplete. The house he and Sharjeela shared with his mother and a sister holds more memories than he can carry in his head.

Aarash does not spend time with other Afghans. Too many of them refuse to learn English; they wear salwar kameez and other traditional clothes, and make only Afghan food. They still arrange marriages for their sons and daughters and expect them to have many children. They live in the old ways. He wants to adapt, but now that his children no longer speak Dari he wonders whether he has adapted too much. Americans have treated him very well, and he enjoys their company, but some of them frustrate him. They understand very little about Afghanistan. When he moved to Seattle he met people who thought the war had already ended.

Aarash was worried about his mother. She had received threatening phone calls because he and Sharjeela had worked for the Americans. He wanted to bring her to Seattle. However, she had not been employed by the US government or military and therefore was not eligible for a Special Immigrant Visa. Then Sharjeela became pregnant. Aarash thought her condition would persuade US officials to grant his mother a visa. Certainly they would understand her wish to be present for the birth of her new grandchild. Family, Aarash reminded me, means everything to Afghans. It is not like the US. In Afghanistan, a husband and wife live with their in-laws, uncles and aunts, nieces and nephews.

However, family has its limits. One of his two sisters recently married. He would need four visas if he tried to help her and her husband, his other sister, and his mother. He thought the chances were slim he would get them all out and decided to assist only his mother. He made no plans to bring Sharjeela's parents to Seattle. Her father, her mother, an aunt, and a sister all lived together. Requesting visas for her parents would have created problems for the two left behind.

He asked me to write a letter to the US consulate in Kabul on behalf of his mother. I agreed. To whom it may concern, I began. I wrote that his mother had not seen Aarash and his family since they had left Kabul. I mentioned the new baby. I added that she could help watch the children while Aarash and Sharjeela were at work. I promised to cover all expenses, including her flight. Within seconds of emailing the letter I received an automated response: *The Visa Unit at the US Embassy in Kabul is not currently offering appointments for nonimmigrant visa interviews. If you have an urgent need for travel to the United States, you may contact the nearest United States Embassy or Consulate in another country to inquire about appointment availability.*

I called Aarash.

I'm sorry, I told him.

So am I, brother, he said.

We stayed in touch. The security situation in Afghanistan, bad when I was there, deteriorated even more. In March 2021, kidnappers killed a cousin of Aarash's father. The next month, President Joe Biden announced the withdrawal of all US forces from Afghanistan and the Taliban began sweeping the country, routing government forces.

I was reminded of an afternoon in September 2015 when Aarash and I met Uresh in his barbershop. He was cutting a man's hair. Four other men sat on a bench waiting their turn. All of us began talking about Kunduz. It had just fallen to the Taliban. Kabul became a ghost town: the streets empty, shops closed, no traffic. Once teeming sidewalks silent, vacant.

Kunduz shows that our security gets worse every day. There's no benefit in fighting, so our army doesn't resist, Uresh said.

When people leave for Europe, the enemy thinks they are afraid, and the government gets weaker and weaker. Now, even the foreigners are leaving, and the Taliban will get in, one of the men on the bench said.

The taking of Kunduz is not just news, another man declared looking at me, but a warning for all people working for the government and with Westerners. The Taliban are not just coming. They are here.

It's time to grow our beards again and carry our prayer beads, Uresh said.

Six years later their dire predictions came true. In August, four months after Biden made his announcement, the Taliban retook Kabul and seized power.

I tried to keep in touch with people Aarash and I had interviewed but they had gone into hiding. Laila Haidari of Mother's House, Uresh, even the owner of the Park Palace Guest House had all stopped responding to my messages.

Aarash was not surprised. His friends had scattered too. He can't relax. He thinks of his mother, sisters, and in-laws. Sometimes when he stands alone in his living room, he gets anxious for no reason. He experiences the fear and worry of his family. In his mind he remains with them. What if someone detonates a bomb? he wonders. At night, he dreams of Afghanistan and relives the terrible afternoon shrapnel tore into his neck and almost killed him, or he sees his mother on the ground amid rubble. He wakes up terrified and calls her to assure himself nothing bad has happened. Then he falls back on his bed and stares into the dark and thinks of Kabul and all that he has left behind and all that is yet to come.

ACKNOWLEDGMENTS

Thanks to the staff of Seven Stories Press, especially my editor, Dan Simon, for taking on this manuscript.

My thanks to everyone at the publications in which some of these stories first appeared. Without you this book would not exist.

Thank you to Chuck Murphy, Roland Sharrillo, Bruce Janssen, Sarah Madges, and Jesse Barker for critiquing early drafts of these stories. I also want express my appreciation to Margaret Dalrymple and her colleagues at the University of Nevada Press for their time, input, and support.

And, finally, my heartfelt thanks to all the Afghan people I had the good fortune to meet. You befriended me and took me into your homes and gave generously of your time and companionship. You took significant risks introducing me to your country. You shared your aspirations, dreams, and sorrows, and your undying love for Afghanistan. I am humbled and grateful. I won't forget you.

ABOUT THE AUTHOR

J. MALCOLM GARCIA has reported from Afghanistan, Pakistan, Chad, Sierra Leone, Haiti, Honduras, Bolivia and Argentina. His beat is the stories that usually go unreported, the lives of people not usually considered newsworthy or important, people who struggle just to survive. His work has been included in *The Best American Travel Writing*, *The Best American Unrequired Reading*, *Best American Essays*, and frequently appears in such publications as *McSweeney's*, *Guernica*, *Ascent* and *N+1*, among others. Garcia is the recipient of the Studs Terkel Prize for writing about the working classes, and the Sigma Delta Chi Award for excellence in journalism. His previous books include *Khaarijee: A Chronicle of Friendship and War in Kabul*. His most recent book is *The Fruit of All My Grief*.